THE LAST RESORT

For Elizabeth, my grandmother, for giving me her Gothic heroes.

THE LAST RESORT

AMANDA HEWITT

echo
PUBLISHING

Echo Publishing
An imprint of Bonnier Books UK
6/69 Carlton Crescent
Summer Hill NSW 2130
www.echopublishing.com.au

Bonnier Books UK
HYLO, 5th Floor,
103–105 Bunhill Row
London EC1Y 8LZ
www.bonnierbooks.co.uk

Copyright © Amanda Hewitt 2026

Cover design copyright © Christabella Designs

All rights reserved. Echo thanks you for buying an authorised edition of this book. In doing so, you are supporting writers and enabling Echo to publish more books and foster new talent. Thank you for complying with copyright laws by not reproducing or transmitting any part of this book by any means, electronic or mechanical – including storing in a retrieval system, photocopying, recording, scanning or distributing – without our prior written permission.

Echo Publishing acknowledges the traditional custodians of Country throughout Australia. We recognise their continuing connection to land, sea and waters. We pay our respects to Elders past and present.

This is a work of fiction. Names, characters, businesses, places, events, locales and incidents are either the products of the author's imagination or used in a fictitious manner. Any resemblance to actual persons, living or dead, or actual events is purely coincidental.

First published 2026

Printed and bound in Australia by Opus Group

Editor: Lauren Finger
Page design and typesetting: Shaun Jury
Cover design: Christabella Designs
Cover images: Summer camp and Summer Camp poster
by Alexander Baidin/Shutterstock; wine glass by Venimo/Shutterstock

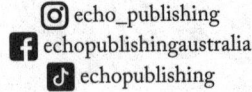

A catalogue entry for this book is available from the National Library of Australia

ISBN: 9781786586452 (paperback)
ISBN: 9781786586469 (ebook)

echo_publishing
echopublishingaustralia
echopublishing

About the author

Amanda Hewitt is an Australian romance author. Based in the south of Sydney, she is a mum of three little guys and wife to a big guy. An expert on guys, she now writes love stories about guys who don't exist. She loves Gothic literature and English period drama. When she is not writing, you can find her knee deep in laundry, or curled up on the lounge with a mystery and a glass of red. *The Last Resort* is her first novel.

Chapter One
Abbey

I was a reluctant holiday-maker. Bedraggled, weary and extremely conscious of being single. But I was in the Maldives and the resort, well, it was lovely. Postcard-perfect. It was all palm trees, nicely swept paths and warm, welcoming lights. The staff were helpful in that 'hotel' kind of way, where they make you feel significantly more important than you are when checking in, but you strongly suspect they will talk about you meanly the minute you step away from the counter. But despite their charm, I could barely muster a polite smile.

It didn't help that the past several hours had revealed that I was a nervous flyer. I never used to be. I was so nervous that the lady beside me suspected I was having a panic attack, and a flight attendant, who looked like Hannah Waddingham, gave me a Valium out of her handbag and a vodka to wash it down. By the time I arrived at the resort, the overwhelming feeling I remember was, well, relief. Followed closely by exhaustion, plus the solid conviction that my life was rubbish, and that going on a holiday by yourself was a one-way trip to Loserville.

The porter (Hot. Model hot. Twenty-five max.) opened the door to the beachfront room, and then we both just stood there while I took a deep, miserable, shuddering sigh. It was the perfect room, literally perfect. I walked into it slowly, taking in the lustrous white linen covering the enormous bed. It was so spacious I could stand there with my black tote held at arm's length, spin around and not hit a goddamn thing. It had better cupboard space than my house, and a gorgeous bathroom with subway tiles, fancy shampoo and conditioner in those exclusive smaller bottles, and a window to let you look out at the ocean from the tub. A bottle of champagne sat cooling in a silver bucket, three-quarters filled with ice cubes and two glasses laid out with their stems crossed in front of the bottle, suggesting there should be a couple staying here.

There were double doors with light-diffusing curtains draped from the ceiling. The doors were open, and a gentle warm breeze flittered into the room, making the soft curtains dance. From the door to where the ocean gently lapped was perfectly pale sand, the kind that squeaks under your feet and gets extremely hot in the sun. To add insult to injury, a full moon hung perfectly low, like a neon welcome sign in the night sky. It was the moon that pushed me over the edge, and I burst into tears and fell on the bed.

I don't know what happened to the hot porter. Perhaps it wasn't every day he showed someone the perfect room, only to have them collapse into a ball of grief and sadness. He had evidently made himself scarce, leaving the emotional wreck alone.

I cried a marriage-worth of tears on that perfect bed, bits of my tubular mascara balling up and marring the perfect white surface. Once I had noticed, I began trying to brush it off, but that just made the smudges much worse, so I simply gave up. Walking over to the champagne bucket, I reached into the slushy ice and wiped a little of the freezing liquid over my eyes. Then I popped the cork and poured out a glass, downing it, failing to care about the not-quite-ladylike burp that came out. Unsatisfied with the glass's capacity, I placed it neatly beside the cooler and drank the next mouthful directly from the bottle.

Internally, I was prepared to acknowledge that it appeared I was bottoming out and having some sort of crisis. Maybe I was entitled to one. Six months and seven hours ago, I had been dumped by my husband of thirteen years. He came home, ate the mediocre dinner I had prepared for him and told me he was in love, just not with me. He laughed in a 'I cannot believe this has happened' kind of way, which reminded me of Elizabeth Bennet telling her father how much she loved Darcy at the end of the love-it-or-hate-it 2005 *Pride & Prejudice* movie. I had laughed too, though I was not amused. He moved his stuff out that day and left it to me to explain to our daughter.

Peter (deadbeat ex-husband) had insisted that I go on this holiday to recover, which I think he felt was a vaguely magnanimous gesture. This holiday, that we were supposed to take together, to reconnect. *Now that is pretty fucking funny.*

My phone vibrated on the perfect side table.

Hey Mum, just checking you got there okay? Miss you. E xx

My thirteen-year-old daughter, Ella. She would be anxious about me being away, even though she would pretend not to be. I took a deep swig from the bottle and smiled to engage my Mum personality, texting her back a bright and cheery message. Anything that did not scream, 'I've just arrived in a foreign country without waterproof mascara and am having a bit of a crisis'.

Here safe and sound, chickadee. It's gorgeous, looking
forward to reading books on the beach tomorrow. Miss you.
Love you. Mum xxx

Another message, this time from my sister, Kate.

Abbey, remember even though you are 42 years old, you're
still bangable.

I stared at my phone, unable to respond to this message. I looked down at my boobs, which were not quite as high as they once were, and my stomach, which was soft instead of firm. I didn't feel very bangable. I felt like an emotional wreck, whose life had been going along fine until a crisis was forced upon me by the one person who had vowed in front of loved ones not to let me down. And, okay, I wasn't heartbroken, not really. It wasn't anything like the same devastation I'd felt when my first boyfriend had dumped me for my friend when we were sixteen. This was more a combination of humiliation and the sensation that my life was falling off the rails. It was miserable.

I tried to pull my shit together for a second, reminding myself that this was a fork in the road or an alternate ending. Reminding myself that I should look for positives. It was choose-your-own adventure time.

Except right now, I could not summon the energy for fresh thoughts.

The last time I had been single, I was twenty-two, hot, and my vagina had not delivered a small human. Now I was cruising towards perimenopause and upping my health insurance to include joint replacements. Could anyone but my grandmother even fall in love over forty? *Fuck. Probably not.*

My misery was allowing me to rapidly make my way through most of the champagne, sitting there on the perfect bed in the perfect room. I raised the champagne bottle to the light, estimating that there was still a glass left – the irony that I was still measuring in glasses, even though I was no longer drinking out of one, was not lost on me. I hadn't bothered to check the label, but it tasted French and expensive.

A stronger breeze rustled through the open doors, drawing my attention to the beach on my doorstep. *You know what? Fuck it. When in paradise, right?* That was as close to a positive thought as I was going to get tonight. I stood up and slipped out of my slides, stretching ruby-red toes in the plush charcoal rug, before stepping onto the sand, clinging to the champagne bottle like an alcoholic hobo in a pretty floral dress.

The sand felt warm under my feet, as if it was still being kissed by the sun even though it was late. My plane had been delayed and then the transfer took forever, so I estimated it must have been around eleven o'clock. Everywhere was quiet, not a soul around. My room seemed to be at the very end of the resort, which reached back towards the left, sprawling towards the restaurants near reception. I peeked at the corner room next to mine, the last room in this section. The beach appeared to go out to a point in front of it. The views must be wonderful from that room. It looked pretty much the same as mine, but larger; the open doors and the fluttering of the white light-diffusing curtains seeming to indicate that I had a neighbour. The horrifying thought came to mind that it might be a honeymooning couple, filled with dreams of happily ever after, who I would have to make small talk with. That made me worry I might not actually survive this holiday, but at least that was a problem for the next day.

I wandered slowly down to the water's edge past several sun

loungers, tables and chairs with folded-down, off-duty umbrellas. I leaned over and planted my champagne bottle into the sand, twisting it back and forth until it found enough purchase to stand upright. Two more steps and my feet touched the water, which felt warm – not bath warm, but not steal-your-breath cold either. I had another nervous look around the empty beach until I was confident I was alone. Peter had bought the holiday in a sale and booked it for the very beginning of the off-season, so it seemed fair to assume that not many people would be here full stop.

I stood in what my sister would call my thinking pose, with one hand on my hip and the other on my grandmother's pendant around my throat. The rectangle filigree pattern stamped into my finger, and I felt along the three small diamonds, centring myself. Grandma Iris was a bloody powerhouse. If she were here now, she would have told me, 'Abbey, stop being feeble.'

Non-feeble Abbey took a deep breath, channelling Iris. I slid the strap of my dress off my left shoulder, then repeated the motion on the other side. I lowered the dress over my chest, wiggled it down my hips and stepped out of it, throwing it back for the champagne bottle to look after.

It should be noted, before we go on, that it was not normally my style to get naked in public. I will blame the aforementioned crisis and the quickly drunk champagne on an empty stomach. My hands reached around my back, unclasping my bra, feeling the sweet relief of getting it off after wearing it all day. I was tipsy enough that I heard striptease music, and I threw my bra back for the French champagne bottle, like a stripper in a Kings Cross brothel. *Lucky you, champagne bottle, I'm still bangable after all.*

The water was black and inviting, and I walked in, throwing myself under. The sound of the sea echoed cavernously in my ears, and I stayed beneath the surface for as long as I could, holding my breath, trying to let go of all the shit I was carrying around daily. It was time for a rebirth, time to let go of the sadness, of trying to hold on to what had been. Time to let go of Peter, or the idea of Peter, or the idea of Peter and me.

I made a vow, then and there, under the water, to come back from this holiday a different person, to reset into someone who could move past disappointment, someone who could set some rules for a better relationship next time. Sometimes life changed in more ways than one, and I knew in my heart that I just had to be elastic and stretchy enough for the changes not to break me. When I was reaching the end of my oxygen, I bent my knees, pushed my feet into the ever-changing seabed and surged up to the surface to come out of the water. I hit my head on something solid. Shocked, I tried to step back, but the solid mass grabbed me, and I took a huge breath into a firm, male chest.

'Christ, are you all right? You were under so long I thought you were drowning.' He dropped his arms to my waist, pulling me against him. His crisp, low voice seemed to almost vibrate in his chest. 'Oh, my God, you're topless. I did not realise that I, ummm, apologise. I'm so very sorry.'

The bright moon illuminated the two of us and the weird, dark light allowed me to take him in. My eyes roamed over shoulders that were broad and a dark thatch of hair I could also feel against my stomach trailing into his shorts. He had a lean throat, and he was breathing as hard as I was. His cheeks were covered in dark hair, not quite a beard, more an overgrown stubble. He had nice white teeth, and his mouth was opened in an 'O' shape as he tried to constrain the adrenaline pumping through him. His nose was perfectly strong without controlling his whole face and his witch-dark eyes, which could have almost been black for all I knew, were piercing me as if he was trying to read my mind. A crop of dark hair rounded him out, water dripping from random curls. My eyes followed one drop down his nose and onto his top lip, where his tongue darted out to lick at it. I felt quite warm suddenly.

I was still breathing hard, trying to get oxygen back into my lungs and I now tried to compose myself rationally by stepping back from the very attractive would-be rescuer, but the height difference between us and the depth of the water meant that his feet were in the sand, while mine were several inches off it. His proximity was overwhelming. I had not touched a man in an age and our chests were pressed together. My nipples were already hard from the water, and I felt heat shoot down low into my stomach.

He moved, taking two steps towards the shore and gently set me down, making sure my footing was stable before letting me go.

'Are you all right?' he whispered, again.

His voice was as dark as the shadows where the bright rays of the moonlight could not reach, and my skin erupted into goosebumps at the absence of his body heat.

'I'm fine. Although, weirdly, I've had "Hotel California" stuck in my head since I arrived,' I stated firmly.

He gave a reluctant, short laugh, as if that was the most unexpected thing he'd ever heard. It was a harsh, raspy noise, as though it had gone unused for a period of time.

I placed a hand in the centre of his firm chest, into the thatch of hair, attempting to push away from him. The lack of oxygen had, apparently, severed the connection between my brain and arm, because my fingers lingered a little, exploring him. He drew a sharp breath and his hand launched up, quickly covering mine, his black-hole eyes boring into me.

Jesus, Abbey, stop touching the man. I moved to put space between myself and the touchable stranger, suddenly hyper-aware that my boobs were out. Uncertain how to remove myself from him while covering this fact, I reasoned that there seemed little point in trying to hide it, although I wrapped one arm around them to give me a modicum of modesty and then walked out of the water. Reaching the collection of items on the sand, I picked up my dress, bra and champagne bottle before yelling over my shoulder, 'Thanks for rescuing me.'

I padded up to the doors of my room, throwing myself under the outdoor shower, removing the sand from my feet and sliding my knickers down from my hips, not particularly caring if my knight in shining armour caught more of a glimpse of my less-than-bangable body than he had in the water. I reached for the perfect towel, fluffy and white and huge, turning off the lights before sliding into perfect heavy cotton sheets. The bed was so tucked in it felt like a straitjacket, but the weight of it, and my inability to move, combined with the bottle of champagne, was comforting. Everything was perfect here … but me. I drifted off to sleep.

Nick

Christ, the glare is actually going to kill me.

It was even more of a struggle to feel the holiday vibes this year than usual. In fact, I couldn't remember a great time on holiday, ever. I'm almost certain it's a curse.

For instance, the year our mother and father took me and my siblings to Disneyland, I caught a stomach bug and ended up vomiting for four days straight. The year they took us to Tokyo, my little sister broke her arm after slipping on ice in the airport car park. *In Heathrow before we left.* Holidays did not bode well for Northbys.

I walked over to the block-out curtains of the floor-to-ceiling doors, which revealed the best view in the whole resort, and pulled them firmly closed, shutting out the handful of couples on deckchairs under grassed umbrellas. The room itself was comfortable, the bed firm, but the breeze in the night that would come through the curtains was the only real bliss afforded here.

Last night, though, something out of the ordinary had occurred and I could not stop thinking about it.

The night had started exactly the way the previous three had: I'd showered, getting rid of the salt on my skin, after having my one swim per day in the late afternoon, avoiding sunburn; I'd drunk a bottle of wine for dinner along with a room-service order of a surprisingly decent hamburger and fries; I'd answered thirty emails in my work inbox that could not wait for my holiday to end. I'd then been walking towards the open doors of my bedroom to close the curtains when I saw her: a woman zig-zagging her way down the beach towards the water.

She was carrying a champagne bottle, which she put down in the sand, taking an inordinate amount of time to ensure it did not tip over. She'd turned her head towards the rooms and I'd frozen, only relaxing again when she'd changed direction, looking up and down the beach.

She'd removed her dress, and I felt my eyebrows rise into my hair. And, yeah, it was probably a little pervy to keep looking at the drunk lady going for a night swim. I am not in the habit of perving on women or looking for some sort of holiday fling, which, I've always thought, sounded vaguely exhausting. But there was just something about her. Like the way her fair, wavy hair was gently catching the breeze, revealing her neck, and I couldn't drag my eyes away from her.

She'd got the dress off with a wiggle of her hips and tossed it back to the champagne bottle. My breath had caught when I'd realised I could see her gentle curves, the outline of her hips, and the swell of her ample bust. She'd stood with one hand on her hip for a moment before removing what I assumed was her bikini top. It wasn't until I saw the lace that I realised it was a black bra. It too was thrown back to the champagne bottle, a little flirtingly, I'd thought, snickering.

When she'd walked into the water, I'd returned to shutting the curtains, but then the worry started. How much had she actually had to drink? Would she be okay? It wasn't safe if she was alone. I stepped outside, trying to hear other sounds from her room, right next door. I just needed to know she wasn't alone in the world.

I was met with only silence, not even the television was on. I felt fear kick in. She'd been under at least a minute so far.

I'd seen enough therapists to know the signs of adrenaline rushing. I could taste it, a metallic flavour invading my mouth. *Fuck.*

I broke into a full sprint, the wine and the hamburger protesting the exertion. I threw off my shirt onto the white sand and briefly mourned my softest jersey pyjama shorts, before leaping into the water like David fucking Hasselhoff. The moon was full and there was an almost ridiculous amount of light, but my search for a shadow in the water was pointless as the water just looked black. I dived to the spot where I thought she had gone under. The panic increased as the sea beat and whooshed, rushing in my ears. I bounced up off the sand bed and took another four steps forward, preparing to dive again, when something collided with my chest. *Oof.*

I felt her try to pull back, but I reached out, firmly grabbing her and pulling her into me, ensuring she didn't go under again.

Even now heat climbed to my cheeks, remembering the feel of her velvety skin, cool and slippery, under my hands, the dawning realisation that her nipples were pressed into my chest. *Of course they were, idiot, you watched her take her bra off.* Her breathing was hard, but she seemed calm, and I had the first inkling that she had not been at risk of drowning. Her wet hair was long down her back, and clear blue eyes inspected me; I felt they saw more than I wanted them to. I stammered out an apology and set her down, feeling awkward that it had taken me so long to let go of her.

Seconds later she hadn't moved or spoken and, worried, I asked her again if she was all right. 'I'm fine,' she had uttered before giving me a wisecrack about a song being stuck in her head. She had put her hand right in the centre of my chest and I felt myself audibly gasp. My heart had thundered.

It's just adrenaline. Calm down, Nick.

Her fingers had moved through my chest hair in this familiar way, and my hand shot up, covering hers to still it. My heart pounded harder, and I was clearly not calming down. Her eyes locked with mine and, I swear to you, it was like some sort of magical thing. I think she cast a spell on me. Water was dripping down her pale skin, and she had this vaguely amused look on her face. She took a step back, eyes cast down, and then draped an elegant arm across her chest and walked out of the water.

I watched her as she grabbed her collection of clothes and her bottle. She finally spoke again. 'Thanks for the rescue.'

Australian?

I stood in the sea for a few seconds, trying to get my head around the last two minutes, and watched her progress to her room. Finally, my body moved stiffly towards my door. About halfway, I could see her little collection on the table outside hers, the sound of her outdoor shower running. She was humming an out-of-tune 'Hotel California'. Better men than me would have dropped their eyes, turned their heads, looked towards their own doors. Good men. Gentlemen.

Three steps further towards my room was all it took to glimpse legs being washed of sand. She was very pale; her golden hair had turned a light brown under the running water. Her legs were shapely, and she pointed her toes like a ballet dancer as she popped one and then another under the water. As she slid her thumbs into the last remaining item of clothing she had on and bent over to remove it, I almost collided with an umbrella. I picked up my pace and marched into my suite next door, dragging sand and water with me through the room, straight into the shower, which I ran on cold. A poor attempt to cool the need she had created in me. To cool the desire.

Crazy thoughts washed down the drain. Recklessness. Abandon. The desire, well, I could not wash that away, no amount of cold water could cool it, and I had to take care of it via another method.

A knock on the door that was heavier than was professional interrupted my daydream, bringing me back to the present. Hunger drove my pace to open the door; I was suddenly ravenous. I stood back, waiting for my 'personal valet', Oliver, to enter the room, which the man did. Without my breakfast.

'Sorry, did you forget something?' I asked.

'My apologies, *sir*. There was a mix-up in the kitchen with your breakfast this morning.'

'Right … well … I will just wait until you bring another.' My tone barely contained my annoyance.

'Very good, sir.'

'Just Nick is fine,' I growled out.

'Do you intend on sitting in the dark in your room for the whole holiday, sir?'

I scoffed at Oliver. 'None of your goddamned business.'

'As your valet, *sir*, it is my job to ensure you sample the delights of the resort. As such, I have booked you into dinner this evening. At the restaurant, sir. Eight sharp. Also, you will tour the private island tomorrow, sir.' The younger man stopped and took a breath before adding in a softer tone, 'It's not good to sit around in the dark on your own, Nick. You know that.'

My head dropped to the floor, where I studied the polished wood. *Fuck me, if he wasn't right.* I looked up, giving his concerned gaze a quick nod.

'Eight sharp. Don't be late. I'll send your breakfast as soon as it is ready.' The young valet smiled. '*Sir.*'

Little shit.

Chapter Two
Abbey

I woke the next morning to a slight headache and daylight that was not soft enough to indicate it was early. I rolled across the enormous bed to reach for my phone, in a manner that made me feel like Chuck Norris's stuntman, to the confirmation that it was actually ten in the morning. The ever-present gentle breeze rustled the curtains of the open door and I prayed there were no holidayers nearby that might have heard me drunkenly snoring my heart out last night.

I could not remember the last time I'd slept past six. At home, getting us up and out the door was a hectic routine. It turned into a veritable production line of tea, fruit, toast, salads and lunch snacks. Like all mothers, I was a passenger to the chaos since having Ella. The minute women return to work after having a baby, there is always an endless list of things to do or things you can't get to and feel rubbish about. Admittedly, it was nice that this holiday was just me, but I was clearly going to have to relearn how not to be on a schedule, seeing as I was experiencing mild panic about the four hours I had lost.

There was a gentle knock at the door.

'Room service.'

I wrestled my way out of the bed sheets and ducked to the bathroom to grab a white fluffy robe to cover my nakedness before answering the door. I was ready to redirect the delivery, as I could not recall ordering anything the night before.

When I opened the door, I recognised the hot porter. He was holding out a covered tray.

'Hi,' I said, a little embarrassed at my crisis last night. 'I didn't order anything.'

He was dressed in the hotel uniform, a navy button-down shirt, tucked into black trousers. He was young and extremely handsome with light-brown hair, tanned skin and bright-blue eyes that closed a little when he spoke, as if he was in a smoky room. He was fit in that does-not-miss-a-gym-session-and-likes-protein-and-probably-has-abs kind of way and, yep, twenty-five max, as first predicted. His English accent was lovely – more Hugh Grant than Michael Caine. The saviour from last night was English as well. It struck me that there were worse situations to be in life than on a beautiful island surrounded by gorgeous Englishmen with posh accents.

The porter's name badge read 'Oliver'.

'Forgive me,' he said. 'You were so upset yesterday. I just wanted to check you were all right.'

'Welfare check?' I asked, raising an eyebrow. I was in the hotel business too.

'Yes. Most people are happy here. I've never seen anyone cry when I showed them to their room.'

My eyes fell to the floor. 'I'm okay. Just an existential crisis.'

'I brought you breakfast,' he added, lifting the plate with the cloche. 'It's on me. I thought it might help.'

'I'll take it, but I insist you bill it to me.' It didn't take a genius or twenty-plus years in the business to know how rubbish the pay was for resort workers. The view and lifestyle were often not enough to overcome the poverty of young workers for long periods. I softened my tone. 'Thank you for checking on me. It was kind.'

He nodded, handing me the tray. 'Have a good day.'

'Thanks.' I shut the door, feeling happy for the human race that not every kid under thirty was a dick.

I carried the tray happily to the table, removing the cloche with enthusiasm. Surprise breakfast was welcome in my life, anytime. The scrambled eggs were unexpectedly piping hot, and the toast was crisp. A plate of fruit and a pot of coffee also greeted me on the perfect breakfast tray. I fell upon it. The minute I started eating, I realised I was completely famished after missing dinner the night before.

Next on the agenda was a shower. I unpacked my toiletries and placed my favourite one-piece swimmers, which sucked me in a whole dress size, and a maxi dress on the bed. My wide-brimmed hat was ever so slightly crushed from the flight, but it was definitely needed to cover my hair, which was at risk of frizzing in the sultriness of the day, and to provide sun protection. I pulled my wet strands into a tight braid to avoid a humidity horror.

Once dressed, I grabbed my phone, picked up my book, a thriller – absolutely no romance novels allowed – and finally crossed the room to push back the curtains and face the day, like a normal human. It was so fucking bright that I had a *Nosferatu* moment, hissing as I stepped back in the room. I picked up sunglasses and sunscreen, steeling myself to try again.

I finally emerged into the daylight and absorbed the breathtaking beauty of the resort. The Indian Ocean lapped gently at the island's white sand, the water a clear turquoise. There was an umbrella ahead with a deck chair that looked perfect for my reading spot for the day, and I walked to it, relieved I had found shade so that I would not end up looking like a lobster on day one.

It was warm, and much more humid than I had expected, so that after fifteen minutes I had to stand up and strip off my dress. There were not that many people about, only three couples sitting under umbrellas like mine further to my left. There was enough space between us all that I did not feel the need to chat or give awkward waves, making this little introvert very relieved indeed.

I did a quick check, interested to see if my mystery knight in shining armour was a half of one of the couples, but all the men were fairer than I remembered him being.

Peter and I had honeymooned in the Maldives. It genuinely felt like a lifetime ago. I remember trying, even then, to establish if I was happy, almost trying to talk myself into happiness. Even though our relationship ended six months ago, it had been decaying for years. Why had I settled for that? Thoughts plagued me as I wondered why I had held on to the misery that everyday life became, wearing us both down. He was right to end it. Part of me understood that.

Deep down, I could admit that staying had felt like a responsibility to the family we had created. But I was also starting to see the part my passiveness played in it. Having a fluid and easygoing attitude often left me sailing along with a tide, rather than fighting against the direction I was headed. A pathological avoidance of conflict meant I would often just move on when I was upset or angry, rather than confront it. To some people, that might seem more than introverted or reserved. To some people, maybe it seemed I was passionless.

I was going to have to limit the amount of time I spent thinking about this crap or Oliver's welfare checks might actually be needed. I stood up and walked to the water's edge, prepared to repeat last night's rebirth every time my head got too negative. The temperature of the ocean was exquisite. I was able to walk right in rather than needing to ease my way. In Sydney, the ocean temperature was always a little cool. This felt tropical and heavenly, and I waded in up to my shoulders and lay back, looking up to a cerulean sky, floating my heart and my head to an easier place.

When my fingers started to wrinkle a little, I reluctantly went back to my seat. The water was refreshing despite its temperature, and I felt significantly better. I resumed my book and had a sip of water to ease my post-booze thirst. God, this was actually bliss. Noticing a QR code on the table, I scanned it to bring up the hotel's menu and cocktail list, swallowing the squeal of delight that sounded in my head. I picked something with coconut, rum and citrus, thinking it was island appropriate.

When Oliver arrived with it, I looked at him, aghast. The cocktail was ridiculous; it looked as if it had arrived from the set of *Fantasy Island* but had attended Mardi Gras on the way. If a cocktail could have a feather boa, this one would have.

What the fuck? 'Is that glitter?' I asked, looking up at him. Pulling down my sunglasses, I studied the drink as if it were an alien specimen.

'Yes.' He paused. 'It's edible glitter. Wait, this isn't going to set you off? It's just a cocktail. Please don't cry.'

'I'm not going to cry over a cocktail,' I scoffed, annoyed. 'Are you the only staff member at the resort?' My relationship with the porter was getting weird.

'I've worked here this summer, an internship if you like. But I'm genuinely worried about you here.' He paused, and I got the impression he liked to consider his words before speaking them. 'You were very sad last night, and you are by yourself. My brother raised me to make sure people were okay.'

'Your brother raised you?'

'Yeah, our mum and dad died when we were younger.'

'I'm very sorry to hear that,' I said sincerely.

'Thanks.' His eyes dropped to the ground. 'Listen, Ms Parker, you shouldn't just read books about serial killers and drink while you're here. Make sure you do things. I've booked you on a trip to the private island tomorrow. And I booked you in for dinner tonight, too.'

I shook my head. 'Oliver,' I said, as if we had known each other for a lifetime, 'I don't need you to babysit me. I'm okay.'

'Ms Parker, you'd be doing me a favour. It is my last fortnight at the resort, and my assignment is to experience being your personal valet,' he added with a genteel shrug of his muscled shoulder.

'Oliver, I didn't pay enough to have a personal valet, so it feels weird, and I don't want to hang out with couples on this holiday. Like, at all.'

'There isn't anyone else booked on tomorrow's tour. It's just you so far. We serve lunch and champagne on the private island.'

The trip went up in my books. 'Well. I suppose that sounds nice. But I'm not sure about dinner.'

'You must. I insist, Ms Parker.'

'You're extremely pushy. It's not endearing. Also, stop calling me Ms Parker. It makes me sound sixty.'

'What should I call you?'

'Just Abbey. Just call me Abbey. I'll go to dinner too. Just leave me be. Okay?'

'Deal. Reservation is at eight sharp.' Oliver grinned at me impishly.

As a mother it made me instantly suspicious. I nodded in

acknowledgement of the dinner reservation, and he left me to drink the rainbow.

By the time I got back to my room in the late afternoon, I was feeling significantly more relaxed than I could remember feeling in the last few months. No, it wasn't just months; it had been years. I looked in the mirror, surprised to see my eyes were bright and clear. My face, with just a hint of today's sun, looked radiant and made my eyes stand out a vivid blue.

I sat on the comfy couch and grabbed my phone. I FaceTimed Ella, checking in and making sure she was okay at the house. Kate continued sending her wisdom via text messages, the latest advising sagely:

Abs, it's okay to sleep with more than one man on a holiday.
It won't mean you're slutty. Just don't forget to use
condoms if you have more than one partner.

Was everyone's sister like this? I suspected not. How many single men did she honestly think were at this resort? And why, pray, would a man want to sleep with me over a twenty-two-year-old cocktail waitress?

I rolled my shoulders and massaged the back of my neck to let go of the tension I was carrying. I was absolutely determined to use that bath before dinner. I ran it, hot and steamy, and sank into it, groaning in joy.

I had absolutely no desire to go to the dinner reservation, but I had agreed to, and the thought of ruining Oliver's work-experience was enough to have me applying my makeup. I unwound my hair from the tight braids I'd put in earlier, the relief on my skull immediate, and it fell into soft golden waves below my shoulders. I had given myself a stern talking-to in the bath, emotionally preparing for dining alone, a timely reminder that feminists had fought for my freedom to do so.

I rolled the dice with the gods of fabric stains, choosing a white dress to wear. *No red wine for you tonight, Abs.* The sleeveless dress had delicate embroidered tiny flowers, and ruffles on the shoulders. It fell just below my knees, and I paired it with some tan heels and a tan bag. The summeriness of the outfit made it look as though I holidayed more than once a decade.

I made my way down the swept footpath to the restaurant, feeling slightly proud that I did not rely on Google Maps or GPS to get me there. There were three restaurants on the island, but Oliver had told me specifically which one I needed to go to and I approached it curiously. It was a teak building that glowed with warm, welcoming light. Jazz hits played softly, the soulful music and décor giving the restaurant a *Casablanca* vibe which my grandmother would have adored. It smelled amazing and my belly rumbled. I had chosen to have another three drinks over any lunch today, meaning the surprise breakfast had been the only thing I had eaten. It was eight sharp, as directed, and I was starving.

'Madame.' The maître d' of the restaurant greeted me. He was a diminutive man with a pristine white shirt and spoke with a French accent.

'I'm Abbey Parker. I have a reservation at eight.'

'Excellent, madame. If you will take a seat here, we will wait for your partner and then we will seat you.'

I stared at the man in confusion. 'Oh, actually, I'm just by myself. The booking is for one.'

'It is Couples' Night at the restaurant, madame. There are no bookings for one.'

'Couples' Night?' I sounded alarmed, and a little grossed out.

'Yes. Romance. Love. You know this?' He looked at me as if

maybe I *didn't* know about love, to the point where I began to doubt I did, too.

'Look. I'm starving. I am not a couple, just seat me somewhere so I can eat.' I added a belated, 'Please?'

'Madame, by yourself you cannot have a table. The last thing a couple needs on Couples' Night is for a beautiful single woman to be in the restaurant. The husband might be looking at the beautiful single woman not *l'amour de sa vie.*'

I felt my fists clench. This guy was pissing me off. 'This is ridiculous.'

The host stood his ground.

'Look, I was part of a couple and, honestly, it wasn't that fantastic. Couples are significantly overrated. Now I insist you seat me.' I was oversharing, a clear sign of my stress, and I could feel I was about to make a scene, which was something I would not normally dream of doing in real life. Why would Oliver book me into a restaurant he knew I couldn't get into?

A couple entered behind me, and the host ignored me to get them seated. When he came back and saw me still standing there, he huffed his displeasure.

'Madame, we cannot seat you unless you are a couple. I suggest you go back to your room and order room service or try one of the other restaurants at the resort.'

I crossed my arms, ready to fire up at the man. 'Listen here, buddy –'

'Is there a problem?' a deep voice echoed behind me.

I turned around to see a tall man in a navy linen shirt and pants the colour of burnt caramel. The colours worked beautifully together, but because he was a man I suspected he had just thrown them on and hoped for the best, rather than making conscious choices. After taking in his outfit, my eyes drifted up his chest towards his face and my breath caught in my throat as I stared, open-mouthed, at my knight in shining armour, Sir Saviour. I felt the heat rise to my cheeks as images of our chests pressed together flooded back to me.

'It is Couples' Night, sir. No single diners allowed.' I could hear an apologetic tone in the maître d's voice, which differed from the tone he had taken with me.

I looked at the host closely, letting him know I was unimpressed.

The stranger, whose eyes, I realised, had not left me, which only caused my blush to deepen, turned suddenly back to the host allowing me time to get my breathing under control and attempt to get a normal colour back into my face.

'Ms …?' He looked back at me.

'Parker,' I offered, struggling to remember my name.

'Ms Parker will dine with me, Antoine.' He turned back to me. 'If that is all right, of course, Ms Parker?'

'Abbey. It's just Abbey.'

'Nicholas Northby,' he said in return. He held out a large hand.

I slid mine into his, ignoring the electrical volt that shot up my arm and landed in my gut. It was a good name. Still, I offered him an out. 'I don't require saving, Mr Northby.'

'Just Nick is fine, Abbey.' He paused and the ghost of a smile rearranged his face, lifting one side of his closed mouth, making me want to see him with a full smile. 'We both need to eat.'

As if on cue, my stomach piped in, grumbling loudly. 'Fine,' I said, resigned.

The small smile graced his closed lips again, and he nodded, satisfied. I followed the host and Nick moved through the restaurant close behind me, a hand on my lower back guiding me. The heat from his large hand radiated hot under my dress. The host led us through the restaurant to a table on the balcony. It had an unimpeded view of the ocean and, not only that, it was the only table *on* the balcony, so although it was Couples' Night, we were completely alone.

Nick held out a chair for me and by the time I had sat down, a waiter arrived with a bottle of champagne, pouring us two glasses. Nick waited silently until the man left. I used the time to study him, sober and in a better light than our previous meeting. His eyes weren't nearly as dark as I had thought. Instead, they were a very light brown, mossy and hazelnut in colour. His hair also surprised me with its slightly lighter shade. It had appeared black when wet last night, but now I could see it was actually brown with tawny highlights from the sun. He was tanned and very attractive, though perhaps not classically so.

'Thank you for dining with me. It would have been a lonely room service if you hadn't agreed, given that I do not qualify for Couples' Night. How is your holiday going?'

Jesus, his voice was lovely.

I threw my head back in the air and took a huge sigh. 'I feel' – I paused, deciding how honest I was going to be – 'like I'm having to try too hard to remind myself that I should enjoy it.' The admission came out way more honestly than I had intended, but somehow the honesty continued as I added, 'It also feels like it has been a long time since I relaxed and that I'm out of practice. Relaxing feels weird, out of character, I guess.'

He nodded slowly, and I could see my answer surprised him. He had probably been expecting me to gush about the resort or something.

'Do you have a busy life at home?' he asked.

'Yes. And yet compared to some, no. I have a child and a job. It's an unexciting life.'

'It's hard to be "exciting" when you're raising kids.'

I waited for him to elaborate, expecting details about his life, but he lifted his glass to his mouth and did not continue.

'So you're here by yourself as well?' I queried.

He nodded.

'How are you finding your holiday? Are you better at relaxing than I am?'

'It's been okay. Work follows me wherever I am and then I had to rescue a half-naked, drowning woman from the water last night, which was admittedly different from previous holidays I've had.' He said this quietly, a smile escaping his mouth.

I gave him a genuine laugh, and he laughed too, his face transformed. His smile was broad, and he looked like a little boy. *Okay, Nick is a certified hottie.*

'I didn't need rescuing,' I pointed out. 'I just needed to leave some shit I was carrying around in the ocean last night.' My honesty had overspilled again. I'm not sure what it was about him that made me expose myself so truthfully, but I decided to stop stressing about it.

'Did it work?' He leaned forward across the table, genuinely interested.

'Yes.' I took a large sip of champagne; the bubbles burned my throat a little.

His gaze was assessing me this time, as if he could tell my answer didn't ring true. 'I don't think it did work,' he said softly.

His ability to read me was unnerving. I had the sudden feeling of being naked in front of him. Again. I stopped breathing for a second under his intense gaze and felt heat flood my cheeks once more. But if he noticed my discomfort, he didn't say so.

'Shall we order?' he asked.

'Okay,' I managed lamely. I picked up the leather-clad menu, fanned myself twice, and then opened it. My mouth instantly watered as I remembered my hunger. 'I'm starving. Do you feel like sharing an entrée?'

'Sure, the tuna carpaccio is good.'

'Ooh, that sounds great. I'll have the seared fish curry for a main.' I looked briefly at my white dress and prayed to the stain gods.

'Perfect. Are you okay if I pick a wine?'

'That'd be great.'

The wine when it arrived was beyond delicious, grassy and zesty. The food came quickly too; I was super impressed with the service here. The tuna was fresh and utter perfection, only topped by the seared fish in the coconut curry and served with flaky flatbread. It was exquisite, piping hot and tasted amazing. I ate everything on my plate and may have groaned several times over the meal, not particularly caring what Nick thought about it.

We finished the first bottle with the entrée, and he ordered a different wine for the main. Our conversation flowed through dinner. He seemed to relax after his second glass of wine. I had offered up my whole life: daughter, sister, grandmother, ex-husband. I told him I'd honeymooned in the Maldives but at a different resort, and then finally he gave me something of himself.

'I come here every year.'

'To this resort?'

'Yes. My mother brought me here when I was a child.'

'Do you ever get tired of coming here? Maybe you should do something else next year? We have great beaches in Australia.'

He grinned at me. 'I have been to Australia many times.'

'Ooh, were you a posh backpacker at some point? Maybe we kissed in the nineties?'

'No.' He laughed, and I liked the lines that appeared around his eyes and the dimples that flashed at me. 'I'd have remembered.'

By the end of the meal, I realised I was having an amazing night.

Inside the restaurant, Couples' Night was in full swing. They had pushed back several of the tables and dropped the lights to mostly just candlelight. Music had started and a bunch of couples were dancing to a playlist that seemed composed of a Google search on the best songs to dance to on a date, which, naturally, included Ed Sheeran.

Nick stood up and held out his hand. 'I'd like to dance with you.'

His manner of speaking, I'd noticed through the course of dinner, was sometimes formal, direct and carried authority. Sometimes it almost sounded like a challenge; him testing the boundaries of how far we could both push this accidental date, his tone checking in with me, an eyebrow rising. I always had a choice and there was something about that which felt safe, as if he was someone you could put your faith in.

'I don't want to be around couples,' I said. There was no way on this earth I wanted to dance to Ed Sheeran next to people who loved each other.

'Ah, a couple-phobe like me. We can just dance here.'

As if someone was hovering, listening to his every word, two waiters came and removed our table and chairs. Nick rescued the bottle of wine and our glasses before they vanished. *Hero complex.*

I finished my glass after taking it from his hand, having enjoyed the contact as our fingers grazed (regency-romance novel-esque). I set it down on the deck in the corner and then moved towards him. The song playing was Chris Isaak's 'Wicked Game'. *Of course it was.* My arm slid around his narrow waist, and I pressed my thumb into his side. He smelled amazing. I picked up herbal and citrus scents, but just his skin smelled great. Even in my heels, I only made it up to his chest, which was as solid as I remembered it being last night. I knew what was under that navy linen, and it thrilled me.

His hand pressed me from behind, moving me even closer, as his thumb grazed the exposed skin of my back. That tiny amount of skin-on-skin contact had me drawing an audible sharp breath, and I felt my body press into him further. His other hand had linked our fingers while we swayed, but he let my hand go, running a single finger up my arm, causing goosebumps to appear in its wake. It moved over my shoulder, continuing to my chin, where he tilted it up so that I was looking at him. His eyes were shining in the light and there was a heat in them that my body seemed to respond to. I had the desire to surrender to him completely.

'This is a nice dress,' he said simply.

'Thank you,' I managed, hoarsely. I hadn't danced with a guy since my wedding day; it was intimate and romantic as hell, and I felt as if I was in a Taylor Swift song. I surrendered to the music and the moment, winding my arm up around his neck and running my fingers through the soft wavy hair at the nape of it. I caught the scent of his shampoo, which may have been the origin of the citrusiness about him.

He leaned his chin into my temple, tucking his head so his mouth rested against my ear, his breathing heavy. My body was reacting with pure desire, something I barely recognised. An overwhelming need to feel his lips against mine overcame me. I wanted that and so much more. Gone was the lukewarm desire that had plagued my marriage – this was searing heat and the urge to give in to it was strong.

Was I the kind of woman who slept with a man on the second night of a holiday? Maybe when I was twenty, before Peter. I was once someone who could make decisions about the opposite sex with spontaneity and casualness. Memories of nightclubs, being pressed against walls, and hot random strangers came to me. The taste of Midori, the sweat from dancing. I moved my body closer to him and his fingers dug further into my side.

The other thing in my mind, though, was that this clearly attractive man could have anyone. He did not need to get involved with a mum in her forties. He could have any woman on this island, someone whose body was firm and fresh, someone who did not have hangups or baggage. Someone not trying to remember who the fuck they were.

The song finished and faded into another, and I pulled back from him a little, trying to clear my thoughts by putting some distance between my body and his. It was hard to think straight in his arms with his intoxicating scent around me.

'Can I walk you back to your room?' he asked with no hint of innuendo, just pleasant manners. 'I think it's right next to mine.'

'Okay. Can we walk by the water?'

He nodded and then we both sat on the edge of the balcony and slid off our shoes before stepping down onto the sand, which was a little cooler tonight. Or maybe the sand wasn't cooler, and it was just that I was so full of heat that it didn't feel as warm as my raging, internal temperature.

We strolled in companionable silence along the beach. He took my hand as my legs tired and led me further towards the wet sand, which was easier to walk on. The water touched our toes. I didn't relinquish his hand.

'Are you planning a naked drunk swim tonight, followed by an outdoor shower?' he asked in a complete deadpan.

'Not this evening. Maybe tomorrow night though,' I replied, and shot him an enormous, dazzling smile.

'I'll make sure I'm free.'

'I can pretend to drown again if you have to fulfil your hero complex?'

'That's exceedingly kind of you.'

'This is me.' I pointed my shoes towards my room.

He mirrored me, pointing to the room next door. 'And that's me.'

'Thank you for dinner. Oh, hey, we didn't figure out how much I owe you. I'll transfer you some cash.'

'You can shout the next one.'

We divided off, our hands reluctant to release each other, holding on for as long as possible.

'Goodnight, Abbey.'

'Night, Nick.'

Inside my room, I collapsed on the bed with a massive grin on my face. What was it about attraction that made you feel like a teenager?

When I finally moved, there was a note from Oliver telling me what time to be at the dock for the trip to the private island. *Still no couples,* it read.

Nick

I stood in the doorway for a long time. I heard her move about her room for a few minutes before she went to bed. It was difficult to comprehend what had just happened. It had felt like a date. But I did not, as a rule, date. Ever.

I could not remember the last time I'd had a nice evening with a stranger over a shared meal. The last ten years, I'd avoided this exact scenario countless times.

There was just something about Abbey. She was unexpected.

Chief among the things I found desirable was that she didn't seem to care what I thought of her. She had this attitude that she was who she was. There was a lack of care to impress me. It was extremely attractive. So was she. She was funny and warm and really,

really sexy. She'd offered me her vulnerability and her bravado in the same breath.

I'd very much wanted to run my hands through her hair, which fell in Disney mermaid waves tonight. I'd very much wanted to slide that strap off her shoulder and look at all the delights that had been pressed against me the night before.

And I'd had a nice time. Would a holiday romance be so bad? It didn't mean white picket fences. There was an endpoint. Rules. Perhaps that was something I could commit to.

Chapter Three
Abbey

Another perfect day greeted me. *God, I love it here.* I had taken the time to tick the little boxes on the room-service menu for an early breakfast of fruit and coffee, and gave myself a huge pat on the back when it arrived.

What did one wear to a private island? I had no fucking idea, so I put my bikini on under cream shorts and a lightweight black shirt. I grabbed the cute, black linen beach bag I had bought for this holiday and packed the essentials: sunscreen, towel, sunglasses and, most importantly, book. I put on a hat before heading to the dock.

As I walked, panic filled my chest about the impending boat ride. My boat stress had started when I was a child. Kate and I had been shoved off to our Uncle Joe's for the day. Uncle Joe wasn't our uncle, he was a friend of the family who would take care of us occasionally when Mum needed a break. Our father ran his own business and was never home. Uncle Joe (balding, gay, optimist) and his boyfriend Aaron (sensible, charming, not bald) decided to take me (nine) and Kate (five) fishing. Mum had jokingly said, 'Don't drown,' as we left.

Uncle Joe, always easily distracted and never the best of

babysitters, had allowed us to go on the boat by ourselves. We were in the middle of the lake in the national park when Kate had stood suddenly, thinking she had seen a fish over the edge. She'd pointed, excited, before losing her balance and had gone in headfirst. I remembered the day with a clarity that only came from being traumatised. I could not remember feeling panicked, at all, because in hindsight I had basically been waiting for this to happen, an inevitability in my mind since Mum's prophetic remark when Uncle Joe had first uttered the words 'fishing in a lake'. Without thinking, I had stood on the edge of the boat, completed a safety dive, and then pulled my sister up out of the water. By the time we reached the surface, Aaron had reached us and we were both lifted to safety. Logically, I should have an issue with Kate and not boats, but here we were.

When I saw the boat that was going to take me to the island, my flight instinct kicked in. I verbalised it strongly in my head and out loud.

'Oh, *nope.*'

The 'captain', who looked to be approximately sixteen, just stared at me. The boat was significantly smaller than any boat taking people anywhere had a right to be. Also, it was wooden. *Shouldn't boats be made from something else these days?* I had no idea what said material would be, but it almost certainly should have been significantly sturdier than *wood*.

Since laying eyes on the so-called boat, I had not moved an inch from the dock where I was standing, safely on land. My body, whilst not exactly happy with this arrangement, was making it clear to me it was damned well not going to be moving any closer.

In my peripheral vision, I caught a flash of white. When I turned, I saw Nick Northby coming down the dock. He looked as if he was in a film clip, or he was Tom Cruise's best mate in some action movie; sunglasses on, backpack slid over his shoulder and his random curls flipping haphazardly over his face.

'Private island?' he asked, offering me a smile. I could see my somewhat pale reflection in the black of his Ray Bans. He wore a white linen shirt that covered his slim figure, and his legs were clad in pink floral boardies that clung to his thighs. I could not imagine another man I knew pulling off those shorts, but this guy, well, the man was beautiful.

'Yes.' I was annoyed my voice sounded a little shaky. I raised an eyebrow above my sunglasses. 'I have a pushy private valet.'

'Me too,' he said, grinning. 'He's annoying as fuck.'

I smirked.

He climbed on the boat so effortlessly that my brain could not compute how he had achieved it. My feet, meanwhile, had not budged an inch.

He turned when I didn't follow him, dropping his backpack and leaning over the side, offering me a large hand, an amused expression gracing his handsome face.

'I don't like boats. I know it's irrational, or maybe it's rational because it could sink. I have a little girl. I'd rather not die.' I swallowed and pointed an accusing finger at the captain. 'This guy doesn't look old enough to work at McDonald's. And this boat looks like the SS *Minnow*.'

He laughed at the *Gilligan's Island* reference, which I appreciated, before he said, 'Everyone is afraid of something, Abbey. I'll be here. I'll look after you.'

I think if someone else had said that to me, I might have thought it was arrogant, a little presumptuous, but on him it came off as calm, common sense. It was just a rendition of Grandma Iris's *Stop being feeble, Abbey*, and before I knew it my clammy hand stretched out, grabbing his dry, cool one.

He pulled me gently into the boat, taking my bag off me with the hand I wasn't clinging to, placing it gently beside his backpack. He guided me to a standing position near the rear of the boat where there was a waist-height edge, placed my hips against the barrier, and then wrapped his body behind me. A strong arm came around my waist, allowing me to grip the railing with a white-knuckled hold, but not before I had run my hand down the strength of his forearms.

As the boat chugged away from the dock, he removed my hat, so it didn't fly away, handing it to one of the boat crew, then he popped his chin over my shoulder. 'See, I have you. I promise I won't let go.'

That sounded, frankly, heavenly, and I remained (tensely) in his arms for the brief journey to the island. Keeping his word, he did not move and instead kept up a steady stream of conversation, pointing out landmarks and distant resorts.

'Do you have a swimsuit on under that?' he asked when the boat had stopped.

I nodded.

'All right, let's get you undressed. We need to jump into the water and walk the rest of the way. Okay? These guys will bring over our bags and our lunch on the dinghy.'

I looked at him with terrified acceptance.

'At least you get to leave the boat.' He shrugged and smiled.

Good point. I nodded again. I was able to get my shorts down without losing touch with the side railing, but my shirt buttons were a two-handed job, and I could not let go.

He unbuttoned his shirt, folding it neatly into his backpack. Then he grabbed my shorts, folded them, and walked back to me. 'Do you need help with your shirt?'

I nodded.

He stepped closer to me, toe to toe, before nimbly undoing my buttons. He lifted his eyes to mine as he got to my chest, keeping his hands a polite distance from my boobs. A finger grazed over my necklace, though, and he studied it while I studied him.

That rocky-riverbed colour of his eyes was so light today they were bordering grey-green.

Underneath my shirt was my bikini, a pair of high briefs and a crop top in a burgundy, which my sister told me flattered pale skin. His eyes lingered briefly, and I saw him swallow.

'Do you have sunscreen on?' he asked.

'Yes, Dad.'

My sassy comment came with a very watery smile, which produced that small one of his, barely changing his face. He reached for my hand, leading me to the ladder on the boat. Keeping hold of it, he climbed down into waist-height water, ordering me to sit so he didn't have to relinquish me, and then I followed him.

The minute I was in the water, I felt my shoulders relax and I let go of the death grip I had on his fingers. 'Thank you,' was all I could mumble.

'No problem. Hero complex,' he said, smirking at me.

The clear turquoise water was heavenly. I could see schools of fish swimming alongside us and a couple of stingrays dancing through the water. The shore was not far off. A strip of sandy beach surrounded a mass of tropical-looking trees so thick it almost looked like a mini rainforest.

Behind me, the sound of the boat's motor kicked in and they drove off. I had a slight panic.

'Where are they going?'

'Just around to the other side of the island. We can walk.'

'You've done this before?'

'Yes,' he said, but did not elaborate.

He was quite the man of mystery, not offering up information unless directly questioned. I held on to the questions that I wanted to pepper him with, for now, acknowledging that part of my interest in Nick was the intrigue of him. I was already realising he was someone who opened up slowly, and I was well aware that, with only two weeks here, it was unlikely I was ever going to 'know' know him.

We climbed most of the way out of the water until it was just at our ankles and then we began walking around the island, pointing out tropical fish to each other. We got to a particular spot he had said he was looking for, although I could not see any landmarks indicating it was important. We must then have walked for maybe another ten or fifteen minutes inland. He helped me over a couple of rocky sections, holding my hand. We walked until I could hear the patter of running water, when we suddenly came upon a waterfall running into a turquoise-green lagoon. It was exquisite.

He scrambled off a rock into a clearing and then reached up for me, letting me slide down his body before setting me on the sand. I didn't move away from him, instead just standing in his strong arms, braced against his hip.

He stepped back though, and I hastily busied myself looking around, not quite sure what to make of him pulling away. Was he feeling awkward? Or just being gentlemanly? You could never tell with the British.

There was no sign of the boat kids, but our bags had already been dropped off and a small table with two dining chairs was set up beside the water. A white styrofoam esky was next to the table and Nick made himself busy pulling out drinks. He handed me a small bottle of water, and we both drank thirstily, before he popped the cork on the champagne bottle and poured two cold glasses.

I was already fluttery in the stomach from the boat ride and, honestly, just being near him, but when our fingers grazed as he handed me a glass, heat surged through me somewhere very low and I downed the champagne with complete disregard for the quality of the wine, which again tasted expensive and delicious. I just needed to take the edge off. My nerves and my desire were combining to make me feel increasingly strange.

I held up my empty glass, and he chuckled at me.

'Bloody Aussies,' he said under his breath.

'Oh, excuse me, sir, from the mother country,' I said poshly, before switching back to the common little Australian I was. 'Just fucking top me up.'

He smirked, downed the rest of his glass, and refilled them both, his eyes crinkling as he laughed.

'My hero,' I said softly, batting my eyelashes at him.

He shook his head, smiling at the sarcasm.

'Wow, it is really beautiful here,' I said, finally dragging my eyes from the beauty in front of me and acknowledging the surrounds. I had never been in a lagoon before, or under a waterfall. 'Are there any crocodiles or anything?'

'No. It is completely safe. Unlike holidaying in Australia, which – as the rest of the world knows – is fraught with danger.'

'A little danger is good for the soul.'

'Pfft. You are full of shit.'

'Fine. I'm *told* danger is good for the soul.' I snorted and finished my second glass. 'You coming in? I mean, I have had two glasses of wine, so anything could happen to me unless a man is on hand.'

He flashed a sardonic smile. I waited while he finished his drink and then we walked to the edge together and dived in.

'Let's go under the waterfall,' I said with the excitement of an eight-year-old. 'I've never done that before.'

I swam until I got to the edge of the waterfall, which was

violently loud up close, and I reached out, feeling the force of it pound against my hand, before swimming behind it. I found a rock ledge, conveniently made by nature, for us to sit on. I did a quick risk assessment of my ability to get on and off it, and then, using my hands, feet and knees, I climbed up out of the water. It was breathtaking and louder than a nightclub in there. I felt my spirit soar, a sense of adventure coursing through my veins.

Nick swam straight under the waterfall and, in a move that can only be described as incredibly hot, used his chiselled arms to effortlessly leverage himself out of the water in one fluid motion to sit down next to me on the ledge. He pushed back his hair, scrunching his fingers in it to get the water out and give it a tousled perfection he seemed unaware of. His body was lean and strong. There were abs, but they weren't made with protein shakes or twice-daily gym sessions. Everything about him was natural, quiet, elegant and strong. He was beautiful.

I sat on my hands to stop myself from reaching out inappropriately. I looked up into his eyes, only to find them already locked on me. He moved his focus down to my lips and leaned tentatively towards me, giving me ample time to pull away before pressing the sweetest, gentlest kiss on me. Both of his hands reached for my jaw, keeping me where I was, and he grazed my lips in short kisses, his lips persistent, sometimes lingering for a second longer to tug at one of mine.

Those micro kisses were driving me wild. I reached for his angular jaw to gain some control. He opened his mouth to me, letting me explore him, deepening the kiss. His tongue tasted like a heady combination of champagne and salt water. I sighed into the kiss and felt his mouth move into a smile against mine. My mouth responded to mirror him.

I don't know when I stopped enjoying kissing in my relationship, but I had not felt like this since Peter and I had first met and, even then, I'm not certain it had felt like this. I could have kissed Nick all day.

But my body was not listening to that thought, at all. It wanted more from him, and I fought the urge to straddle him on the rock after his hand started exploring my exposed skin. First, I was a little overwhelmed that our flirty heat had turned into heat-heat so fast. Second, I was not prepared to have sex on this rock. Sex in nature was always much better in theory than reality. I also wasn't one-hundred-per-cent confident there weren't snakes around, of the animal variety.

I kissed his mouth again, then reluctantly withdrew. 'I need to eat,' I said, diving under the water before he could talk me into staying. I swam back to the beach.

I was dried off, unpacking lunch supplies, before he left the lagoon. His desire under the waterfall had been evident, and the time he had taken to collect himself was flattering.

I flicked my circular towel down on the sand and topped up our glasses, using the lid of the esky to balance them on. Lunch was a delicious cold lobster salad, packed into dry ice to keep cool. It was perfect in the heat of the day, and we were silent as we took our first few bites, sitting cross-legged, knee to knee, like children.

'I love holidays,' I said, waving my fork around at our surrounds. 'They are freeing. You can literally be whoever you want to be.' Though weirdly, I felt more myself than I had in years. 'Or you can convince yourself that you can do anything.'

'What can you do on holidays that you can't do normally?' he said, sitting forward, interested in my philosophy. 'What personality traits change for you?'

I started a list, counting them off on my fingers. 'Well, I'm starting to relax. I can feel it in my shoulders and neck. Even after the boat! On holidays I eat with reckless abandon.' I pointed to the demolished salad and licked the finger I held out, which was covered in dressing. 'I drink with reckless abandon.' I finished my glass of bubbles and held it up. Then I met his eyes. 'On holidays, I swim topless under the moonlight and get rescued by gorgeous men.'

He grinned at that.

'On holidays I have a personal valet, who's a little overfamiliar and really, very bossy.'

He snorted, and I watched delighted as his proper smile emerged and lit up his face. He shook his gorgeous head, his hair doing miraculous things.

Moving onto my other hand, I continued. 'On holidays I'm not a mum whose husband of thirteen years left her after meeting the love of his life at work.'

He looked at me with that searching, piercing look.

'And maybe I'm someone who can sleep with someone without having feelings attached, because it's all going to end anyway,' I finished softly, looking into his eyes. I took another bite of my salad as he refilled my glass. 'So, what about Nick Northby? Does he change on holidays?'

He started a list of his own. 'On holidays I'm someone who eats and drinks with reckless abandon,' he said.

I raised an eyebrow at him.

'Okay, okay. On holidays I worry less about the people I'm responsible for.'

This insight felt as if it was a gift for how honest I had been so far. I smiled in gratitude.

Warming to it, he kept going. 'On holidays, I can forget that I have chosen a career over so many other things in life. I can kiss a beautiful woman under a waterfall.'

Our eyes met and the look he gave me made me feel exposed.

'On holidays, I can pretend I'm the kind of man who could fall in love.'

Ha! *Oh, here we go.* Typical men. This is what I had to look forward to as a single woman. I put down my salad and fork. 'You can't fall in love in real life, or you choose not to?'

He shook his head. 'Both.'

'Wow. I feel like if we spend more time together, I am definitely going to want to unpack that.'

He reached across and kissed me again, in a delicious lobstery, champagney kiss. 'Say you'll have dinner with me tonight?'

'I don't want to be around couples.'

'Christ, me neither. Come to my room. We'll get room service.'

My heart thumped a little at this proposition. The inevitability of what having 'dinner' in his room would mean. *What the hell, Abs. You're forty-two, single, bangable, distinctly not feeble and – fuck – you are on holiday and a gorgeous man wants to have sex with you.* I steeled myself. 'Okay,' I said, as casually as I could.

I showered and dressed carefully, my floral dress tied at the shoulder, which I suspected was as close to sexy an outfit I had here. I put on my black bikini underneath, just in case we swam. Also, I did not own lingerie as such. I had bras and knickers, but my underwear was serviceable, not sexy.

I stood outside his door, debating on knocking or running for a full minute. My arm decided for me, giving a sharp double knock, and then my hand flew to my necklace to fidget with. I took a deep breath to combat my weird, nervous giddiness.

Nick opened the door, and I had the briefest acknowledgement that he looked incredible in a plain black T-shirt before he launched his lips at mine, his hand finding its spot on my jaw, guiding me safely to his mouth.

Once I was kissing him back with the same enthusiasm, unsurprisingly straight away, he dropped his hands to my hips, attaching them to his and then walked backwards, allowing the heavy door to close. He used the same method to guide me back against the closed door.

I tried to formulate cohesive thoughts underneath his ministrations, but his passion was so thorough that none came to me, and I let go of control, surrendering to my desire for him.

His mouth inched down my neck. He stopped for a second, finding my eyes. My chest was heaving, and my half-lidded eyes opened because he had stopped.

'Abbey.' He whispered my name like a fucking benediction. 'Is this okay?'

'Is it okay?' I was confused. I was almost certain my hands were gripping his T-shirt, holding onto him with enough force to ensure he couldn't remove his body from mine if he tried. But then my head caught up. The times had changed. I had to consent in more than one way. 'Yes,' I replied.

'I have been thinking about kissing you again all afternoon.'

He rubbed his thumb against my lip, and I took it between my teeth and let my tongue roll over it, earning a low sound from him that might have been a growl. This time it was me who launched my lips at him. He took his time now, exploring my mouth, his hands running down my side. He grabbed the back of my hip and pulled me into him, letting me feel him hard against me. *Good God.* He walked me backwards again, further into his suite.

I opened my eyes as his kisses moved down my neck and saw a long lounge room that had enormous sliding doors leading to a private pool. The actual bedroom part was familiar, set up very similarly to my room next door, the same white, light-diffusing curtains fluttering. But here there was an unimpeded view of the point of the island. It was breathtaking.

I pulled at Nick's T-shirt, got it off and then ran my hands confidently down his chest, as though touching random men was something I did often. He made short work of the ties at the top of my dress, and it fell into a pool of mixed colours at my feet.

His lips moved down to my collarbone and I moaned his name when his tongue touched the hollow of my throat. His hands were expertly undoing the butterfly clasp on my bikini top, my brain registering that this was clearly not his first rodeo with the tricky clasp. The minute it was off, his hands were all over me, feeling the swell of my breasts and licking, sucking and pinching at my nipples.

'Abbey.'

He was so intense and just so fucking hot. I reached for his stomach and then lower, feeling his erection through his shorts. He felt so hard. Jesus, I wanted him so badly; I started pushing impatiently at his shorts. He pressed me back and my knees bent when I hit the edge of the bed. I lay back on it. He shook his head and gave me a quick smile, but that was quickly replaced with a dark, worshipful look at my body. He slid down my bikini bottoms, lifting my knees. He kneeled and rained kisses along my legs until his tongue found a molten, soft core. I was so wet … it had been almost twenty years since I was this turned on. He used his mouth and fingers, expertly moving until I screamed his name and lifted myself further into his mouth as I came.

He reached over to the bedside and grabbed a condom out of the drawer. He rolled it down his length and entered me, filling me, before my breathing had regulated. I kissed him again, tasting myself on his mouth. Whispering his name, holding his hips, surrendering to him with an abandon I barely recognised.

His lips were everywhere, his hands all over me, the sensations completely overwhelming and delicious. His teeth grazed my earlobe, and he said my name –'beautiful Abbey' – as if he was praying to some divine goddess. He felt so good inside me, I didn't want it to ever end. Our two bodies made perfect sense together.

I felt him tense and his breathing change, his fingers digging into my hip as he surged within me.

Gradually he caught his breath, with his nose in my hair, bracing his weight so he did not squish me. He pressed a kiss into my neck before finally withdrawing. His eyes met mine, and he gave me an awed, assessing stare, as if he was trying to figure out exactly what was happening between us. I held his gaze, offering a small smile, feeling slightly self-conscious for the first time with him.

Nick smiled, and a breath came through his nose. He kissed me again with those short kisses I could not get enough of and then added one to my forehead, which lingered, before he got up.

He busied himself cleaning up and there was a knock on the door, a familiar voice calling out room service. I was naked, still on the bed, unable to move. My thighs were still quivering from the intensity of the second orgasm I'd just had. Nick shut the bedroom door to give me some privacy while he opened the room's door to Oliver.

Jesus. It's been a while, Abs. I stretched like a satisfied cat, a huge grin on my face, my hand shooting up to cover the squeal of joy that wanted to erupt. Holiday sex was *amazing*. Then I bounced up and pulled on my dress, not bothering with my bikini. I used Nick's ensuite and then slipped into the lounge area, which was massive, spacious, utter perfection.

Oliver looked up, noticing me, and the flitter of a smile crossed his face. 'Ms Parker,' he said quietly in greeting as Nick signed for the bill.

'It's just Abbey, Oliver. Jesus, please tell me you haven't signed me up for activities tomorrow.' I grinned at him.

'No,' he said, quietly amused, giving a snort of laughter. 'I hope you enjoyed the island, though.'

'I did,' I said. Nick looked up at this and smiled at me, and I almost tripped over. Something in my stomach did an impressive flip.

'Good evening then,' Oliver said. He smiled outright as he left the room.

'Drink?' Nick said.

'I'm parched.'

He poured me a huge glass of red wine, handed it to me and then, taking my hand, led me to the pool. Pulling at the ties of my dress, I watched his breath catch when he realised I was naked underneath. He climbed in first, sitting down on a step. As I walked in, he pulled me onto his lap, wrapping his arm around my waist.

My body, full of surprises this evening, startled me again when I relaxed back into Nick and for a few moments we sat, simply watching the ocean and the stars.

He kissed my back, sweeping aside my hair to give him better access to my neck. 'You are very unexpected, Abigail Parker.'

I shot him a grin over my shoulder, and he kissed my lips.

'How was your holiday today?' he asked.

'Significantly improved. I think I'm getting better at it,' I said confidently, before adding, 'I have ... never had a holiday romance before.'

'Holiday romances are good. They have end dates, rules everyone is aware of. No heartbreak. Just fond memories.'

I thought it was interesting that he was setting boundaries with this statement. I mean, I knew one night in paradise did not mean happily ever after and I don't think I believed in love over forty, anyway. Plus there was the glaring issue that we lived on the other side of the world from one another.

'Did you get this suite on Groupon, like I got mine?' I asked, turning back to him.

He paused, bemused. 'Umm. No.'

'It's very nice.'

He nodded and then returned to kissing my neck, pressing his lips into my jaw and occasionally letting his tongue sweep across my skin. I let out an involuntary sigh, which made him smile. His hand rose from my waist, between my breasts, and he touched the necklace around my throat. 'This is beautiful. It looks art deco.'

'It's my grandmother's. Her name is Iris Cavendish, she's a character. She's ninety-four and has had seven husbands!'

'Wait, people get married more than once?' he said with pretend astonishment.

'Husband number seven, Giovanni, passed away several years ago. Her first husband, Ray, bought this for her in London after the war. Also, after my grandfather, Harry, husband number two and Ray's best mate' – I paused for effect – 'she never changed her name again.'

'My goodness, she must be some kind of woman.'

'Mm-hm. She has spent years telling my sister and me that all Cavendish women are spectacular mates and lovers. But I am almost divorced, and Kate is single, so I'm not sure. Love over forty seems unattainable to me, though Gran had three husbands after she turned forty and she married Giovanni when she was eighty-three.'

'Wow, that is fantastic. Is she done? Or is husband number eight still to come?'

'Well, I'm not certain because there is this old guy, Lionel, at her nursing home. Lionel has a pink rose delivered to her each pension day.'

'Bloody hell. Those are some decent moves, Lionel.' He gave me one of his rare laughs. 'Okay, Abigail Parker, tell me three more things about yourself that you haven't already.'

'Three? Well, I told you I have a little girl. Her name is Ella. Nick, she's amazing, she just doesn't see it yet. She has decided this year that she wants to be a surgeon and work in an ER.' I paused, considering the next one. 'Umm, oh, I know, I've worked for the same guy for twenty years. He retired before I went away and now I'm a little bit panicked by the future.' I considered the last one. 'Christmas is my favourite time of the year. Ella and I line up a classic film each day we can. We play carols in the car for the entire month. If I could put up a Christmas tree and start playing carols in November, I would.'

'Urgh, Jesus, a whole month of Christmas carols?' He shook his head, laughing at me, and I got the impression it sounded like his worst nightmare.

'Why do you think you can't fall in love in the real world?' I really should have asked Nick to tell me three things about himself because getting information out of him was difficult. It was as if that expression about getting blood from a stone had been made just for him. But my question had been on my mind since he'd uttered that sentence on the island. I'll admit I also intentionally asked it suddenly, hoping to catch him off guard.

He swallowed, and I felt the tension in his jaw next to my head.

'I don't know. Trust.' He took a breath, and it seemed as if it hurt him. 'Faith. Control. I wouldn't want to love someone so much that if something happened, I couldn't recover.'

'That seems like a pretty fatalistic view.'

'Life doesn't always work out the way you think it will.' He said this without emotion, like someone who had learned hard life lessons. 'Now, stop talking and turn around.' His voice had turned seductive and chocolatey, but it was still commanding.

'You are very bossy.' I stood as directed and turned to face him, straddling his legs.

He wrapped a hand around the back of my neck, holding my gaze. His eyes glittered. He was so … smouldery.

'Are you hungry?'

'Is that a euphemism?'

'Ha. Noooo, but I wish it was now.'

'I'm always hungry,' I said.

'Well, I'm going to feed you and, if you like your dinner, maybe you'll think about staying the night?'

'Well, I have to sleep somewhere, I guess.'

He kissed me reverently, pulling me into his chest, and I felt desire stir again, so I pressed myself into him further. He pulled away from me suddenly.

'Just so we're clear, sleeping has nothing to do with what I am thinking of.'

I laughed – a throaty, feline sound I could not ever remember hearing from myself – and then kissed him with enthusiasm. It had been an age since I felt sexy or desired. I liked the feeling very much. I liked Nick Northby even more.

We dried off, heading back into the lounge. Dinner was in a warming-cupboard contraption that was a part of the trolley, which turned into a dining table. Nick whipped it out with great fanfare, doing an excellent impression of Antoine in the restaurant, which had me in fits of giggles. There were tender slices of steak covered in salsa verde, there were sweet potato fries and a simple rocket, pear and parmesan salad. He poured us out another glass of Shiraz each.

Later that night, he took me to bed and we took our time. He looked into my eyes and told me again how he had not expected me, that I was beautiful. I breathed breathy smiles into his unshaven cheek, marvelling at our bodies and the feelings we were both able to give and take. We fell asleep fitfully, tucked into each other.

We spent the rest of my holiday together, holding one another's hands, staring into one another's eyes, moving in unison, answering for one another, constantly in contact – just like one of those annoying couples you see on holidays.

Nick

I felt the emptiness of the room after Abbey had left. I could still smell her.

Earlier, I had taken her to the airport and brushed away her tears as we said goodbye and then watched from the terminal as she walked to the plane.

My heart was being traitorous. It ached for her. Nick Northby didn't do things like this. He didn't date random women he met on holiday. He certainly did not develop feelings for them. It was a holiday romance, and it was over.

It was time to get back to work; to focus my mind on the one thing I was good at. The company was where I found the structure and endless hours to fill my time. I had inherited it from my mum and in the time I'd been at its helm it had grown exponentially.

A therapist once told me that I could not continue to use the business to provide me with the tools to ignore any emotional crisis I experienced. She was so wrong.

I closed my eyes, taking one last lungful of Abbey's scent. Her image appeared, her blonde hair caught in the warm breeze, her oceanic-blue eyes. I had become addicted to her, that's all it was. Abbey was all easy smiles, self-deprecating humour and honesty. God, she did not give a fuck about what I thought about her. Why was that so appealing?

We had had plenty of conversations, getting to know one another, but none of them had focused on work … ever. She had never pressed me for details, always happy just to let me unfold in my own time. I told her I owned a company, a family business. She told me she was an executive assistant. Every day I waited for the questions that inevitably would come from women about what I did for a living, the size of the company and how much money I had. Abbey Parker never asked me anything remotely like that. Abbey did not see the business. She seemed to only see me.

She'd told me that she did not use social media. I knew this was true because it was absolutely clear she had not googled me. Abbey had said that she thought life was better without it. She was a teenager in the nineties and deeply wished she could return to 1996 when the world was a better place and people didn't stare at their phones constantly. I'd told her I thought that was naïve, and she had giggled at me. Every time I'd picked up my phone, she'd said, 'Put your fucking phone down, Nick.'

I will admit, I was going to miss her. But I did not make plans to see her, even though I knew we would be in the same city next week. If I saw her, I would want to be around her, I would want to hear her laugh, I would want to touch her hair, my body would crave her. I needed to not see her, to protect her, to protect myself.

There were two types of people in the world: people who respected boundaries and people who didn't. Abbey respected boundaries, but she had this way of cruising past mine. As though they were invisible to her. Everyone else saw the clear, unmountable walls I had built.

It was a holiday romance, a great holiday romance, and now it was over. Time to get back to work. Time to get back to reality.

Chapter Four
Abbey

Home. The holiday joy had left me by the time I came into the arrivals gate at Sydney Airport. My tears started at the sight of my daughter and sister. Ella was ginormous, having somehow grown several inches in two weeks. There they stood, my little family, holding a handmade, glittery, cardboard 'Welcome Home' sign.

Ella, seeing me crying, burst into tears herself and ran to hug me. I could not remember a hug that huge from her since she was four, and I felt the loss of the little girl she once was, who had been replaced by this teenager. Kate joined in a second later, throwing her arms around us. My sister looked at me closely and then took pity on my fragility by bundling us all into my white Toyota Corolla and getting us home to our shared house in the not-quite inner-city suburb of Tempe.

I had an overwhelming joy flare up from being in my house. Being home. After Peter had left, I became obsessed with making it a place that reflected me. We'd started outside, ripping out the English cottage garden, which my mother-in-law, Henrietta, had planted. Neither Peter nor I enjoyed gardening and so the entry always looked like shit. Kate had sensibly selected some agaves, succulents and plants that could handle the pollution and saltiness of Sydney air, without needing anything from us but a once-a-week water, which was about the only kind of commitment I was prepared to make with a plant. The garden looked chic now – and, okay, my renovation commitments had eventually stopped, mostly because I could not afford them – but standing outside it, the place really did feel like mine, and not mine and Pete's.

I walked arm in arm with Ella. Kate carried my bag inside and then topped the list of my favourite people ever by pouring me a massive glass of red wine. I dumped my suitcase onto my bedroom floor. The room was exactly as it had been when Pete lived here and, returning to it after a break, I suddenly felt within myself that the time had come to change that, as a massive priority. Being with Nick these past two weeks had taught me that I wanted someone in my life, eventually. And that meant letting go of the past.

I fished the small presents I'd brought back with me out of my bag. And when I say small, I mean small – the Maldives had what they had. I had come home with a seashell bracelet for Ella and a rock painted with a beach scene for Kate. I remembered my mother bringing little things home from trips away when Kate and I were little. It was nice to think that your loved one had been thinking of you, even for a minute, when they were away from you.

The holiday was well and truly over, though, as I was headed back to work on Monday. Before then I had an elaborate 'catch-up day' Ella had planned and filled me in on. I told her I couldn't wait, but as it was after 9 p.m. I took her to bed, kissing my beautiful golden-haired girl goodnight, and promised to share all the details about my holiday over lunch the next day. Obviously, I planned on omitting the gorgeous, dark-haired man with whom I had spent the majority of my holiday.

Kate, on the other hand, would want to know everything and I knew there would be no escaping a debrief. She'd gone to some effort; starting a fire outside and placing our comfiest outdoor chairs in front of it. The bottle of red was on a small table and there was even a small cheese platter. I noticed a spare bottle of wine under the table in case it was required, and I thought for the umpteenth time this evening that she was a much better husband than my ex-husband was.

Kate was younger than me by four years, a registered nurse at one of Sydney's largest hospitals. She was truly beautiful, with blue eyes and hair that was a deep chocolate, which she had expensively highlighted so it sheened golden under lights. She was taller than me by a few inches and slimmer than me, well ... by heaps. Kate was competent, bossy and my best friend in the world. We lost our mum when we were barely grown-ups and we relied on each other. Grandma Iris was always there, cheering on our growth as we turned into young women.

Gran and Kate had this grab-life-by-the-throat attitude, and they adored each other as kindred spirits. I was often their shared frustration. My grandmother told me once that I was like water, bending to whatever shape I needed to be for anyone who wanted something from me. She said she worried for me. She never worried for Kate. Kate was like a stone, solid and stable, unbendable. I used to worry about being water, but then in year 9 I learned about erosion, and I realised water had its own power.

Kate had had a string of lovers and boyfriends over the years, but none of them ever met her exacting standards for long enough to survive. When Peter left me, I was in dire straits financially. Kate had moved in, mostly to help me cover the mortgage so I could buy him out of the house, but with the added benefit that she could also help with Ella. Ella adored Aunty Kate. They were soul sisters in directness, a fierceness that harked back to our grandmother that had clearly skipped me.

I sat down, taking a huge sip of my wine, tilting back my head to look at the sky. I wondered what Nick saw when he looked up at the sky he was under. Privately, I could admit I was missing him. Telling yourself not to catch feelings did not mean you wouldn't. We'd exchanged numbers, but I knew how he felt about attachment, and I was determined not to call him. Well, other than forwarding him 'Kate's Pearls of Wisdom', as he had deemed my sister's messages after reading one over my shoulder one day.

It had read:

Abbey, I packed your vibrator. Don't be afraid to use this while having sex. He'll enjoy it and so will you.

Delighted, he had insisted on reading them all out loud, giving me one of his rare laughs while calling them 'sibling gold' and floating the idea of turning them into a self-help book. I cried with embarrassed laughter which sobered the minute he insisted on me fetching the said item out of my suitcase and getting naked immediately.

A smile came to my face as I thought about the particular activity that followed that.

'So are you going to tell me about him?' Kate raised an eyebrow at me.

I sighed, shaking my head. 'How do you know there was a "him"?'

She met my eyes with an expression that read, 'Do not even attempt to leave out details'.

So I told her everything. Absolutely everything. We had told each other everything since forever, and this was no different. As we made our way through the bottle of wine, I started from the top, the rescue, the boat, the suite, the dinners, the drunk times dancing and singing, the nights. *Oh, my goodness, the nights.*

I told Kate about how hard it had been to make him laugh, truly laugh, how difficult it had been to extract the little details of his life. I told Kate how he didn't believe he could love or fall in love, but the way he looked at me and the way he clung to me at night – with the desperation of a man who needed love above anything else – had told me that maybe he wasn't being honest with himself.

I told her about realising I had lost Grandma Iris's necklace on another trip back to the private island, and how he had spent a whole day looking for it.

And I told Kate about the goodbye. How it was heart-wrenching, and that I had shed tears that he wiped away with his thumb while kissing me.

'He sounds hot. Maybe he has a brother?' Kate said, making me laugh. 'What are you going to do about it?' She handed me a biscuit loaded with brie.

'Nothing.' I shrugged, shoving the biscuit in my mouth. It was creamy and delicious, and I waited until I finished it before adding, 'There is nothing to do about it. He lives in London and, even if he didn't, he made it pretty clear what his parameters were in terms of what we were doing. He made himself *very* clear. It would be disrespectful. Like I wasn't holding up my end of the bargain.'

'Well, cheers to Nick fucking Northby then, hey?'

Cheers indeed. I clinked my glass against hers. We moved on, Kate filling me in on the two weeks I was away, including that Ella had started hanging out with a girl called Bella (sweet Jesus) and that Grandma Iris had finished the novel *Bonds of Sin Broken, Again* and rated it 5 stars on the spice-o-meter.

Cracking into the second bottle of wine, we put on a playlist of angst and sang at the top of our lungs. I worried briefly about the neighbours, but the thought was gone as Heart's 'These Dreams' came on. Kate and I excelled at a duet.

When I almost fell asleep into my glass, she hopped up and started packing things away.

'I fucking love you, Kate Cavendish.' I was suddenly filled with fierce family love, and I hugged her with Ella's airport-hug ferocity.

'I love you too, Abs. Hey, remember there's a hot doctor at work. I'm going to set you guys up.' She kissed me on the forehead as if she was our mum. 'I'm glad you had sex, hon.'

Me too.

On Monday morning, I very reluctantly swung back into work mode. Getting Ella ready for school, preparing breakfast, lunches and dressing before making the twenty-minute train ride into the city. Feelings of pressure and stress had stolen any remaining holiday joy from my system.

I had been promoted to my job when I was twenty-two, having been the random personal assistant who took a phone call from the school where the company's CEO, Eric Linden, sent his kids. His daughter had hit her head in the playground and needed to be picked up and taken to hospital. The Lindens, who owned a waterfront property with a jetty and large boat, were out on a sailing trip and their nanny was at the dentist. I attempted to call them, but they were all out of service, so I arranged with the principal to collect little Libby Linden from school. I took her to the hospital to check out her head (slight concussion) and then took her home to wait for Nanny Francesca to get back from her root canal. I finally got a call from a satellite phone from Eric and

Lynne, incredibly stressed after getting random reception at sea and having their phone ding for some three minutes with messages that their daughter had been injured. Eric was so impressed with my efforts that he created a position for me the following Monday: Executive Assistant to the CEO for Delacqua Hotels.

Eric had retired just before I went on holiday and I didn't know what happened to the executive assistant when the CEO retired. I was relatively confident it was like being the King's wife: I fully expected the next guy would bring his own queen. It left me feeling less than secure. My life six months ago was not perfect, but at least you could say it was secure. These days I felt as if I was on a boat drifting, untethered. It was terrifying. I very much needed a job; I had a mortgage to pay. I was prepared to walk away from Delacqua to find a new one, but I hoped I wouldn't need to.

The minute I arrived in the office, I knew something was off. There was a buzz in the building, a hum. People were having whispered conversations in the lobby and that was ... unusual. The hum had a bristling excitement about it, and I had the distinct impression people were looking at me as I walked in. I frowned a little as the sea of office workers parted to let me into the lift. I knew some of them and I was surprised when I didn't even get a *how was your holiday, Abs?* I took a spot in the back corner of the lift, a habit of old to hear gossip, anything of interest. Part of my job was to always know what was going on.

I heard two young women whispering and caught the dreaded words 'new owners'. My stomach bottomed out. *What the fuck? Was that possible?* Delacqua was owned by an overseas parent company. Was it possible it had been sold? The crowd thinned as the floors climbed until it was just me left, panicking, in the lift.

When the doors opened at my floor, the place was empty. The executive offices were on the top floor of the building and there were usually twelve assistants seated at desks in the centre. But today there were none and nor was there anyone in the offices round the edge, the space feeling like a cavernous, echoey hole.

My desk was at the far end of the floor. I pushed back my shoulders and walked towards it, my heels muffled on the grey carpet. The silence was eerie, reminding me of years gone by when I would come in on the weekend to complete projects or finalise something for Eric. It was also giving early *Walking Dead* vibes, when no one knew a zombie apocalypse had started.

When I finally reached my desk, I was greeted by a box sitting on top of it and all my things packed up. *Right. Cool.* On top was a picture of Ella when she was three. Peter had taken the photo on a weekend away in the Blue Mountains. Ella was holding out a wildflower she'd picked for me.

Life was changing so rapidly; I had to close my eyes and take a second to breathe. I was a firm believer in personal evolution. People needed change in their lives to grow, but it was completely overwhelming the sheer number of alterations taking place. It felt as though nothing was certain anymore. As if I was standing on sand, which was constantly moving, finding it hard to get my footing.

'Ms Parker.'

I opened my eyes and was staring at a beautiful, ice-blonde woman in the most exquisite navy-blue suit I'd ever laid eyes on.

'My name is Alana Sales. I'm the lawyer for the new owners, Hartwell Holdings. We would like a word with you in the boardroom.'

In my bag, my phone buzzed. I looked at it in case it was Ella's school, but it was Kate.

Have you seen the news?

The lawyer cleared her throat. She had spoken with a European accent I couldn't identify, no friendliness or politeness in her tone. She seemed hard, like Nordic ice.

'Now?' I asked, surprised my voice was still working.

'Yes.'

I popped my handbag in the box on my desk and took off my jacket. The stress was making me hot. I had dressed very carefully this morning, assuming I was starting a new role today. I was head to toe in black tailored pants, a sleeveless black blouse, with black heels. My hair was in a tousled high bun, with a few golden strands out, to soften it. I'd felt powerful and attractive, right up till the moment I met the lawyer.

I walked on stiff legs towards the boardroom, a room where decisions and careers were made, where I'd been part of so much success and joy over the years and so few tough times. At the mahogany boardroom table, there appeared to be three men in suits, with their beautifully tailored backs to me. Two of them sat side by side next to Alana's empty chair and another man was further around. Alana opened the heavy glass door for me. On the table opposite her empty seat, a glass of water, a notepad and a pencil were laid out, and I walked towards it, not looking up until I was seated.

The man next to Alana was in his fifties, with grey hair blending into a designer grey suit.

'This is my associate, Mr Jeremy Liu,' Alana began, pointing to her right.

I nodded at him and then my eyes travelled down the table to the other two men and I stopped breathing momentarily, my mouth opening. Alana's voice kept going, but it sounded distant.

'The owners of Hartwell Holdings and my clients, Mr Nicholas Northby and Mr Oliver Northby.'

Oh, shit.

My eyes moved to Oliver. The personal valet was gone. His hair had been cut, and he was clean-shaven. He was dressed elegantly in a navy pinstripe suit, a crisp white shirt and a burgundy tie. Our eyes met briefly, but there was no warmth or recognition. He kept his face impassive.

Nick was … *Jesus*. I pushed away images of soft white curtains fluttering in the warm breeze, of him wrestling with sheets, laughing as he ripped them off the bed, of his eyes filled with desire and longing for me, and the feel of the large span of his hands on my body.

The man in front of me was not the same man. He sat like a beautiful statue, impassive and cold, his navy suit cut to perfection but straining slightly against his broad shoulders, wealth and privilege wafting off him. How had I not noticed that before? He too had shorter hair and his almost-beard was gone. He was cleanly shaven, leaving rosy cheeks that made him look younger than I knew he was.

There was no greeting, no look of recognition. Nothing at all. Not a single acknowledgement of two weeks spent exploring one another's bodies, living together and sleeping together.

'Ms Parker,' Alana began.

I jumped a little. 'It's just Abbey.' I did not take my eyes off my anchor in the room, my person. Nick.

'For the purpose of this interview, I think it's best we remain quite formal,' Alana said with a little bit of acid, dragging my attention.

I blinked at her hostility.

'Ms Parker, when did you last speak with Eric Linden?'

'Eric? Umm, well, I've been on holiday for two weeks.' *With those two guys.* My eyes drifted back to Oliver and Nick, who still were not acknowledging our connection. My heart was pounding in my chest and I had no idea what was going on here or why I was being interviewed about Eric. 'I saw him on the Thursday before I left. We had a retirement party for him, in here … Umm, in this room.'

'You've not spoken with him since?'

'No.'

'You worked for him for a long time.'

'Yes, twenty years.'

'Were you his lover?'

What? If I'd had liquid in my mouth, I would have spat it across the perfect surface of the table.

The attack from this viper had come so quickly that my first thought was that I had misheard her. 'I beg your pardon?' And by that I meant: *no fucking way*. Eric was old enough to be my father.

'Were you having sex with Mr Linden?' the lawyer rephrased, saying the words slowly, as if I was a child or an imbecile.

I looked directly at Nick, who had been making notes on a piece of paper and whose hand had stilled at the question. I waited for him to stop this interview. It was offensive and personal and attacking, but he did nothing.

'No,' I said firmly.

Alana looked at me as if she didn't believe that. My thumping chest was so loud in my head I worried they could see or hear it. *What the fuck was going on here?*

'We have reason to believe Mr Linden embezzled funds from this company, Ms Parker. Almost twenty million dollars have been misappropriated over the last thirty years.'

What?

'What?' I shook my head. 'There is no way Eric would do that. He's got a family. He's a good person. He's kind. He has always looked after me. He was a great boss. There's no way that is right.'

'Ms Parker, let me assure you he has done this. As of this

morning he is in police custody, and his assets have been frozen. What we are trying to ascertain is how he did this, and to what level you were aware of it or aided him.'

'What?' That came out loudly and my head spun directly to Nick. 'You think I took money?'

'You did take money, Ms Parker. Your bonuses were paid from his slush account.'

If I thought my heart had been pounding earlier, I now had chest pain and thought I might vomit. This was utter madness. 'Oh, my God. I cannot believe this.'

'We have forensic accountants looking into this, Ms Parker. We will find what we are looking for. We wanted to allow you to confess to wrongdoing before the police are involved. The new owners are being generous and are prepared to be lenient if you disclose what you know. We know you have a daughter.'

I could feel my breath rising and falling now. I looked at the two men I knew sitting opposite me. Yes, I'd only known them for two weeks, but I had spent nearly every second of that time with one of them. He knew who I was.

But he did not move, nor did his expression change. I was angry about the situation, but his indifference made me want to, mostly, just cry.

I reached for a glass of water and was not surprised to find my hand trembling. I sipped the cold liquid, feeling it slide down my dry throat, using the time to try to formulate cohesive thoughts. I desperately wanted to put the cold glass against my hot red cheeks. Instead, I put it down firmly on the table.

'I ... I can't help you,' I said, as strongly as I could. 'I don't know anything about this.'

Alana shook her head. 'It's funny. I looked at you and thought you would be smarter than this, Abbey.'

Fucking viper. I tried to channel my inner 'new-non-holiday Nick', mirroring his body language with its arrogance, wealth and privilege. I tipped my chin up an inch and said icily, 'I'd appreciate it if you would keep it formal and address me as Ms Parker.'

'You are suspended, pending this investigation.' Alana tilted her head before adding a drawling, 'Ms Parker.' She was enjoying this now.

My attention was caught by Oliver writing down something and passing his notepad to his brother. Nick looked at it and then pushed the pad to Alana.

She looked annoyed by whatever was on that piece of paper. 'You will continue to be paid during this suspension, Ms Parker. We'll be in touch.'

Alana and Jeremy got up and walked out. Nick followed them without looking back. Oliver sat there staring at the table before he met my eyes. His face softened, and I thought he was about to speak, but then his phone rang and he answered it, leaving the room. I put my head on the table, feeling the cool, polished surface against my skin.

What the fuck? Had Eric taken money? I could not get my head around it.

'Abbey.'

He had never said my name like that, cold and professional. It was one of my favourite things about him, how silky and round my name sounded coming from his mouth. When I raised my head and looked at him, I knew sadness was written on my face. Tears were stinging my eyes, threatening to spill. I wanted to run to him and bury myself safe in his arms. My Nick though. Not this guy. Who was, what? My boss? Though, maybe I didn't have a job anymore.

'I need a minute,' I said hoarsely. I did actually need a minute. There was no way I was going to approach him feeling needy.

'Will you come to Eric's office before you leave, please?' It was phrased as a question, but issued as a command.

I acknowledged him with a nod, but refused to meet his gaze.

I sat there for a full five minutes, willing the anger to come and take over the sadness. But it didn't. I was shattered, scared and sad. I wanted to climb into my bed and never emerge again.

I walked past my desk to Eric's old office, where Nick was standing at the window. He had taken off his jacket and I could see through his shirt the outline of the arms that had held me, as the city's blinding bright sunlight poured through the window. He turned around and walked to the front of the desk, leaning against it, legs crossed at the ankles, looking at me. I stood mute, waiting for him to speak.

'Hi,' he finally uttered. He blinked at me, once, slowly.

Hi? Hi? He just accused you of taking money and now hi? This finally ignited my anger.

'Did you need something?' I said, perfectly professional and polite, but with a distinctly heaped tablespoon of Alana-like acidity.

'I need his password.' He gestured towards the computer on the desk.

I walked to the desk and pulled out Eric's notepad and a pencil and wrote it down.

'I want you to put it in.'

'You don't trust me to write down the correct password?' I huffed then and moved around the desk, roughly moving the leather chair out of the way, and waited for the computer to boot up. He moved behind me, not touching me, but I could feel the heat of him. My traitorous body reacted to the proximity of him and his gorgeous scent. Naturally, I ignored it.

I typed in Eric's password: *LynneandLibby1959*

'Thank you, Abbey.'

I spun on my heels to look at him. I could feel my emotions surging back. 'Nick, please tell me you don't believe I had anything to do with this. That you don't think I'm that kind of person.' The words were out of my mouth before I could think them through. I hated the pleading sound in my voice.

I saw something cross his face, but it wasn't there long enough for my brain to compute or articulate it.

'Nick,' I whispered. I reached out a hand to the groove of his rib cage where it fit perfectly, contacting the solid familiar mass that was his warm, cotton-covered chest.

It was there for barely a second when he moved as if I had burned him, flinching visibly. He stepped away to the window, turning his back on me, facing the view.

'Go home, Abbey.'

I think there was a tortured sob, which I could only hope was in my head and not in the room as I fled the office, grabbed my box and went to the elevator, which mercifully was waiting for me. I congratulated myself that I did not let a single tear drop until I was in the cab.

Nick

I'd run my mother's company since I was twenty-four years old, and today's meeting was the only day I ever hated my job. The only time I wished I was anywhere else, doing anything else.

I'd met Eric Linden about six months ago, in London, when Hartwell was first moving to buy the Australian hotel chain. Linden was a schmoozer, typical Australian blue blood, raised with a firm belief that he was better than anyone else. It wasn't a personality type I was unfamiliar with; it was just interesting to see that Australian snobs were as unlikeable as English ones.

We had found the issues with the funds prior to purchase and managed to get a significant discount on the business, as a result of the PR scandal that was likely to ensue when the press found out a top hotel executive had stolen from the company he'd helped run for decades.

When I opened the email from Alana with the list of names of Delacqua employees to be investigated, an Abigail Parker had been at the very top. I'd had my assistant pull her HR file, certain there were hundreds of Abbey Parkers working as EAs in Sydney, not believing the coincidence. *What were the chances?*

But when I saw the HR record, I knew it was her. In my gut, I knew. By then I was back at the resort after dropping her off at the airport. I could still smell her, still feel the pressure of her lips on mine, feel how perfectly her body curled into me.

I closed my eyes against the filtered glare of the office in Sydney, desperately trying to find memories of her fingertips pulling lightly at my hair or her spontaneous hugs. What came, though, were not the happy recollections of our holiday, but her shattered expression from that horrendous meeting. Her whispered plea, 'Nick.' I'd never heard her voice sound like that before.

Holiday Abbey was happy and confident. She was easygoing and the most honest person I'd met. I could not reconcile it with the shattered woman from today. But neither could I understand how Eric Linden had pulled off fraud of this magnitude without help. I swallowed the emotion. Acquisitions were tough at the best of times. I was probably jet-lagged and just three days ago I had woken to her warm body wrapped around mine.

My brother made his way into the office. He'd turned into a man before my eyes and it sometimes surprised me, even though I see him every day that I can, that he was no longer a boy. He's a handsome lad. He looks like our mother. Her sandy hair, blue eyes and olive skin. He was clearly agitated. He almost ripped the heavy door off its hinges and his hands were balled. In fairness, he had spoken to me about Alana before we started, and he had specifically told her that he did not want to piss everyone off.

'It *was* your Abbey.'

'She's not *my* Abbey, Ollie.' I was annoyed with myself that my tone was so defensive.

'I'm not happy with that meeting, Nick. I couldn't let Alana not pay her. She has a daughter and a mortgage; we both know that.'

I'm not certain when my brother became wise and emotionally mature. It's a recent acquisition. I looked at him with suspicious admiration.

'I know. I agree.' I agreed so much that I had fired Alana on the way to the lift.

'There is no way on this earth Abbey had anything to do with this. I thought she was going to pass out in that room. And Alana accusing her of sleeping with her boss was well out of line – it wasn't anything we discussed. It was wrong and unprofessional. She risked our reputation in that meeting. The last thing we need is a wrongful dismissal with the addition of discrimination on our first bloody week here.' My younger brother's blue eyes flamed with his impassioned defence of a woman we barely knew.

'I know.'

'Nick, we need to fix this. We both know her.'

'I said, I know. I'll take care of it.' My legs were twitching under the table. I had the urge to get up, stop what was happening and go sit beside Abbey and hold her hand. The urge to protect her, it made my heart pound, and it fucking terrified me.

I would fix this. I told myself it was for the business; it was for Ollie. It was important to find out what happened, so the company could move on. It was important for his future success because Delacqua would be his one day. It had absolutely nothing to do with that shattered woman. Nothing to do with what I'd felt when her hand had touched my chest. Not a thing to do with the internal struggle I'd had of being in the same room with her and not taking her in my arms.

    She did not need rescuing.

Chapter Five
Abbey

Ella's keys jingled in the door at a quarter to four, and it was literally the first time I had moved since arriving home, box in tow, at eleven. I had been catatonic on the sofa all day. My box sat next to my suitcase on the floor of my bedroom.

But when I heard my daughter arriving home, Mum mode kicked in, making me jump up and pretend to be my usual self. Like an American mother on a sitcom, I went into overdrive, fussing over after-school snacks, listening to Ella's endless story about her new best friend Bella. *Ella and Bella, Ella and Bella… Jesus Christ.* I opened a bottle of red 'to make dinner' and drank the contents before ordering a pizza. Kate was on a date after work so, mercifully, I was spared having to run through the day's events.

That morning, before the absolute train wreck of a meeting, Kate's message had been to tell me that Eric had (very publicly) been arrested. When I told Kate I knew, and about the meeting I'd had, it freaked her out enough to start making calls to lawyers, hoping to find someone reasonably priced to ensure her innocent sister did not go to jail.

'I mean, you don't know her, but I can assure you she is borderline naïve,' I heard her saying on the phone to one lawyer. 'Takes people at face value, does not have social media ...'

After pizza, I walked to the kitchen to open another bottle of wine, thankful my membership from a Hunter Valley vineyard (currently being paid for on Peter's credit card) had arrived at my door. The happiest of deliveries, only made awkward by me hugging the delivery driver.

Kate and I met with a lawyer on the Friday, a slimeball named Rutherford Milson, who stared at my boobs and asked Kate out at the end of the meeting. He advised a wait-and-see approach, given there was no knowing if the new owners had any evidence of any wrongdoing on my part. He advised me not to answer calls from the Lindens, which I hadn't anyway. They had not called.

My belief in Eric's innocence vanished that night when I heard on the news that Lynne and Libby Linden had made the trip to a non-extraditable country and that Eric had arranged for all their assets to be transferred to Libby before being arrested.

When Pete picked up Ella from school on Friday night, sensations of relief washed over me, closely followed by guilt. But I was honestly just happy to be alone. Happy that I could be as sad as I wanted to be, free to wallow in my unemployment and my apparently imagined holiday romance.

I wallowed for approximately four hours and then I pulled my shit together. A visit to Grandma Iris would result in the restoration of my gumption, so I arranged to take her out for a coffee at a beautiful café just down the street from her nursing home the next morning.

My grandmother had never mastered the concept of casual dressing and she looked at my jeans and Fleetwood Mac T-shirt disapprovingly while she sat resplendent in her wheelchair in wide-legged slacks and a white shirt with the collar up. The shirt was so crisp, the collar standing so firmly, I could only stare at it in amazement. Gran's still-long hair was gathered up in a sleek bun. She had once modelled her look after the 'Great Kate' – Katherine Hepburn – and, honestly, she still looked like an ageing Hollywood icon.

'Mrs Cavendish!' The café owner had marked Iris a VIP at some point over the last few years, and so she escorted us to Iris's favourite table in the window.

Gran had visibly aged since I'd been away and my heart clenched as I wondered how many more trips to the café there would be.

'Good morning, Cherie. It is a lovely day. We'll have the usual.' My grandmother liked English loose-leaf tea in a pot, and scones with jam and cream. 'Oh, and how did you go with that book I recommended? *The Duke's Dark Desire* – wasn't it marvellous?'

Inwardly, I groaned at Gran recommending romance that was bordering on porn to strangers. But maybe I needn't have worried.

'Mrs Cavendish, I read it in four hours.'

My grandmother nodded knowingly.

I sat down after sliding in Grandma Iris's wheelchair and placing my handbag on the spare chair beside us.

'Abigail Cavendish.' Gran had never been a big fan of Peter and preferred to use my maiden name when addressing me. 'You have colour. Did you have sex on that trip?'

I looked around the café to catch Cherie's head shooting up. Our eyes met, and she shot an enquiring brow at me. I felt heat rush to my cheeks.

'Oh, my God, Gran.'

'I must say, it seems to have put a distinct glow in your cheeks, child. Was he Maldivian? I have never had the pleasure. Was he circumcised?'

This is where Kate gets it from.

'Gran, keep your voice down.' I shrugged my shoulder. 'He was not Maldivian, for your information. He was English.'

'Lovely. I bet he had lovely manners. One does not always want lovely manners in bed, but still, it is nice. Of course, my first husband, Ray, was an Englishman, and he was a wonderful lover. Not quite as skilful as your English grandfather, though, Abigail. Harry was a once-in-a-lifetime love. Englishmen are lovely. But one wants to avoid discussions about cricket with them. It isn't polite to brag.'

My heart filled up with her; she was such a fucking delight. I let out a happy sigh. I loved it when she ran through the husbands and then gushed about my grandfather. I didn't have many memories left of him, as he died when I was four. She'd married another five times and, somehow, she loved each of them, but she never loved them the way she loved Harry.

'Now, dear, Kate called me. Are you going to prison? I must say, Abbey, this is rather a turn. Going criminal. Have you ever seen that film, *Chicago*?'

'Gran, I didn't do anything wrong. I most certainly have not "gone criminal".'

'Yes, dear. That's exactly what they say in the film.'

I felt the tears come only a moment before I was crying. My grandmother reached into her handbag, which was small and leather – like the one the queen always carried – and pulled out a handkerchief with her initials embroidered on it.

'Abigail dearest, Cavendish women do not let life get to them. Do not be feeble. You, my darling girl, are enough for any job, at any time. Sweetheart, sometimes things are not in our control. We must simply find the things that are. So enough tears. What are you doing with what you can control, my darling?'

Just as I'd suspected, two hours in the company of my beloved grandmother was all that was required. I came away from her feeling stronger and calmer, and with a list of spicy-romance-novel recommendations I absolutely would not read.

I could not control Nick. Or what was happening at work. I could only control my response to it.

Part One of Operation Recovery included finding a new job. So I spent the weekend putting together a resumé and applied for several roles I'd seen advertised. The response was good, and I had three interviews lined up for the week after. My only stress was around who on earth to put down for a reference, but I would cross that bridge when I came to it.

Operation Recovery, Part Two, was a bedroom makeover. My bedroom looked exactly as it had when Pete had left. My plan for the weekend was to paint it all white. I invested money I was not confident I had in light-diffusing curtains and added some light-wood accents to try to recreate the perfection of my blissful Maldives hotel room.

Saturday morning dawned bright and sunny. A good omen for painting, I told myself, making a start as soon as I'd breakfasted and had enough coffee. I had bought out the hardware store of brushes and drop sheets. They'd seen me coming, but it did not stifle my enthusiasm for the job.

I aimed to get a coat of paint on before lunch. It was, in fact, incredibly soothing work. I had a playlist of classic eighties songs

I could sing badly while I painted (badly). Kate woke in the early afternoon, walked in like the bloody foreman and critiqued the job I was doing. Sure, my cut-off jean shorts and white singlet were completely covered in paint and when I had gone to the loo I could plainly see it was also in my hair and on my face and body, but I had enjoyed the first coat immensely and reconnected with Pat Benatar and Hall & Oates.

The physicality of the work had stirred my appetite. I planned on getting the second coat started after I ate. I carefully opened the wet door, happy to breathe less-toxic fumes, and headed to the kitchen. The sound of voices met me in the hallway. I was a little annoyed because I didn't realise Kate had a friend over and, given what was going on, I wasn't super keen to socialise. My stomach rumbled in protest, though, and I pushed aside the worry, deciding to brave it for food.

It wasn't until I was in the room that I realised the conversation was confrontational. I caught the end of Kate saying, 'I'm not really sure you're welcome here, or that you have any right to ask to see my sister.'

I could see that Kate's hackles were raised. Her arms were crossed and her cheeks were red. Her body language screamed defensive and the look on her face read 'Don't fuck with me, buddy'. Her tone was no-nonsense, pure authority, the one she used for patients who were being non-compliant. I silently sympathised with the stranger who was facing her wrath. I looked at him. *Oh, nope. Not a stranger.* My sympathy vanished.

'Look, I understand she may be angry with me. I promise I'm not delivering bad news.'

Nick Northby's tone was almost Holiday Nick, charming and persuasive, and though he wasn't facing me, I knew he'd be wearing a charismatic smile. He was trying to work his way around Kate, whom he considered to be the gatekeeper. He had no idea what he was dealing with. Kate may be younger than me, but she had long ago made herself my protector. Kate thought I was too soft. A pushover. Too pliant.

'Listen here, pal –'

I cleared my throat to let them know I was in the room. When Nick turned around, my breath caught. It was right up there with the most annoying reaction I've ever had to someone who was clearly my sworn enemy. Why I still found him attractive – after this last week – was beyond me, but my eyes drank in the sight of him. On the island he had worn only shorts, but now his long legs were clad in black jeans. They made him look taller somehow, and well, very hot. He also had on a grey T-shirt and gorgeous – and expensive – brown boots.

'Abbey.' The cold, business tone was out of his voice. Instead, he sounded excited, like the time we had gone fishing and one of the lines had started jumping. 'I worked out how it was done,' he said, eyes gleaming.

My heart sank. My worst fear was that I had inadvertently played a part in Eric's crime, somehow. I mean, I signed things for him, took calls and deliveries and responded to hundreds of emails a week.

Nick was watching me and when my face fell, he rushed to reassure me. 'No, no. It wasn't you. I found out how *he* did it. I can prove you weren't involved.'

I didn't fully take that in as I continued to stare at him with sad eyes, thinking about having to sign over custody of my daughter to my sister and what that would mean for Ella to have Kate as a parent as opposed to me. Would I be allowed to see her in prison?

He had a document wallet on the bench, and he opened it, pulling out four different bulldog-clipped, highlighted documents.

I walked closer. He smelled like freshly showered goodness. Delicious.

The first was a general ledger segment from the Delacqua Adelaide and then one for the hotel in Sydney. Then there was a bank statement from what I assumed was Eric's slush fund and the business account. There were several highlighted amounts circled in red pen and I picked up the pages to look at them.

'Okay, see here. Why would he pick the Adelaide business?' Nick asked.

I have no fucking idea. But then I thought for a second, and there was a simple reason Adelaide differed from the other hotels. 'Because it was losing money and had to be supported by head office,' I said.

'Exactly. It was already being supported so it would be easier to hide the trail. And he took money from Sydney because it had the highest profit margin. He started off eight years before you worked there, small amounts being siphoned from the transfers, first a few thousand dollars, but he gets bolder later on.' He points to a large amount from just three months ago.

I still couldn't understand. 'How was it not picked up by the end-of-financial-year audits?'

'That took a bit of working through. We've let go of the finance director, at any rate. It was poor management at the least, and I'm not convinced he didn't know.' He opened the fourth document and flicked quickly to the page he was after. 'But Linden was quite clever. He actually has it accounted for in the Sydney P&L, but not in the head office P&L. It's under a category that Delacqua called "projects". There are a couple of other dodgy things too, a cleaning company that doesn't exist and an interior-design business that pays for artwork. The company is fake and there are no artworks, there are no projects. Plus, the business was still profitable, so accounts weren't specifically looking for it. It was cleverly done. If we hadn't bought the business, he probably would have gotten away with it.'

'And, my bonuses?'

'Paid from that account, but they were also paid by payroll. We assume that every time he paid you or anyone a bonus, he would add around ten to fifteen per cent on his request, have it transferred over and then pay you the original amount from the slush fund and pocket the rest.' He swallowed. 'I know you didn't do anything. I need you to come back.'

I guffawed at him and dragged my eyes away from his kaleidoscopic ones. I couldn't let myself get lost in them and miss what was being said. 'Why would I do that?' I felt anger flare and could hear it in my voice.

Kate heard it too. She gave me a sharp nod and felt free to leave the room.

'Abbey, this last week I have seen meticulous record keeping, supreme organisation and, honestly, excellent leadership, not from Eric's desk, but from yours. You are fantastic at your job, and you have managed to do that for years without pissing a single person off in that business. They all love you. I had twenty-five emails from other employees, saying there was no way you had anything to do with any of it, including one from a guy in accounts called Mike who wrote a four-page message.' He paused, and gave me a fleeting smile, as if he was trying it out for the first time. 'I think Mike's in love with you.'

Oh, being personal now, are we? Fuck you, Nick. I shook my head. 'Mike's gay.' My anger burst white and hot as I remembered my 'interview' the other day. 'You sat across a boardroom table from me and let that Nordic viper of yours accuse me of stealing money and fucking my boss.'

'She was just doing her job.' He shrugged. 'She's actually Dutch.'

'Oh, how *fascinating*. Are you sleeping with her?'

'Excuse me?' he bristled. 'Two weeks of paradise, Abbey, does not give you the right to ask those questions.'

I interpreted that as maybe they'd had sex in the past. 'I see, but it's okay for you to have your minions ask *me* that? At my place of work?'

His eyes had the grace to fall to the floor even if he couldn't verbalise an apology.

'I don't think the two of us working together is a good option,' I said, more calmly than I felt. I took a deep breath and shook my head to clear the random thought I had of him pressing me against a desk. *Not helpful, brain.*

'You don't have to work for me. It will be Oliver. The company is for him. He's green. He could use your help. He finished his uni degree and then I had him do various jobs across the companies we own. He's done everything from janitor work to personal valet work. Theoretically, he can run a company. But he needs experience next to him. You're going to be that.'

'You're going to give a twenty-five-year-old a chain of hotels worth millions? You're mad. Little nepo babies running the world,' I ranted as I walked away, heading back to my bedroom.

'He's thirty-five.' He followed me down the corridor and stopped when I turned suddenly, almost colliding with me.

'Thirty-five? Shut up! Really?' I was genuinely surprised and bewildered by that. What kind of skincare did that man use?

'He looks like a kid still and up until a few years ago he was acting like one. But then he did something I didn't expect him to do. He put himself through university and came to me when he had graduated with honours, asking for a job.' Nick sounded proud. *I was raised by my brother,* Oliver had said.

I was still not buying his bullshit. 'Find someone else. It turns out that being an EA for a criminal is an underrated skill. I've been headhunted by three other CEOs this week and one high-ranking politician.' I spun and continued to my bedroom and started preparing for the next coat of paint. *Honestly, if someone had told me it was going to take this fucking long to paint a few walls, I would have hired a man to do it.*

'Look, Abbey, I understand you're pissed off with me. Coming back from holidays, there was no way in the world I expected to run into you.'

'The irony that the only boss I've ever slept with is you, hey? Nick, I don't know who you are. And you may not have expected to run into me, but you did know you were coming to Sydney. For the whole of the two weeks, you knew you were going to be here in this city, where I lived.' I turned away from him, trying to get the hurt out of my voice. Also, I was going to dissolve into a complete, blubbering mess. And I really didn't want to do that in front of him. I still had a fucking whole coat to paint.

Get your emotional shit under control, Abbey.

'Oliver needs you,' he said.

But what I heard was: *I don't need you.*

He doesn't want you, Abbey.

'I've drawn up an offer, Abbey. I want you to take it.' He walked over to where I was standing and reached for my arm to make me face him.

As soon as our skin made contact, a chain reaction occurred in my body. First heat flooded me, pooling somewhere at my centre; second, my breathing changed; third, my eyes looked briefly up to meet his whisky-coloured ones and then dropped, focusing on his mouth, the narrow top lip and the pouty lower one. I had the overwhelming urge to remind him of those two weeks. How they felt, what they meant.

'There is only you. I need you,' he breathed.

I closed my eyes, wishing desperately that he'd said that about us, about me. 'When do you leave?'

'I'm here for a bit. Maybe a couple of weeks, maybe a month. It depends on how successful we are.'

His hands were still on my paint-covered arms. I wanted him closer, so much closer. His thumb brushed over a bit of dried paint.

'Are you painting by yourself? Do you need help?'

What the fuck was that? We weren't friends.

I pulled my arm back. 'I don't need anything from you.'

'Abbey,' he breathed. Silk. Chocolate. I watched him stiffen and swallow whatever he had been about to say. 'The offer is generous, Abbey. I need you back.' The CEO was in the room.

He turned to leave, and I felt my eyes gravitate to his arse in those jeans as he walked away. *Hot fucker.*

'Nick.'

Shut the fuck up, Abbey. Do not even think about saying that, under no circumstances are you to throw this man a –

'I miss him.'

He turned and looked at me with a wariness in his dark eyes. 'Who?'

I looked at the ceiling, the battle I was having with my brain and what was about to come out of my mouth would surely be on display in my face if I looked at him.

'Holiday Nick. I miss Holiday Nick.' My hand covered my mouth after that came out. I dropped my eyes to meet his and, for the first time since I had seen him again, I could almost see the man I'd known.

I thought I saw his jaw move for a second, as if he were going to throw me a smile and march over to me and pull me by the waist of my jean shorts into his mouth. But his gaze dropped, he opened his mouth and closed it again, deciding not to speak whatever was on his mind. Then he squared his shoulders and turned and walked away.

And I picked up the roller.

The second coat was a torturous chore that no eighties pop song could improve, and I laboured until it was done. When I finished, I could have collapsed and slept for a week, but I also had shit everywhere, so I huffed and commenced the clean-up. Finally, I threw myself into the shower to wash off the paint and dirt and got into clean pyjamas, preparing the sofa bed to sleep on that night.

Kate was dressed in scrubs and ready to start her shift at the hospital. She deemed it an appropriate time to broach the visitor from earlier.

'Old mate' – she pointed towards the door – 'is gorgeous, if a bit of an arrogant prick,' she stated. 'Google says he's loaded. Fantastic arse, by the way. How the fuck did you not google him in the first place?'

'I don't google people. I didn't know about his money, although maybe that was lack of perception on my part, and his arse ... oh, my God, I know.'

'He gave me this to give to you.' She handed me a large white envelope.

It wasn't sealed, and I knew Kate had already read it, which honestly annoyed the shit out of me. I seethed inwardly at my sister's bulldozer tactics with my life. I pulled out the contract and after a quick glance I think my mouth fell open in shock. I sat up a little on the sofa bed and reached for a lamp and my glasses. *Fuck.*

'It's a very generous offer. He wants you,' Kate said in a sing-song voice that sounded like *Abbey and Nick, sitting in a tree ...*

'It's ridiculous.' Nick fucking Northby wanted to double my salary to get me back to Delacqua. 'Also,' I said, a little enraged at the complete unfairness of the situation, 'it's a babysitting job. It's ridiculous.' I was repeating myself and my voice had become a little shrill.

He had trapped me. That money would completely change my life. I could afford the house without my sister and Kate would be free to go live somewhere else and have a life of her own, instead of interfering with mine. Maybe I could buy a new car. It was so much that maybe Ella and I could go on our own holiday.

I threw the contract down beside me, lifted my knees, and put my head on them.

'You don't want to take it?' Kate said, reading my mind. 'Why, Abs?' Kate was nodding, working it through. 'You have feelings for him.'

'I ... Maybe I thought I did, but I didn't know him. I don't have feelings for him.'

I sounded unconvincing as fuck. Even someone who didn't know me would have known I wasn't telling the truth, so my sister snorted at my denial. I tried again.

'I don't want to take his money.' That part was honest.

'Abbey, you should talk to him about how you feel.'

'The only thing that has changed since we were on that holiday, Kate, is him. I don't know this version of him.'

She tilted her head sympathetically. 'I have to go. Listen, Gran has figured out how to tweet.'

I raised an alarmed set of eyebrows.

'Yup. A young nurse showed her. Now she's talking to some impoverished author who is encouraging her to write reviews on Amazon.'

'Ah, Jesus. I cannot imagine.'

'Gran feels we've been holding out on her. *Did we not know she was a supporter of the arts?* Anyway, I'm on night shifts for a bit, so can you call around and show her how to use her Amazon account?'

'Because I'm unemployed and have nothing to do?'

She shrugged a shoulder and blew me a kiss as she walked out the door.

My phone was in my hand.

I hovered over his name for ten minutes. Then I texted him.

Fine.

His reply came straight back.

Okay.

Passive-aggressive fucker.

Nick

After I left her, I walked to the house next door, out of view of her front window, and leaned back against the dark-brown brick fence. I fought the desire to return, bang the door down and take the paintbrush out of her hand.

Her house was cute and clean and had a warmth I knew came directly from Abbey. It was significantly more modest than I had expected. If the numbers didn't tell me she had no involvement in Eric Linden's crimes, her house certainly did. She hadn't a penny she didn't work for.

Her sister was a lioness. Protective and strong. What that told me, from personal experience, was that she considered Abbey weaker than herself. More susceptible to arseholes like me.

It would be arrogant to think that in the short time I'd known

Abbey, that I knew her better than Kate did. But the thing about Abbey was that she was strong, she just wasn't aggressive.

Three offers? She would take the deal I'd offered her. I had made it impossible for her not to. If one of them outbid me ... the thought made me anxious. It made me want to go back in and grovel, apologise for not calling, apologise for remaining silent during that meeting ...

It was best not to spend time analysing the need I felt to have her back in the business. She was the best person placed to help Oliver succeed, and that was that. Purely professional.

Unlike my desire to paint her fucking walls.

She missed Holiday Nick. *Fuck* – I did too. How did I tell her that Holiday Nick wasn't real? That he wasn't someone who appeared at that bloody resort once a year. That I had actually never met *Holiday Nick* before ... before her.

There was another Nick once who was similar, but he did not survive his marriage.

And then Regular Nick's driver was parked looking at him, waiting for him to get off a fence in front of a girl's house and get in the bloody car. So I did.

Our apartment in Sydney is fantastic. We own the top floor of a harbourfront building I got for a steal. I'd bought it years ago and then had it renovated when I realised how much time we might need to spend there, with the acquisition. When the neighbouring apartment had come up, I bought it for Ollie, though he is mostly at mine. So I was not surprised when I opened the door and saw his feet on my dining table.

'How'd it go?'

I rolled my eyes. I had expected her to text a *yes please* by now. 'Fine.'

'So she'll come back?'

A short breath escaped my mouth, and I nodded and then shook my head as I reluctantly admitted, 'I don't know.' I went and sat at the table opposite him, also putting my feet up on it. He slid a glass of single malt to me. 'She's getting other offers, and she was …' I drank. 'Upset with me. With us … Mostly with me.'

'Well, *we* can hardly blame her. We both sat there and acted as though she was a stranger to us, while an employee of ours accused her of being a slut and stealing money. She might be able to forgive me … I'm charming and handsome, but you were her lover on that holiday, and you are an ugly, miserable old bastard and therefore *you* are fucked.'

I ran my hand through my hair and pulled at my T-shirt, uncomfortable with how accurate and blunt he was.

'Did you speak to her … on a personal level?' Ollie asked.

'We have nothing to discuss of a personal nature.' My voice was clipped.

'You get to lie about that now, Nick. But the minute she signs that contract, you will disclose to me if that changes. You will follow the Northby rules. Am I understood? It will actually be my business, so I'll need to know if you are having … feelings … of a personal nature.'

I scoffed. Clearly he had forgotten the Northby rule about who was the actual boss around here. And that I would never mix personal with business, and that I was a fucking master of control.

Determined to make a liar of me, Abbey popped into my head. I don't know why I thought to say what was on my mind to Ollie, but it just came out. 'She was painting her bedroom by herself and there is something about her house that is so warm, so her. Oh, and her sister is fucking terrifying.'

'Really?' Oliver laughed. 'I don't know why that surprises me.'

'How did you find Bondi Beach?' I asked. He had declared this morning that he was going for a surf and had to purchase a board – apparently, he thought the minute one arrived in Australia one could surf.

'Fucking horrendous. The ocean here is angry all of the time. The views were lovely though,' he said, finishing his glass with a knowing smile, and standing. 'As a result, I have a date tonight with Marissa from Maroubra.'

'Well, I wish you luck with that.' I lifted my glass at him.

'Why don't you come? Australian women love our accent. And all women love our money.'

I shook my head. 'No thank you, Ollie. Have a lovely evening.'

'Nick.' He looked at me with a serious expression. 'You can take risks in life as well as business.' He shrugged a shoulder at me, then gave me a slap on the back. He left, not waiting for a response.

I sat there, drinking Scotch, watching as the sun set with Hollywood-film-like perfection and then, as the evening darkened, the harbour was lit by a thousand glittering lights. Waiting.

Fine.

I sat up, reaching for my phone. I snorted and my heart pounded. It was such a passive-aggressive response, and it had come hours after I'd expected it. I could feel how pissed off she was at sending it. She'd wanted to say no to me.

Okay.

I smiled. Inside, my gut did a little victory dance, but my shoulders and heart sagged in relief.

Chapter Six
Abbey

I started work almost two hours earlier than I needed to, restocking my drawers with stationery and sorting my desk. I checked the CEO's office, which was now Oliver Northby's office, and ensured it had everything he needed. The office also had a butler's pantry and an ensuite, which I gave a quick once over, ensuring things had not fallen apart in the weeks I was away.

Oliver had messaged me on Sunday night.

> Abbey, I'm thrilled you are on board and look forward to us working together. We'll have Nick in my office for the first two weeks, and then we'll fly solo. Wouldn't mind you joining the executive meeting, if you are free? I'll chat to you about it tomorrow. Oliver.

I came back to over a hundred emails, and I worked through them diligently to see what changes had occurred. The Northbys, it seemed, had retained everyone with the exception of our old financial controller, and given what had been occurring that seemed only fair.

Eric had always been an early starter, but I must admit it took me by surprise when Oliver arrived early. He was carrying two coffees and breakfast for the two of us.

'Uh, I'm pretty sure this is my job now. That I am essentially your *personal valet*,' I quipped.

'Old habits,' he said, grinning. 'Thank you for coming back. I need to apologise. That meeting was fucked up. Nick let Alana and her team go. I want to assure you they won't be around anymore.'

He had immediately endeared himself to me by apologising and swearing, but I confess I was surprised by the decision to part ways with their lawyers. It made me feel slightly better knowing I wouldn't have to bump into that viper of a lawyer in the hallway. I was also pleasantly surprised that Oliver the CEO was exactly the same person as Oliver the valet.

He was dressed very stylishly in a bespoke dark-grey suit. His crisp shirt was a light blue and his navy tie knotted perfectly at his throat. He looked more like a model or heartthrob than a CEO, but richer, and I was instantly aware of the amount of buffering I would have to provide for him, running interference from would-be admirers. That would be interesting.

'Well, then, shall we get started?' I asked.

We cheersed our coffees and spent the first hour of the day on either side of his desk, eating breakfast and speaking about the business and his vision for it. It afforded me the chance to observe him closely and predict the potential strengths and weaknesses of him and his management style. Oliver was a great guy; he was affable, cheeky and easygoing, but drive and a desire to prove himself tempered this. He seemed to be a natural leader.

Nick arrived at eight on the dot that morning. That first

morning, God, that first morning was hard. I was still so mad at him. I had relaxed with Oliver over coffee and a bagel (honestly the best bagel I've ever had) and, to some extent, I could see that he and I working together was going to be fine. But then *he* walked in.

Nick floored me. He looked beautiful in a mid-blue suit. His shirt was the same colour as Oliver's, but he had a light-green tie which made his eyes sing. His brown accessories matched perfectly and my gaze was drawn to the undo-ability of that belt and how perfectly tailored his pants were to his thighs. It was difficult to remember I could undress him (and not just mentally) two weeks ago and I dragged my eyes up and reminded myself that I loathed the man.

Truth was, Nick was stirring huge emotions in me, and that made me uncomfortable. Our two-week fling had left us in a weird place. Were we exes? Or were we just pretending it hadn't happened and were now just colleagues? I'm not sure either of us knew how to navigate it and so it was, naturally, awkward as fuck.

'Morning,' Oliver said as Nick walked in.

Nick said nothing. He just looked at me. The silence stretched for way longer than I was comfortable with and, not coping with it, I broke first by standing up to leave.

'You ready for the exec meeting?' Nick said to Oliver.

'Sure am. I invited Abbey to attend. I need a radar on the room, what they're thinking of us, how the temperature feels from somebody we trust who was here before,' Oliver said confidently, shooting me a dimpled, lopsided grin as I stood at the door.

'I'm not sure that's necessary,' said Nick, his eyes dark, looking pointedly at Oliver and clearly trying to communicate something to his brother.

'I'm sorry, Nick. Is there something you want to say to me?'

Oliver asked in a firm challenge. He stood and put his hands on his narrow hips. I had no idea what they were talking about, other than it was obviously about me.

Nick did not answer. He turned his head sharply towards the window, opened his mouth and closed it. I took pleasure in seeing him uncomfortable and struck dumb for words. I hid my grin.

'See you at nine in the boardroom, Abbey,' Oliver said smugly.

The executive meeting started badly, in that I was late and so was Oliver, but everyone else was on time. I wish I could say that we were late because of something important, but he had called IT because he could not get a password to work for the accounting system. He needed to learn to call me instead.

I walked into his office without knocking to give him a five-minute reminder for the meeting and he looked at me helplessly, pointing to his phone on speaker. I walked over and popped his end on mute.

'How long?'

'Nine minutes so far.'

'You don't call IT for IT problems,' I told him.

'I don't?' He looked bewildered.

'No.'

'Tell me, Abbey, who should I call for IT problems if not IT?'

'You call me for everything. Am I understood, Oliver?'

'—and so, Mr Northby,' the voice on the phone said, 'we have lost three full-time staff members in the last six months, and we are seriously under-resourced, so I'm very glad you called. The IT system needs a full upgrade, as we are at risk of new cyber threats. Honestly, these guys are learning new ways every day and our security systems are a little archaic and, oh, yeah, can I ask you about pay increases, while I have you, sir?'

I unmuted our microphone. 'Who am I speaking with?'

'Evan,' the man on the phone said quizzically, as though he was uncertain what his name was.

'Evan, hi. It's Abbey Parker, Mr Northby's assistant.'

'Hi, Abbey.'

'I'm so sorry, Evan, Mr Northby had an urgent phone call he needed to take. I am going to put you in touch with Kate Miller in the HR department. You can let her know if there are any issues. Your feedback is very important to us, and Kate will debrief us about your call later.'

'Oh-kay.'

I forwarded the call to HR and hung up the phone.

Oliver looked at me. 'I still don't have a password, Abbey!'

I pulled out my phone and called down to security. 'Bernice, hi! It's Abbey. The new owner and CEO, Mr *Oliver* Northby, is having trouble with his password to Fisc. Can you reset it for me?'

Bernice was sixty years old and had worked for the company as the secretary to the head of security the whole time.

'Abs, no drama at all. Is that the broody one or the model?' Bernice asked.

She was on speaker, and I shot Oliver an amused look. 'The model,' I said, silently laughing.

A delightful blush crept up his cheeks.

'We've had worse-looking bosses,' Bernice said before giving me a crazy-arse password that was sixteen letters long, with three special characters.

I typed it straight into his computer and then reset it for him. 'There we go. Now, we're late.'

'Ah, shit. Nick will be annoyed.'

Fuck Nick. I wanted to say. Instead, I picked up our notebooks and the report he wanted and led him to the boardroom.

Nick shot Oliver a dark look as we entered the meeting and Oliver (bless his heart) looked suitably chagrined. But the look Nick pinned me with was something else entirely. Admittedly, I was probably reading things in his displeased smoulder, but it burned into me and made me long to be naked with him, listening to him whisper the ways I was going to be punished in my ear. There was something in his eyes that let me know he knew exactly the effect he was having on me, and I broke out in goosebumps and flushed.

There were two seats next to Nick, and I expected Oliver to take the chair beside his brother, but he sat in the far one, leaving me sandwiched between them, significantly more aware of one than the other.

Then I knocked Nick's pen, which rolled on the shiny surface of the table noisily before dropping off and landing on the carpet between us.

'Sorry,' I said, avoiding his eyes after quickly glancing at him and finding them accusing me of having done that on purpose.

'Sorry,' he said in a *this is your fault* way.

'If you just ... I, uh, oh, sorry, I ...'

'Abbey,' he whispered in exasperation.

We had both bent at exactly the same time, bumping into each other, but the pen had continued rolling, and had landed near my foot. I could not see it because his head was in the way, and he attempted to retrieve it while I bobbed around behind him. Eventually, he grabbed my stockinged leg and lifted it, which caused me to sit up straight and sustain a loud gasp, grasping the arms of my chair.

I caught Mike's eye across the way, and he was barely suppressing his mirth. Meanwhile, Oliver had hidden his grin behind his hand.

Nick sat up, readjusting his tie and his hair. His cheeks were as flushed as mine now and he took a deep breath, calming himself after this mortifying start to this meeting. I knew everyone else in the room, and earned a couple of sympathetic smiles. Most of them had been in their positions for at least a year except Mike, my dear friend, who was the newly appointed financial controller. But there was a weird nervousness and tension in the room, which originated from the two unknown quantities present. The Northbys.

I turned to look at Oliver, waiting for him to break the tension with his irrepressible charm. But it was Nick who started speaking first.

'Right, well, now that everyone has decided to join us,' Nick drawled, 'let's get down to it.' He opened his notebook, and I could see a full page of meticulous notes that I suspected carried on to the next page. 'We enter into this new phase of ownership with a change of direction. An increased focus on professionalism, integrity and service delivery will make Delacqua *the* hotel chain travellers think of when they are choosing where to stay in Australia. Oliver's direction for this company is new and fresh. He will drive this business to meet my standards. And my standards for our management team are extremely high. We won't be carrying passengers.'

I looked at him, struck with awe and a little impressed by how much authority he was carrying in his voice. And while it wasn't an effusively warm welcome, given that a single manager had swindled a significant amount of money from the business, it seemed important to set the tone and expectations. New Nick was a force to be reckoned with. But he also came across as a bit of a prick, as he spent the next forty-five minutes of the meeting interrogating everyone about their departments.

Whenever anyone would say something dumb, which inevitably

everyone did given how nervous they were, he would roll his eyes and write a name down on his notepad, before peppering them with questions about figures, which there was no way they could have memorised. Eventually, Oliver would intervene, taking sympathy on the red cheeks and stammering of his management team.

'Are you seriously telling me that you do not know off the top of your head what your budget for last year was, Christine?' Nick fired the question towards our executive housekeeping manager, Christine Anderson (legend, mid-fifties, divorced, came out as a lesbian two years ago).

Christine would normally know these figures, and she was also a fiery bitch. I fully expected her to put him in his place. Instead, she looked as if she was about to cry.

'Right, well, I think that will do for today. We'll do this again at the same time next week. I'll have Abbey send an agenda and some notes for what we are expecting,' Oliver said.

I almost heard the internal groans.

Nick was up and out the door before anyone else even moved. Then they all filed out, dejected. Ollie tried to make small talk with a couple of them to soothe them, but the clock read five past ten on Monday morning, and his entire team was devastated.

'I'm going to go get a coffee down the street. I'm on the mobile if you need me, Abs. Did you want one?' he said as we left the boardroom, handing me his notes from the meeting.

'I can get you one?'

'No, I like to walk. It's a nice day. Gives me time to clear my head.'

'Okay.'

I headed back to my desk and saw that Nick had taken Oliver's seat. I walked into the office, putting down Ollie's notebook while his brother's dark eyes surveyed me. He stopped typing. I could see tension in his shoulders, so I walked through to the butler's pantry and put the kettle on.

The kitchenette was so much nicer than my kitchen at home that every time I stepped foot in it, it made me want to move in. The back wall was all attractively modern cabinet storage. There was a wine fridge hidden in there, glasses, towels. The actual kitchen side was a white marble galley. There was even a dishwasher. I reached for the good china teacups and a pot.

He walked in and leaned against the benchtop, arms folded, lovely legs crossed. The room was completely screened off from the office and we were alone together for the first time today.

'Where's Ollie?'

'He went to get a coffee.'

He snorted as if that was a weakness he did not understand. I tried not to shake my head.

'What are you doing?' he asked.

'I'm making you tea.' I scooped out three teaspoons of tea into the pot and poured in the boiled water, watching the leaves dance about before shutting the lid.

'Why?'

'You're stressed, and I haven't seen you drink or eat this morning.'

'Did you make tea for Eric Linden?'

'No.'

'You have something to say, Abbey. Go ahead and say it. I didn't appreciate your eye rolling during that meeting.'

I folded my arms and took a step towards him. 'I'm a professional, Nick. I did not eye roll once, though the urge to kick you under the table a couple of times did arise. If you felt my disapproval, maybe that was your inner voice telling you to step it back a notch. What was the point of alienating everyone in the room?'

'I know exactly what I'm doing, Abbey.'

'Was making everyone terrified of you your aim?'

'Yes.'

I shook my head. 'That is not who you are, Nick.' *Fuck.* I dropped my eyes to the floor mortified. I had promised myself not to get personal with him.

He tilted my chin until our gazes met. His eyes were shining. 'If they are terrified of me, Oliver can build relationships with them that work on a much better level. It's a classic good-cop-bad-cop move. Understood? I don't need them to know *me*, Abbey.'

I swallowed at our closeness and nodded. I could feel the warmth coming from his body and I inhaled him deep in my lungs. I almost crumbled and put my arms around his narrow waist under the gorgeous jacket. But then I remembered where we were and who we were now, and I took a step back. Waited for his tea to brew.

'I want to hold a launch party next Friday night,' Nick said. 'Would you mind booking the ballroom and organising an invitation for the staff and their partners? Make it black tie. Give everyone the chance to dress up.'

'Done.' I poured him a tea, added a dash of milk and gave it a stir, handing it to him with a biscuit on the side.

'I don't need you to make me tea.' He sipped and then groaned over it. Tea from a pot was a winner. 'Thank you,' he said quietly.

I nodded and left.

The first week was done before I knew it. Nick and I had a couple of awkward moments, stepping through doors at the same time and then apologising. An interminable elevator ride.

I had to fight hard against Holiday Abbey. She was my enemy with Nick. She noticed everything about him. She could see stress in his shoulders and wanted to massage it out. She wanted to push his dark curls back off his face and slide into his lap while he drank his fucking tea. Holiday Abbey wanted to ensure he ate three times a day and laughed at least once an hour. Holiday Abbey dreamed of Nick and not just Holiday Nick anymore, and it was terrifying. And what was most terrifying was the knowledge that there was no Holiday Abbey. There was just Abbey. And Abbey wanted Nick.

Still, his brother and I were a bit of a crack team. We got on well, getting through enormous amounts of work and managing to have a laugh occasionally. I don't know if it was from our time in the resort, but I felt this genuine warmth and friendship from Oliver.

He had a good head for numbers, had a strategy he wanted to see the marketing team employ, and was engaged, with an excellent work ethic. His drive gave him high expectations of people, but they were the same expectations he placed on himself. He was a hard guy not to respect or like. By the end of the week, we were taking turns buying breakfast and making coffee.

I had lunch with Mike on the Thursday and he gave me the lowdown on the week I missed, and we ended up – naturally – talking about the entire company's current obsessive topic: the Northby brothers.

Mike Malik was my best bud at work. I actually could not even remember when we had first become friends or why, but I think I needed to do a financial report for Eric for some big meeting and Mike had taken pity on me. He was thirty-four and the salt of the earth, with a Pakistani dad, and a mum from Penrith, and he had this gorgeous, rugged poshness about him that got him laid constantly. He was swarthy and handsome, the most adorable human on earth.

'Let's talk about the Northbys.' He pushed my leg as he said this, and his eyes enlarged to the size of planets.

'Oh, God.' I shook my head, not wanting to engage. 'Can we not? Jesus Christ, remember the good old days when we talked about our shared love for Jon Snow.'

Mike ignored me. 'Sir Brood-a-lot and Prince Charming. They are like a walking, fucking romance novel. I don't know about you, but I always imagine Englishmen in period costume. Puffy shirts and tight breeches. And, Abs, Sir Brood-a-lot is a Darcy, which is hot once you get past the fact that he's an arsehole. But Prince Charming, fuck me, I would definitely give that a crack.'

'I think Oliver is into girls, babe.'

'How disappointing. Why?'

I shrugged.

'Right, Abs. Let us talk about frocks for next Friday's party. I have this emerald velvet tux, which is going to dazzle, hon. What about you? You wanna be my plus one?'

'Urgh, I don't think I'm going to make it. Things are a bit tight this week and I have nothing to wear. And I don't know about mingling, I just … hate shit like that.'

'You cannot leave me alone at that party, Abbey. We are work wives and we are the only single people on earth.'

Don't remind me.

I walked out of the office on Friday afternoon feeling fantastic about the fact it was Friday afternoon, but also pleased about what Oliver had achieved that week. This ended when I reached the lobby and saw it was absolutely bucketing down outside. I looked in my handbag and, sure enough, there was the world's tiniest umbrella, which had not a fucking chance of keeping me dry.

Sydney had two types of rain. The non-existent-for-up-to-six-months-drought kind and the fucking-bucketing-down-total-annual-rainfall-in-a-week kind. This was clearly the latter. I looked out nervously before deciding I had to get home one way or another and stepped out into it in the direction of the train station.

The rain was one thing, the gale-force southerly was another, and five steps into my journey, my tiny umbrella – pink with black polka dots, RIP – blew inside out, dumping more water on me than I could possibly have imagined it could hold. I looked at it and dumped it in the bin beside me. *Fuck it.*

A honk of a horn next to me had me raise my middle finger. *Who the fuck was honking at me?* Only a psychopath would have a laugh by honking the horn at a woman who was impersonating a drowned rat, for fuck's sake.

The window on the fancy black sedan rolled down.

'Need a lift?' a hot English accent said to me.

Fucking fuuuccckkk.

'C'mon, Abbey, in you get,' Nick commanded. 'I promise I won't bite.'

The car was warm, and I awkwardly tried to get off my drenched jacket, but the thing had me in a vice-like hold. Eventually, he leaned over and joined in the battle, and together we managed to free me.

He handed me a towel from his gym bag, which I kind of grossly hoped would smell like his sweat (*I know*), but was equally delighted that it was clean and dry. When our fingers grazed one another's, our eyes flew up and locked. Christ, the man had eyes like opals. Whatever light they were in, they gave you different things. Today they shone amber and a grey-brown. My mouth opened and closed as I peered into them, and I swallowed heavily. He reached out and pushed a strand of hair in wet ringlets behind my ear. His thumb brushed along my jaw and his eyes dropped to my lips and I leaned towards him, surrendering to this thing between us.

'Where to, Mr Northby?'

Oh, shit, the driver. We were not alone.

Nick sat back, blinking slowly, and he gave his driver my address.

My phone vibrated in my bag and, seeing Ella's name, I picked it up, looking out the window.

'Mum, oh, my God, the most exciting thing ever happened.'

'Hi, honey, are you home?'

'Mum, I got selected. I am so excited. For the junior student exchange program. I get to go to Canada for three months.'

'What?'

'The junior student exchange program, Mum.'

'Ella, I genuinely think you are too young to go to Canada by yourself for three months.'

'Mum, the host family are doctors. I'm going. It's only four thousand dollars. That's only two thousand each from you and Dad, and that's all I need for this once-in-a-lifetime experience.'

'Four thousand dollars?' The incredulousness in my voice arose from having savings totalling around two hundred and fifty dollars. And, okay, old mate next to me had increased my salary by doubling it, but I was in week one of my new employment contract and it would take me an age to save that kind of money. 'Ella, we'll talk about this later, okay?' I hung up and felt my head pound. I put my hand to the back of my neck and rubbed it, feeling my wet hair against my fingers.

'You okay?' Nick asked.

'Just a headache.'

He reached into his gym bag again and pulled out a bottle of water and some ibuprofen, handing them to me.

'Thank you.'

We sat in companionable silence.

'What high school is Ella at?'

'St Joseph's. It's an excellent school and she's bright.'

'I, uh, I didn't realise you were Catholic.'

'Oh, umm, I'm not. Peter picked the school.'

'I see. How is Iris?'

'She's well. I taught her how to post reviews of romance novels on Amazon. She's busy.'

He laughed quietly and it might have been the first genuine smile I had seen on him all week.

'You should do that more often.'

'What's that?' he said, quirking an eyebrow at me.

'Smile.'

'You haven't RSVP'd to the launch party.'

'I wasn't planning on going.'

'You have to.' His voice sounded strained. 'For work,' he added.

'I have Ella next week and I don't have anything to wear for your black-tie dress code.'

'You have Ella *this* week and I'm certain you have something to wear, or Kate does.'

It was annoying he knew my schedule with Ella.

'Abbey, if you need … you know … money …' He leaned forward, his eyes and voice imploring.

'Nick. Stop.'

'I'm just trying to—'

'Just here will be fine,' I said to his driver. We were at the top of my street. I needed to get out of this car. 'I do not need to be rescued, Nick. Thank you for the lift.' I climbed out and shut the door firmly behind me. And ran down the street to my house. Why were people trying to fix things for me? Why did they assume

I couldn't sort out my own dramas? It was infuriating.

I stood in the rain, digging through my handbag for my bloody house keys and saw them in an actual pocket, astonished that at some point that day I had put them in an easy-to-find place (where I would never look) and not in the central compartment I was digging around in.

When I looked up, he was in front of me.

'Can Holiday Nick talk to Holiday Abbey just for a second?'

The water was dripping down his face, making his hair dark and shiny, reminding me of that first night we met. It felt like a lifetime ago.

I shook my head. 'If Holiday Nick arrives, I won't want him to leave me. And Holiday Abbey, well, the problem there ... is that she is just me. Just Abbey ... So no. Not even for a second.' I put my hand into the hollow of his chest where it fit. And then I went inside, leaving him in the rain.

Nick

This work situation with Abbey was going to kill me. I'd told Ollie I would step away after Friday night's party. I promised myself I would not get personal with her. I almost kissed her in the bloody car.

People who make vows never to fall in love again should avoid spending enormous amounts of time with Abbey Parker. Abbey was ... she was pretty fucking wonderful.

At work, she was just ... fantastic. On Tuesday, she was absolutely flattened underneath the pile. She seemed to be the company 'community brain' and they would ask her for things instead of thinking for themselves. I watched her carefully, waiting to see how she would react, keeping hold of anything I needed from her myself. I did this so as not to add to her day, though I could tell this irritated her or she read something else into it because she took the time to shove passive-aggressive tea at me. I watched, impressed, as she politely managed items off her desk. The freeloaders left with simple instructions and a smile, and I was astonished. She practically ran the place, giving Oliver and me the space we needed to focus on the takeover and changing the things he wanted to change. I wanted nothing but to be close to her, to study her carefully.

She still had not RSVP'd to the party, which was bloody well driving me crazy. I was thinking about her non-stop and I was doing ludicrous, and I mean, absolutely barking shit all over the place. For example, on Monday I rang her child's school principal and made an anonymous, eight-thousand-dollar donation, to ensure that Ella and some other fucking child I do not even know can go live with Canadian doctors for three months, without cost to Abbey.

That, sadly, was not the limit of my madness. Worried the lack of RSVP was actually about a dress, I was forced on Thursday to wander around a Sydney department store to pick out something for her. Thankfully, the staff were extremely helpful, and the store was searched for a colleague who was Abbey's approximate height and weight. And Amelia from the kitchen department was extremely patient as she tried on every gown in the bloody store until I found it.

I then, awkwardly, had to get her sister involved.

I knocked on their door on Thursday afternoon, when I knew Abbey was safely ensconced at her desk in the office, and Kate answered it with a coffee in her hand. Her hair was up in a messy bun and her activewear told me she'd been to the gym.

'Is Abbey okay?'

'Yes. I'm so sorry to come uninvited. I, uh, I need your help.'

She arched an imperious eyebrow at me and then stood aside.

The hallway was narrow; the bedrooms coming off it, the two walls completely blocking out the rest of the house. There were family photos dotted, pictures mostly of Ella growing up. The house still smelled faintly like paint, and I stopped at Abbey's bedroom and stood in the doorway, taking in her decorative efforts. It was instantly recognisable as the resort room. Even the curtains, even the gentle breeze coming in her window. It was peaceful and calm, and it smelled like her perfume over the paint. A black-and-white photo of a beach graced the wall next to a floor-length mirror. A pair of her work shoes were neatly beside it. I've never looked at a room and wanted to go lie down on a bed more.

Kate cleared her throat. 'Did you just come here to stare at her room, 'cause that's pretty fucking weird.'

I gave a sharp laugh, but heat came to my face because I had been standing in that doorway for a long time. I had been thinking how on the holiday, her tinkly laugh would echo through my suite, bringing an instant smile to my face and I could almost hear it as I stood there.

Kate walked me through to the kitchen. 'Is this a coffee or something stronger discussion?'

I blew a snort out of my nose and then raised my eyebrows. 'Something stronger.'

She nodded and pulled out a bottle of gin and without asking poured me a healthy one with tonic, surprising me by adding a sprig of rosemary from a pot on the windowsill.

'What's in the bag?' she asked.

I appreciated her directness for once.

'You might think I'm behaving badly or maybe inappropriately. I'm not certain what I think about it myself, really. I, uh, don't usually … um, but …' I paused, taking a gulp of the drink. It was bloody strong. While I recovered from the first sip, I practised what I was trying to say, as it seemed I was having difficulty trying to string together a coherent sentence.

She drank too, but waited silently for me to continue, a tactic I used often in business.

'We are having a launch party tomorrow night,' I started. 'Abbey said she wouldn't come. It seemed to be about a dress, so I thought I would attempt to, uh, you know, rectify that.'

'You bought her a dress?'

I drank again. 'And shoes, just in case that was an issue, too.'

'I see.'

'You do?'

'Maybe better than you,' she said into her glass. 'Well, let's look at it.'

I got unusually very nervous. I hooked the bag over the door frame and opened it carefully, pulling out the dress and then removing the dust bag to leave it hanging on the door. I picked up my gin and downed it, while Kate stepped forward inspecting it.

'It's a good dress,' she said, still looking at it. 'Abbey will look beautiful in it.' Her eyes travelled sideways to give me an assessing stare.

'I can give you the, er, receipt in case it doesn't fit, or she hates it.'

Kate nodded.

'Will you help me by talking her into going?'

'Her not buying a dress, that would have cost her significantly less than you have spent on this, Nick, *is* about money, but not in the way you might think. She's a single mum and every cent she earns is accounted for because her arsehole ex-husband gives her the minimum of what he has to and anything else Ella needs is on *her*. Abbey denies herself many things to provide for her daughter.

'That is why you accusing her of taking money from that company, which has given her fuck all for over twenty years, is so upsetting. And that is outside of what happened between the two of you on that holiday. When you add that in, your behaviour, Nick, is pretty fucking hard to forgive.'

I forced myself to meet her eyes while she laid that exacting judgement upon me. Nothing that she had said was untrue.

She walked back around the kitchen bench and reached for my glass, which I handed her. She poured another two huge gins and handed me one. We both leaned back against the wooden counter, staring at the gown in the doorway.

'But fuck me, Nick. This is a nice dress.'

She clinked my glass, and we drank. And I found my first friend in Sydney. Kate Cavendish – gatekeeper, lioness and all-round queen – and I, on a Thursday afternoon, over two gin and tonics and a designer dress, formed an alliance to get Abbey Parker to a ball.

Chapter Seven
Abbey

Another week, another awkward-as-fuck, good-cop-bad-cop exec meeting, with Nick grilling everyone and Oliver soothing. I somehow managed to restrain myself from rolling my eyes. From what I'd seen of Ollie in his first week, he didn't need this kind of nannying.

I spent the rest of week two organising the itinerary for Oliver to tour all our hotels, which was pretty simple work, in that I was mostly just booking travel, drivers, meetings and accommodation for him. Given that I had just got home from two weeks away from Ella, the timing wasn't great for me, so I also arranged for various assistants to go with him to each state. His first visit was scheduled for the end of next week, with him flying out to Brisbane on the Friday.

There were a bunch of projects from Hartwell Holdings, including the review of every wine we had in every single hotel. I sat in on a phone call with Oliver and their head buyer, Louise Carlow, who wanted to utilise the local wine industry in a more boutique way. Oliver wanted the same thing to happen regarding the restaurants using local seasonal produce.

Nick avoided me. There was no other way to put it. While Oliver would spend the day calling me or utilising me in some capacity, Nick had moved himself into the boardroom and barely looked in my direction. Occasionally, rebellion would overtake me, and I would very deliberately take him in tea, which he would pretend he did not want, before groaning over the cup as I left.

I was in complete denial about my feelings for him, and if I'd somehow imagined spending more time with Nick would cure me of them, I was sadly mistaken. The man was a powerhouse. He would rock up every day in his bespoke suits, distractingly fitted to his body with a perfection that made me jealous of his tailor. His workload was enormous and his passion for his business was unmistakable. He vibrated with the culture and ethics he spoke about. And yes, he was tough, but he was also approachable.

Mike had not had the benefit of a handover in his new role, and Nick carved out a whole day to work with him and the rest of the finance department. At lunch the next day, it was evident Mike's crush had switched.

'He's just so ... understated and down to earth. Much more so than you'd expect from a guy with that much money. And, honestly, he is way smarter than me. What is going on with his hair? Is it product? Can I get mine to be so fucking touchable? Also, Abbey, his arse ...'

Jesus Christ.

I'd also had glimpses of the love and care he had for his brother, such as on the Wednesday night, when I might have been pacing outside Oliver's office, waiting for a meeting of his to finish up.

Nick approached me, his hands stuffed into his pockets. 'Who's he on the phone to?'

Oh, hey! Hi, baby. You wanna come to my place for dinner and then spend the rest of your life with me? Thankfully, that did not escape my brain and I said, 'Sydney City Council.'

Nick had suggested Oliver contact them over the no-standing zone directly out the front of the Delacqua Sydney. It meant guests had to be dropped off further back and walk to the entrance, and that was not good for business.

The discussions were in their second hour.

Nick opened the office door without knocking and held it back for me. I ducked under his arm, entering ahead of him, and took a seat across from Oliver. Nick sat beside me.

Oliver looked tired; he had all day. I was getting emails throughout the night from him and Nick was too.

Nick stayed quiet, listening to the discussions, which had turned from the parking to possible refurbishment of the interior of the hotel, to the mayor of Sydney worming his way into the launch party on Friday night.

Nick was itching to jump in. I could feel him virtually vibrating in his seat, but he managed to stay silent.

Oliver finally hung up.

'You okay?' I asked.

'Politicians …'

'How did it go?' Nick said seriously.

'They're willing to discuss it, but also want to talk about subsidised accommodation when the mayor travels, as well as subsidies to surrounding businesses when we renovate and sponsorship of the mayor's Staycation campaign. Our discussions went in a fucking circle and got us nowhere.' He ran his fingers through his hair roughly. 'That's two hours of my life I'll never get back.'

'It wasn't pointless, Ollie. You've opened up a communication stream. You can continue it Friday night,' Nick said.

'I should have let you speak to him.'

There was something vulnerable in that. Nick was obviously Mr Fix It in his family.

I was about to interject, but Nick beat me to it. 'You did everything I would have, though I may have ended it an hour earlier,' he joked, a genuine smile lighting up his handsome face. 'You're doing a good job, Ollie.'

Oliver yawned. 'Abbey, what are you still doing here? Go home.'

'I didn't want to leave in case you needed me.'

Oliver smiled and closed his eyes, rubbing them with his hand. 'I'm exhausted.'

'Let's go get a beer and some dinner,' Nick said. 'You've been killing yourself for a month. Phones and laptops down, okay? Abbey, you are all done here. Thank you. Head home,' Nick said, turning his dazzling smile on me.

Inwardly, I sighed and basked in it.

'Unless you want to join us, Abs?' Ollie stood, putting on his jacket.

I looked at Nick, who raised an eyebrow, wrinkling his forehead. I read this as: *you can if you want to*. But I had other commitments.

'I'm all good. Ella has cooked, which is vaguely alarming. Still, I'm curious.'

'Good luck with that,' Nick mumbled.

'I suspect I might need it,' I returned.

After that, we were slightly more comfortable with each other. Oliver worked from home and Nick did not come in on Thursday, which I confess I was a little disappointed about because I had definitely felt the ice thaw and I had wanted to see him. Either way, I had a pretty chilled day, which one can never complain about.

I was in a good mood when I got home, but it quickly turned to rage when Kate presented me with a dress. A dress bought by Nick.

The designer bag hanging in the kitchen prompted me to

interrogate her, and she confessed to gin and tonics with my boss/ex-lover or whatever – the flare of irritation I felt in my gut had nothing to do with jealousy, of course – and that she had agreed she would 'get me to the ball' on Friday night.

Naturally, I stamped my foot, telling her in no uncertain terms that that was completely and utterly unacceptable. I refused to even look at the dress or even think about discussing it with *him*. The gall of that man.

I would return the dress over the weekend – an absolute pain in the arse, by the way – and give him back his bloody money the next week.

I avoided him at work on Friday by spending the entire day at the hotel. The Delacqua Sydney had been rebuilt two years ago, and it was big, glassy and shiny. I found it vaguely depressing and lacking personality and, apparently, so did the Northbys, because I had taken notes on Monday in a meeting with their architect where Nick had called it cold, unwelcoming and lacking in character. But the ballroom had the benefit of a large balcony and views overlooking the city and harbour.

I headed home just after four and walked in the door, dumping my bag on the floor of my newly renovated room, which looked like just the slice of heaven I needed this Friday night. Sliding my shoes off my tired feet, I padded into the lounge room, only to be confronted by all three of the Cavendish women. My daughter sat next to my sister, who had pulled in her trump card, my grandmother. It was an aggressive move and could only have been my sister's idea of an intervention.

Iris looked as if she had just climbed down from the deck of a yacht. She had on a thick cream jumper over navy culottes and canvas sneakers, definitely channelling Lauren Bacall.

'Abigail.'

I walked over to her, kissing her and wrapping her into me. She was warm, smelled like Chanel and she made my heart ache with love and devotion.

'Hi, Gran.' There was a warning in my tone, but I could not hide the warmth and affection I felt for her.

'Mum, Aunt Kate says you're not going to a party tonight because you don't want to wear a fancy, expensive dress someone bought you.'

'Ella, dear, will you please go pop the kettle on and make tea for Granny?'

'Of course, Gran.'

'Thank you, child.'

We all watched Ella leave the room and waited until we heard the kettle start.

'Kate, this is completely unacceptable,' I hissed.

Kate lifted her chin and looked at the ceiling.

'Abigail, darling,' Gran said, dropping her voice. 'You have been holding out. Kate says your new boss is also your Maldivian lover. How very serendipitous.'

I looked at Kate, horrified. 'He's *English*. I'm not sleeping with him … anymore.' I was mortified as I realised how sad I sounded.

'And, Gran, there is this fancy-arse party tonight that Abbey is refusing to go to. She claimed she had nothing to wear and then a dress appeared for her, and she won't even look at it.'

Kate was dobbing me in as if she was eight, making me want to pinch her. I threw what I hoped was a dignified, daggered stare at her instead, and she folded her arms and huffed.

'Abigail, when a man buys you expensive presents …' Gran said, shaking her head.

'He is being manipulative. He accused me of taking money from the company and almost fired me over it. And now he is trying to pay off his guilt. He has already doubled my salary, and now this.' I pointed accusingly to the bag.

Gran and Kate shared a look.

'Open the bag, Kate,' Gran ordered.

Kate gave me a wide berth as she moved to the dress.

'And, Abigail Cavendish, instead of going to this party this evening, where presumably there will be decent champagne and music and lots of men in tuxedos, what will you be doing, my love?'

'I thought I would have a bottle of wine for dinner and watch a murder mystery,' I retorted, fed up with their interference.

Iris rolled her eyes at me.

'Here it is, Gran.'

I turned around and got my first look at the dress.

'Oh,' I said. My impassioned denial of this gift was suddenly silenced. 'Nick chose this?'

Kate had helped Gran up and the three of us stood there, silently staring at it.

'I have not seen a dress that fine, since … Well, it has been a long time. That is a fabulous dress. It looks like you, Abigail.'

The dress was divine. No, it was honestly the loveliest thing I'd ever seen. There was a whimsical simplicity to it. It was a dark-gold metallic fabric, with a sweetheart neckline and a bodice that ran to the waist. A pleated skirt draped softly to the floor and a thigh-high split saved it from being too sweet. If I had endless money to spend on a dress, I might buy this dress. The bag read *Made in Italy*, which to us regular folk means *unaffordable*.

'Wait, there are these as well.' Kate practically skipped to the corner and pulled out a shoe box.

I recognised the brand. I recognised that these shoes could pay my mortgage this month or go pretty bloody close. I opened the box and a gorgeous pair of black suede slingbacks in my size stared back at me. They were perfect. The heel was not too high, which was considerate, and they were unadorned enough that I might have the chance of wearing them again.

'Jesus.'

'Well, go try it on,' Iris ordered.

Kate and I looked at each other. 'Go on, Abs, at least try it.'

I nodded. I did have to; I might never get the chance to wear designer clothes ever again.

Kate walked me to my room, and I put on the dress. It fit as though it had been measured for me. I slid my feet into the shoes and stood looking at myself in the mirror. I looked elegant, taller, slimmer than I normally did. I swept my hair to the side and realised no matter what I did, it looked good. *Jesus Christ*. Was this what life with him was like? There was not a girl in the world that could not get used to it. Germaine Greer popped into my head and slapped my face, but still … a girl could dream.

My phone vibrated. I knew it would be him before I even looked.

I still don't have your RSVP.

Jesus, what was happening? It was confusing. Was he trying to tell me something? If Holiday Nick had been allowed to speak the other day, what would he have said? I began to think about him in a tux and it all became very, very tempting.

There was no way on earth I would get away with not showing Gran and Kate what the dress looked like on, so I dutifully walked out to the lounge room. The twirl I did upon entering was a bit of showmanship. *Ta da*.

'Holy fuck, Abbey. It looks perfect.'

'Oh, Mum, you look so beautiful.'

'Of course, Cavendish women always scrub up rather nicely.'

'Jesus, Abbey. Where are you off to?'

I turned to see my ex-husband standing in the doorway. I was instantly irritated. I looked at him and at that moment attempted to establish what I had seen in him that had made me want to marry him in the first place. He was wearing funky cuffed cargo pants, expensive sneakers and a T-shirt, which was a brand I was not cool enough to recognise. His hair was longer than when I last saw him, and I wondered if he was attempting to look younger than he actually was. He had helped himself to my fruit bowl and was crunching loudly on an apple.

Why had I given up my youth for him? I remember thinking he would be an amazing father and he had a great job. When I was twenty, he seemed to be a man, responsible and willing to be a grown-up.

But I didn't notice how much I changed for him. He liked to have an opinion on everything, including how much I ate (women don't normally eat that much, Abbey) and what I wore (you wear too much black, women who are mums should wear colour). I thought it was normal.

The fact that he did not love me was, surprisingly, not the source of my antipathy. I didn't love him either. The affair … the affair bothered me; it was deceitful and disrespectful of the love we had once shared and the child we had created. I would always maintain a relationship with him for Ella, but we were not friends, and I did not appreciate him being here at this particular moment.

'Peter,' I said politely if not warmly.

'Dad, Mum is going to a party for work. Doesn't she look amazing?'

'Geez, bit old to be showing so much leg, Abbey. And a bit much for work, isn't it? You hate those dos.'

Peter completely failed to notice the death stares he received from both Iris and Kate. But I was having a fucking epiphany. How many times over the years had he done that? Planted the seeds of doubt in my head? I had just looked in a mirror and I knew I looked good. I felt confident, and yet with one sentence, he had tried to alter that and encourage me not to go. How many times had I just given in, in an attempt to please him, instead of doing what I wanted? Instead of living my life?

'Peter, you can just call Ella's phone and wait out the front from now on. There's no need for you to come into my house.' I gave Ella a quick apologetic look, but she just nodded, approving of my suddenly firm spine. I turned to my sister. 'Kate, any chance you could help me with my makeup?'

A proud smile appeared on her beautiful face.

'Peter, what the devil is wrong with your hair? Good lord, you look like one of those middle-aged men trying to look younger.' My love for my grandmother grew exponentially. 'It's borderline ridiculous. You will take me back to the nursing home and we shall leave the girls to get ready. Ella darling, grab your bag. Your *father* needs to get going ... to a barber, preferably.'

I covered my snort with a cough and walked over to Iris to kiss her goodbye.

'Love you, Gran.'

'You look like an absolute knockout, child. Nothing feeble about that outfit.' She dropped her voice for just my ear. 'Dance, drink champagne and have sex with a stranger tonight. It'll do you good.'

Jesus Christ.

Two hours later I was in the back of an Uber, looking out the window. The rain from the week before had cleared, leaving beautifully warm autumn days and chilly evenings, and Kate had lent me her black faux-fur bolero to ward off the chill. Gold and black earrings sparkled, dangling against my neck. Kate had swept my waves to one side and had insisted I wear a red lip colour, making me feel slightly unlike myself.

There was a nervous energy inside my stomach, which I did not want to acknowledge but could not deny. I wanted to see him. I wanted to see him in a tux. I wanted him to see me looking like this. We were both doing a pretty good job of avoiding our holiday romance selves, but how long could that hold out for?

After everything that had happened, I was as drawn to him as I had been on that island. And there were times at work when I would look up and find his eyes resting on me and the only reason I knew was because I was looking for them.

Whenever he entered a room, my body knew it before I did. We were two individuals, connected gravitationally, an inexplicable magnetic force between us. And though we had drawn a huge line in that white sand to mark the end of our affair, it felt as if he might have flirted with the edge by buying me this dress. And the question was, now that the barrier had been crossed, would it hold? The thought that it wouldn't … well, I could not deny … it thrilled me.

The real question was, could I keep my feelings separate if he offered me more? I honestly did not know the answer to that.

My Uber passed through the familiar, almost abandoned-looking, suburb of Tempe into Sydenham, the two suburbs marked only by how low the planes passed over, an Ikea the size of a suburb and a train station that could take you anywhere. Through St Peters and onto King Street, Newtown – still clinging on to its bohemian soul despite the multi-million-dollar housing market – and into the city.

Sydney glittered. It always seemed to me like the little sister of other major cities in the world, unsure of who she was, until you got to the harbour where it all just made sense and her genuine beauty shone.

I got out of the Uber down the street from the hotel, as the no-standing zone in front of the Delacqua had left a row of cars dropping people off that stretched down the road. I walked the short distance to the hotel lobby. Even if I hadn't just spent the day here overseeing preparations, I had been in the company so long and visited often enough to be a well-known figure. Larry Bertram, the legendary doorman and porter, kissed my cheek when he saw me and then raised his eyebrows, shaking his head, whispering that I looked 'pretty as a picture', which filled me with renewed confidence.

I took my place in the back corner of the lift and fidgeted nervously, my hand rising to the spot where my pendant should be, mourning its loss. When the lift opened, the occupants poured out into the glowing foyer. The room itself was lit gently by candlelight, chandeliers and a soft turquoise colour I had picked from the lighting team.

The Northbys stood at the entrance, welcoming guests and making small talk, briefly, before moving on to the next person. They were both flawless and for the first time, looking at them from a distance, I could see a resemblance, which I realised had to do with their mannerisms.

Oliver was perfectly turned out, cream jacket gleaming against the lights. There was something modern and red carpet-esque about the look. I could see women in front of me murmuring appreciatively and adjusting their dresses.

The way Nick sensed me brought to mind a teen werewolf flick; I could have sworn he sniffed the air. I was still five or six people deep in a queue, but his eyes found me, and I saw genuine surprise. I had done the unthinkable and caught Nick Northby off guard. His face broke into a lupine smile.

As I moved closer, person by person disappearing between us, my heart pounded. I had taken off my jacket in the lobby of the hotel and checked it into the cloakroom, but the goosebumps that graced my arms had absolutely nothing to do with the temperature.

'Abigail Parker.' Oliver gave a low whistle. 'You are a triumph, and if I weren't your boss' – he gave Nick a quick side eye – 'I would say something wildly inappropriate.'

He took my right hand, spinning me and then kissed me on the cheek, making me laugh. Why did it feel as if he was *my* brother?

Ollie released me and I moved towards Nick, who had shoved his hands in his pockets and looked like ... well, heaven, or perhaps more divertingly somewhere darker, lit only by flames. His eyes were sharp, and they roamed over my body, and I swear to you I could almost feel them, as if his hands were travelling over me.

'You found a dress,' he said, holding tightly to keep the grin from spreading across his face.

'Oh, what, this old thing? Just something I found at home,' I said, sounding bored.

'You didn't RSVP.'

'Is there a naughty corner?' I raised an eyebrow at him.

'Jesus, I hope so,' he uttered.

I laughed, a sound neither of us had heard in weeks. We held eye contact for a moment more and then I moved into the room, but I could still feel his eyes on my back.

Inside, Mike waved to me and handed me a champagne before making delicious noises over my dress. 'Is that Dolce?'

'What? No,' I lied, gulping my champagne. *How on earth did he know that?*

'Fine, keep your secrets.'

We mingled for about thirty minutes, and I was thankful to have Mike there, keeping conversations flowing, as it allowed me to keep my eyes on the room, watching the Northbys circulate. They'd split up and were working their refined charm on the who's who of the Sydney social scene. There was an endless supply of politicians, retired sports stars, and B-grade celebrities fawning over them. Thinking I would not be here, I had assigned an assistant to each of them for the evening and they did me proud keeping the boys gently moving, whilst running interference on would-be admirers.

They eventually slipped away, as Oliver prepared to welcome everyone and launch the business, and I followed them into a little room behind the stage.

Oliver was more nervous than I would have ever imagined, and Nick shot me a look that begged for help. I stepped backwards and asked the waiter for a bottle of single malt and three glasses, then marched up to Ollie.

'Oliver Northby.'

'Ooh, I feel like I might barf, Abs.'

'Nonsense. Remind me to take you to visit my grandmother Iris at some point.' I fussed with his tie and pushed a strand of hair back from his forehead until the whisky arrived. Then I poured us a glass each, and we drank.

'Iris would tell you …' I paused. 'Actually, she would say something incredibly inappropriate and hit on you. But she would say to me, "Abigail, do not be feeble," and that is what I am going to say to you.' I reached out to put my hand on his arm. 'You are Oliver fucking Northby, and this company is yours. You are charming as fuck, handsome and rich. Don't you dare be feeble.'

He held my eyes and then nodded once and threw back the rest of the alcohol, and the three of us walked to the door.

Oliver entered the ballroom and I almost took one step through, but a firm hand pulled me back by the wrist. Nick's lips were on mine. It was swift, ephemeral and it felt so good to be in his arms again that I would have given up anything asked of me for one more minute. He was not freshly shaven and his whiskers were not yet soft and, honestly, I would have scratched off my own face for more. He pressed a 'Thank you,' into my ear and I wiped lipstick off his mouth with my thumb before we walked out to take our seats.

I sat next to Mike and Nick took his at the head of a table of VIPs, including the mayor of Sydney and his daughter. I swear to you I listened to what Oliver said, but I did not hear a word. I clapped at the right times and then ate the food when it came around, but my eyes kept gravitating towards Nick. His eyes were drawn to mine, and I had the odd sensation that I had the power to compel them to me. But I had competition, and she was right next to him.

Miss Mayor was a renowned Sydney socialite and occasional model. She travelled in a pack of kids her age who had as much of a leg-up in life as she had. She was twenty-five years old, stunning and blonde, with legs that came up to my ears. And she had her eyes set on the good-looking, rich, English guy in the nice tux. Nick Northby. He was busy talking to her father until Oliver joined them. After that, she had his undivided attention.

I watched as she coaxed reluctant smiles from him, listened enraptured as he spoke and put her hands on his arm or his thigh when she tittered. He laughed at one point, surprised by something she had said, and I had the feeling I was watching a successful first date. All I could do was to drink through it. At least, I congratulated myself, I was managing to drink the champagne from the glass this time.

Music started after the dinner was cleared, and the party hit the dance floor. Little Miss Mayor dragged out a reluctant Nick and I was one thousand per cent certain an Ed Sheeran song was around the corner. I knew he was doing his job; I just didn't want to watch it. We were in this grey place, somewhere between former lovers and lovers, which was … hard. And I'd thought I could feel him taking a step, emotionally, towards me. And more than anything, I wanted that.

'Come dance, Abbey,' Mike said.

'I'm just going to get some air, I think,' I said, smiling at him.

At the very least, the night had been successful, especially for something that was short notice. It showcased both our restaurant and our wines, as well as our real trump card, our charming new owners.

The balcony was empty due to the coolness of the evening, and I walked slowly to the balustrade, breathing in the sea smells of the harbour. Underneath us, Sydney sang; horns honked, crossing lights pulsed, and the sound of voices laughing and having a wonderful Friday night filled my ears like a favourite band.

What was I doing? Why was I here?

'Ah, someone else avoiding the dance floor?'

I turned to find a handsome guy in his early fifties in a plain black tux. I smiled politely.

'You're Abbey, right?'

'Yes. I'm sorry. Do we know each other?'

'I'm Patrick Conlon. Umm, the mayor's assistant. We spoke on the phone the other day.'

'Oh, right, hi! Nice to meet you.'

'You too.'

'It's cold out here.'

'Yeah.' He looked out at the view and then down to his hand on the balustrade, before meeting my eyes again. 'Do you, uh, I know we are both avoiding that dance floor by being out here, but you wouldn't want to dance with me, would you? At least it's warm in there.' He smiled.

A handsome man in a nice suit wanted to dance with me. Maybe I should take Gran's advice for me this evening. Maybe I should stop being feeble.

Nick

This glamorous young person was all over me like a rash. There was a time in my life where I would have been flattered, but that was a lifetime ago and, at the moment, all I could think was that she had picked the wrong guy. Why not choose Oliver? He was so much lighter than I was. Same childhood, but considerably less adult trauma.

And even if I could have somehow mustered the energy to say she was *very* attractive, my head would not let me, because all I wanted to do was to ascertain the whereabouts of a particular girl in a particular gold fucking dress.

I caught a glimpse of the dress from behind and spun the pretty blonde, whose name had vanished from my head – Alicia? Alison? Fiona? – so I had a better view.

And there she was. Abbey. Dancing with a solid, attractive bloke. He looked older than me, stronger than me and possibly taller than me. He was annoyingly handsome in that 'I got handsome as I got older' way, which I am not certain is happening with my looks. Not that I think about that sort of thing.

Abbey was dancing and there was this glorious radiant smile on her face, which was flirty and earthy and – *fuck me* – if she was not the only woman in this room. *I am lost.* I had allowed my control to slip earlier, and I had kissed her. Now that was the only thing I could fucking think about.

Not this party, not this woman in my arms, nothing but her.

And there she was dancing with this other guy because I couldn't be the man she deserved.

But what am I doing? I would not be living here beyond a couple of weeks. *I do not want a relationship. I don't want to hurt her. This is the last work function I have on. The last duty I need to fulfil for Delacqua. Tomorrow I am just Nick. Just Nick in old Sydney town for two weeks, just in case Ollie needs me. Just Nick ignoring the callings of home. Holiday Nick.*

I have two weeks. And if that is something she might want, I wonder if ... Why wouldn't we? It felt as if something had shifted and the heat we'd been ignoring for the last few weeks was finally breaking free. It felt as if the two of us crossing boundaries tonight was inevitable.

I should leave her alone. I could not offer her what she wanted. I think she has feelings, and I am definitely having feelings. I absolutely do not want her hurt. Abbey is sweet, generous and kind. I do not want her to feel pain. It would be better if we stopped. If I stopped ...

I excused myself from the blonde and walked to the DJ with purpose, insisting that the next song was an Ed Sheeran song, and then I waited by the door.

The song switched. I watched as she listened and then shook her head at the handsome stranger and extricated herself from him. She grabbed her bag, took one last look around and walked towards the door.

I had a quick word with our security guy and had him hold the lift I walked into. I listened from the back corner, out of sight, as he ushered another couple towards the other lift. She walked in and, gorgeously, just smiled and rolled her eyes as she saw me. I pointed towards the camera. She nodded.

Her face became serious as her eyes met mine and locked. I saw her breathing change and watched as her chest rose and fell. That dress on the lady from the kitchen department had looked good, but I had no idea what the perfect dress for the perfect woman would look like, and it was so much better than I could have ever imagined. Abbey is small and curvy. Perfectly curved. Soft, supple, silky. My hands remember exactly how she feels and the memories haunt me. I remember how she feels every single night; I remember her mouth and the curves of it. I remember her sounds. I very much wanted to hear them again.

It was the longest fucking lift ride in the world. She had more makeup on than I had ever seen on her and when she bit gently on a red lip I thought I'd combust. Thankfully, the lift dinged, and we walked out. I waited as she grabbed her coat, and we left the building, walking about a block. Finally, we were far enough away from that fucking hotel, and I dragged her into an alleyway and kissed her much harder than that stupid, mad kiss in that little room.

Her lips fit perfectly to mine and we found an instant rhythm. She tasted like champagne and crème caramel, and I wanted to devote myself to the combination. My hands started exploring her in that dress, what it felt like around her waist and how it felt over her arse. I pulled her hips into mine and I knew there was a fucking split there somewhere and that I could get to skin, but it evaded me at first and then she moved her leg a little as she pressed her body into me and there it was, her warm soft skin under my palm, where it should be.

Dangerous thoughts, Nick. Very dangerous thoughts. What would it look like? The two of us?

Her hands were in my hair then and I'm pretty sure the first noise came from me. My hand was roaming over her breast and the other was climbing under her skirt. She whispered, 'Nick,' into my ear and I kissed her harder, silencing her before I gave in to the desire to fuck her against this wall. I have never wanted anything more in my life than this woman at this moment.

She was vibrating. No, she wasn't vibrating, her phone was.

'Abbey, your phone.'

'Oh,' she said, dazed.

I waited for a second as she found it in her purse and then I started kissing her neck and her collarbone as she squinted to read it.

'Oh, fuck. It's Gran's nursing home.' She put her hand into the nook on my chest to get me to stop.

I placed my hand over it and pulled away.

She took the call.

'Speaking.'

She listened.

'Oh. Okay.' She swallowed. 'Is she okay? I'm on my way.'

Chapter Eight
Abbey

I ordered an Uber, and he held me for the two minutes it took to arrive. He opened the door for me, and I turned to press one last kiss to him.

'You should go back to your party,' I said into his cheek.

'And miss the opportunity to meet the great Iris Cavendish? Not a chance on this earth. In the cab, Abbey.'

I didn't have the energy to fight the situation. I wanted him to want to come. I wanted Gran to meet him. I lifted my dress, sliding along to the far seat, and he hopped in after me, folding his long legs into the compact car.

The call from the nursing home had been to let me know she had fallen. This was the third one this year. Previously, we'd had success with rehabilitation, but at the moment she didn't have the energy to get through a two or three-hour program. We had arranged for a private physio to visit her once a week, but when I had called to check in on how she was progressing, the physio had said she wasn't making any gains. Tonight's was the good kind of fall apparently: what they call an 'assisted fall'. She'd had her back to a cupboard when she'd gone, so she had slid down it and then called out to them from the floor. Though she was sore and bruised, she had not hit her head.

My hand was on my throat searching for my pendant and he reached across to me, taking my hand in his and giving it a comforting, warm squeeze.

We arrived at Iris's nursing home a little after ten. Ashford House was a beautiful Victorian mansion in Randwick, an affluent area, where it was leafy and green. Iris had lived in nearby Paddington for most of my life, so she was familiar with the area. The house had been converted into an attractive-looking nursing home in the last ten years and housed forty or so residents. Iris had been here for three years. Though I had offered for her to live with me when she'd decided she could no longer live alone, she had refused, saying she would kill Peter in a fortnight.

The amount of money she paid to live there was a king's ransom. It had eaten most of the money from the sale of her Paddington townhouse.

We were let into the locked foyer by a nurse, and I stopped at the base of the stairs, leaning on Nick to remove my slingbacks. I picked up the skirt of my dress and ran up the stairs. At the top of them, he removed his jacket, leaving him in a waistcoat and a gleaming white buttoned shirt. He had removed his tie in the car and looking at him in the light I stared at his throat for, well, too long.

Iris's room was at the far end of a long corridor. It was the best room in the place because it had a corner window that dappled light spilled into during the day. Three years ago, when she had still been able to see the print, she could read her books by it. We eventually switched her to digital and audiobooks as her eyesight had worsened.

I was a little apprehensive as I entered her room. She did not enjoy being fussed over and preferred Kate to me in these kinds of situations because Kate was all level-headed and I would become emotional. That Kate was not here told me that whatever had happened to Gran, medically at least, Kate was not worried about her.

Iris was on her bed, her covers pulled to her waist, her beautiful pale face against a perfect white pillowcase. I could not see a single injury on her. She looked as if she was lying in state, like a queen, her long white hair that she refused to cut spread out onto her pillows in soft shiny waves. Her pale-blue nightgown, tied with a ribbon at her neck, had a ruffled collar and ruffled cap sleeves, which somehow added to her queenliness. Lionel was beside her on a chair, holding her hand.

His soft brown eyes crinkled to greet me as I walked into the room, Nick close behind me. Lionel stood and reached for my hand. His was clean, dry and warm and felt like paper, the soft and cherished kind. He was a love letter, creased and treasured. He was dressed in clean, brown-checked flannelette pyjamas and a navy-blue dressing gown.

'You look fabulous, Abbey,' Lionel whispered.

'Abigail Louise Cavendish.' Iris's voice rang out strong, like that of a Shakespearean thespian. 'If you are going to bring gorgeous men into my room, I would appreciate you calling ahead. I might have liked to have put a little colour on my lips.'

A relieved sigh escaped my mouth. Clearly, the fall hadn't dampened her spirit.

'Gran, Lionel, this is Nicholas Northby. He's my uh … well … he and I met on holiday, and he is my, erm … boss?' Nick raised a dark eyebrow at me. 'Nick, my grandmother, Iris and her uh …' I searched for a word to describe Gran and Lionel's relationship. 'Friend … Lionel.'

Fuck me, but life is complicated.

Gran extended an elegant arm to Nick, who astonished me by bowing over her hand and kissing it with a courtly flourish.

'Mrs Cavendish. Lionel.' He shook Lionel's hand.

'It surprised us all enormously that Abbey took a lover on holiday. And then I was quite confused, thinking he was Maldivian,' my grandmother said, raising a gorgeous flush on Nick's cheeks. 'Of course, England is lovely. I myself have had two English husbands. My Harry was English. He had very *gracious manners*. I was quite swept up with him. I can see why my granddaughter likes you and, of course, that is a very nice dress.'

'It is nice to meet you too, Mrs Cavendish. I have heard a great deal about you.'

Gran gave Nick an assessing stare. 'Abigail, did you take my advice this evening?'

'No, Gran.'

'Hmm, well, the night is still young, I suppose.'

'Gran, are you okay? The nurses said you had a fall.'

'I didn't fall.'

'Iris, you did, remember? About an hour ago, dearest,' Lionel said gently.

'Oh, well, I just wanted tea, dear. I just wanted to make tea.'

'Gran, if you use your buzzer they will bring you tea.'

'Nicholas.' Nick took her hand again. 'Tell me about you, young man. I am exceedingly pleased to see colour in Abbey's cheeks. I don't suppose she has spoken to you about Peter. Abbey turned herself into a brown little mouse to match him. Boring, you were, for a bit, Abbey.'

I chose to ignore the mouse jibe.

'Now her colours are back. She is a Cavendish again. Full of spirit. And once a woman finds her spirit again in her forties, well, we become thoroughly unmanageable, but magic.'

'I've always found Abbey very colourful,' Nick said.

It made me grin and my chest swell with pride. I had thought that being 'beige', as Gran called it, was what the perfect mother looked like, what the perfect wife looked like. I had been kind, likeable, easygoing, falsely happy. I did not flirt and had fun moderately. I spent years gushing about how happy my life was. Ignoring the big question in my head: *Is this it?*

'Yes. That is pleasing,' Gran said knowingly. She smiled, but then she closed her eyes for a few minutes.

God, I found it hard to imagine that she might not be here forever. And when someone was this much of a person, so vibrant, so big, what kind of void did that leave in the world? I felt the sadness travel from my face into my gut. Nick reached out and tucked me into him.

We stood for a minute more.

'Well, get out dears. I'm exhausted.' She said this without opening her eyes and I almost laughed.

Nick moved towards the door, leaving me to say goodbye.

'Oh, and Nicholas darling.' Nick stopped as she spoke. 'There is a live model art class here on Tuesdays. I don't wish to speak for all the ladies, but I have just noticed your pleasing assets at the back there, dear. Puts me in mind of a ripe apricot. You would be welcome. They pay thirty dollars per hour for the models, dearest.'

I saw heat rise in his cheeks once more and I could not help but give him a challenging, amused smile.

'Oh, um, well, I'll think on that. Thank you, Mrs Cavendish.'

I snorted, unable to contain my laughter. The idea of women in their eighties and nineties painting a naked Nick was absolutely priceless.

I bent over my grandmother, kissing her head. 'You are incorrigible.'

'That man is lovely, but Abbey, hold on to your spirit. Guard it. Don't let men take it, Abigail. It is too precious,' she whispered to me. 'You are worth it. Know that within yourself.'

I felt tears in my eyes and then got them under control. When I stood, my shoulders were set ever so slightly squarer, for – as usual – it was exactly what I had needed to hear.

He ordered the car and put in my address. It was a short wait, and I shivered a little in the night. He noticed straight away, draping his coat around my shoulders and pulling me into his body heat. He was such a gentleman. I was completely overcome with him, and my heart sang at having him close like this.

'So you going to take Gran up on that modelling job?'

He chuckled, a lovely soft sound. 'I think I'm in love with her.'

'There isn't a man in the world who is not susceptible to her charms. Not even the great Nick Northby.'

'Abbey …' Nick started.

I met his eyes and my heart gave a shuddering lurch. I was in over my head here. I wanted to make very bad decisions with him. I wanted to show him all of my colours.

'Did you want to come to mine for wine?' I said.

He swallowed. 'Certainly. Yes.'

There was a tension in the car. We did not touch each other. Occasionally, his dark eyes glittered at me, making my heart pound.

He got out of the car at my house and then helped me out. My dress slid, and the slit revealed my entire leg as I climbed out and he reacted by moistening his lips and inclining his head. The minute I closed the cab door, his lips launched at me.

I walked backwards through my gate, groaning as he started

touching me. One of his hands was on my waist, the other had pushed down a dress strap and then ran down over my chest.

Time with us not together was time wasted. I adored him. We should do this forever.

I found the keys in my little clutch and put them in his hands, so I could keep my lips busy with his jaw.

We stepped further back into the cool, dark house. I found the switch for the air conditioning and heard it fire up. In the dark hallway of my house, the hall that had every single bedroom off it, Nick and I were against a wall and content not to move.

He felt so good under my hands, both familiar and solid. It had been too long since I had felt him, and the time we had spent together these last two weeks had been tortured and angsty, full of pain and longing. I craved him. He was so confident touching me that my body was readying itself for him, a low heat burning through me and settling deep in my stomach. I could feel wetness between my legs and I pushed his hand off my erect nipple, which he had gained access to by pulling my breast out of my dress, and moved it with intent down in that direction.

He needed very little encouragement. Lifting the skirt of my dress, I leaned further back into the wall for support, easing my leg slightly wider for him as he pushed my underwear aside. His other hand was against my throat, angling my jaw where his mouth wanted it, and he pulled away, tilting my chin up until I met his eyes before running his fingers along my seam.

I moaned, closing my eyes and sliding my hand over his hard cock.

'Do not close your eyes, Abbey. I want to see you.'

They sprang back open.

He plunged two fingers into the pool of moisture he had created, and I ground my hips down onto him, moaning.

'You have no idea how much you are going to enjoy the next

two weeks, baby,' he said as he pulled out of me, circling my clit. 'I am going to make you come so many times.'

I was trying desperately to maintain focus on unzipping his fly and freeing the object of my desire, but he kept his thumb on me while sliding his fingers into the soaked desperate mess that I was, making it hard to think of anything but how it felt.

'Nick,' I breathed.

'Do you feel how wet you are, Abbey? I cannot wait to fuck you, honey. Holiday Nick and Holiday Abbey for two more weeks.' His fingers kept up a steady movement against my grinding hips and I found my breathing becoming less frequent and heavier.

My orgasm crashed over me like a wave. I gripped the back of his neck, keeping him where he was, silently giving into it. But as I came down, at some point, his words came back to me.

'What do you mean about the two weeks?' I whispered.

'I'm officially free, discharged of the last of my duties with Delacqua. I'm here for two weeks, I'm on holiday. I can be Holiday Nick, for you. Holiday Nick for two weeks.'

He went to kiss me again, and I kissed him back, instinctively, but then I pulled away. Disappointment dropped into my stomach, like a massive sinking stone.

'Nick, I …' He kissed me again. 'Wait, wait … stop.'

'Abbey?'

'No.'

'No, what?'

'I don't want that.'

What the fuck, Abbey? Why? Why do you not want this very, very hot man for two whole weeks?

'Why?' he asked.

'Is that what this is?' My grandmother was echoing in my head and part of me was cursing her.

'What?'

'Holiday Nick? Is that who this is?'

He looked at me, so confused. 'That is what you wanted, Abbey. "I miss him, Holiday Nick." That's what you said. I thought that was what you wanted.' His voice was gentle, but I could hear shock as well.

'Jesus, this is too much.' I felt overwhelmed and I couldn't articulate what I was thinking, because I thought I already had. There shouldn't be a Holiday Nick, there should just be … Nick. I was just Abbey. Any notion about the feelings I thought we shared, well, that was just a bit too much to think about, a bit too shattering. For him, this was clearly just sex.

'Hey.' His thumb grazed against my ear. 'I bought that dress because I want her. I miss her. Holiday Abbey.'

What the fuck did that mean?

'What the fuck does that mean? You bought a dress so you could have her? For two weeks? This is the cost of fucking you for two weeks, is it? Oh, that is lovely, mate. I need to get this off.' I pushed away from him.

'Wait, no. Abbey, that is not what I said. You're putting words in my mouth. I thought … I thought this was what you wanted. Or I thought we could at least discuss if this might not be perfect?'

I walked into my room, which did not smell like paint anymore, heedless of whether he followed. I tried to get the dress off, but I couldn't reach the zip and after watching me contort myself, he marched over and roughly unzipped it.

'You can have your goddamn dress.' I picked it up off the floor and threw it at him. I was topless underneath with tiny, soaked knickers on. I picked up my Fleetwood Mac tee, dragging it over my head. 'My grandmother warned me about shit like this.

Don't let men steal your spirit. You are fucking unbelievable. Two fucking weeks!'

'Abbey, stop it. I'm not trying to take your fucking spirit. You're being ridiculous and, honestly, fucking offensive.'

'I'm offensive? You know what, Nick, if you want someone to fuck for two weeks, why don't you go fuck that twenty-five-year-old?' *Now ... that ... was offensive.* 'You can fuck anyone you want to. They will adore you and your floppy hair and your posh accent and your fucking money. And you can give them whatever segment of yourself, whatever version you want to. Holiday Nick or Arsehole Boss Nick or Can't Fall in Love Nick. Leave me the fuck alone.'

He threw the dress on the bed. There was colour in his cheeks and a curl had fallen forward over his brow. His breathing was rapid, and his eyes were flaming at me. I had never seen him angry, and I knew it was madness, but I felt quite proud that I had made his control slip enough to show it to me.

There was a second or two where I felt like we might just walk until we crashed into each other. Apologise. Kiss softly. Foreheads together.

He shook his head. 'Goodnight, Abbey.'

I heard the front door close firmly a moment later. I fell back onto my bed.

Fuuuuccckk.

Nick

What the actual ...? I was so fucking angry with her I wanted to march back in there and have it out. *What the fuck did she want from me?* I thought I was giving her what she wanted. I had bent over backwards for that woman over the last two weeks. *You know what? Fuck her.*

Christ. She made it sound as if I was trying to purchase her services for two weeks. As if I was hiring her like a common prostitute by buying her a dress. That was not what this was.

I had told her from the start that I could not fall in love. It wasn't a thing. I'd made myself clear.

Why couldn't she see we were perfect for each other in that regard? We were both old enough to understand that love was bullshit. Love required the rose-coloured glasses one only owned in their twenties. Sometimes naïve people kept them in their thirties. I had actually never owned them. I'm pretty certain I was born with a healthy amount of pessimism. Maybe I borrowed a pair once upon a time. There had been a period when I had been more open. I had believed in hope; I'd had faith in others. I gave my heart away and did not think of the consequences. Then I was broken.

I know what she thinks, of course I do. She thinks she wants all of it. All of me. But Abbey and I are just physical. It's good physical; it might be the best physical I have ever had. I was thinking about her all the time, constantly aware of her; I always knew the minute she entered a room. Sometimes, when she was close, I had to shove my hands in my pockets to stop myself from reaching out to her.

I'm drawn to the sound of her voice and to how expressive her eyes can be when she is communicating something important. I know her movements and I have learned to read them like a foreign language. When she's anxious, she touches her grandmother's pendant, though it is no longer there. When she is thinking something that she's not prepared to say, she bites her bottom lip. Tonight, I saw her fuming and even that was beautiful. All colour.

And it helped that she was funny and cute. Smart. Competent. Dedicated to her family. It helped that she was amazing with Oliver. Better than I could even have predicted. I mean tonight … he was about to freak out and she just settled him right down, with her gentle, no-nonsense common sense. Do not be feeble. What fucking brilliant advice! I would have copped one on my chin if I had said that.

And what Iris said about Abbey having her colours on. Christ, I cannot imagine her being beige, and it makes me wonder about her ex-husband. The kind of man who doesn't let a woman like Abbey shine. She is so luminous. Everything about her gleams. Tonight she shone and watching it was like looking through a fucking kaleidoscope, shards of crystal light moving about. I could not have stopped looking at her if I had tried. There is a part of me that wants to stand in that light. Permanently bask in it. *It's terrifying*.

Abbey doesn't seem to see that I am a black hole absorbing light. That my darkness can completely stifle her. Yet sometimes, being next to her, I feel her light pierce through my dark. I crave it and I don't know how I feel about that.

This is why, Nick. This is why you should not do shit like this. I don't do this. I don't get involved with women. Not physically and definitely not with feelings. I don't do things like this, ever.

Which Abbey … does not know.

I was pacing out the front of her house waiting an inordinately long time for a fucking Uber, having a moment of genuine clarity.

Fucckkk. I think I've fucked up here. That sinking feeling entered my stomach.

I woke up the next morning and wished I had drunk more at that party. If I was hungover, at least I'd have an excuse for moping about my apartment in a hoodie and track pants.

I had not stopped thinking about how badly last night had gone. I couldn't stop thinking about how I'd worked that out, standing in front of her house, and how much of a prick I was that I did not go back and apologise straight away. Not that she would have opened the door to let me.

Why didn't I do that?

Fuck.

Oliver walked through my front door and headed straight to my fridge.

'What are you doing?' I said.

'What?'

'You have your own fucking fridge. Get out!'

'All right, cranky. Keep your bloody wig on.'

'Jesus, you are an annoying little fucker.'

'You wound me.'

I sat down on my sofa and stared at the glory of Sydney while I continued to obsess about the horror of last night.

'Mike said you and Abbey left about the same time. Do you have anything you want to tell me?' Oliver said as he sat down with a carton of orange juice and an apple.

'Can you get a glass?'

'Don't attempt to divert.'

'No, I did not leave with Abbey.'

'Bollocks. Nick, I've known you my whole life. Do you honestly not know that I know when you are full of shit?'

'Fine, her gran had a fall, and I accompanied her to the nursing home because she was upset.'

'Oh, you accompanied Abbey, did you? Did your tongue accompany her throat? Wait, is her gran okay?'

'Her gran is fucking magnificent. Her name is Iris Cavendish. She's extraordinary. I want you to meet her.'

'That sounds unnecessary.'

'Do you have plans today, Ollie?'

'Yes.'

'Cancel them. I'll shower. Let's go for a drive.'

We pulled up to Ashford House and my brother shot me a glare.

'Nick, you cannot be fucking serious.'

I ignored him, signed us in, and walked up the stairs to Iris's room. This seemed as mad as the dress purchase, admittedly, but I just wanted to check on her, to make certain she was well. There was also the hope that, maybe, Abbey would be there, and I could … I don't know … I just wanted to see how Iris was.

'Ah, Nicholas. I must say, this is a surprise.'

I bent over and kissed her crinkled, soft cheek. She smelled amazing, like a young woman, no lavender or rose or anything one would expect of an old lady. In fact, it could have been Chanel. Our mother used to wear it and I'm not certain if my siblings remember that about her. I inhaled Iris slightly more and hugged her, feeling the ache in my heart.

'Mrs Cavendish, may I intro—'

'Call me, Iris, Nicholas. Then I won't feel so old when you introduce me to the gorgeous man next to you.'

I gave a soft laugh and noticed a flush climb up Ollie's neck. 'Iris, my brother, Oliver Northby.'

Ollie slid his hand into hers. 'Lovely to meet you, Iris. I'm so sorry to disturb. I was supposed to meet Abbey's grandmother, but you cannot possibly be old enough.'

She laughed – a tinkly sound that was joyful and put me in mind of wind chimes. It further belied her age.

'Oh, young man, if I were ten years younger …'

The two of them were instant friends, both masters of flirt. She had him eating out of her hands in approximately two minutes flat and, like me, he was an instant devotee.

Lionel came in and sat down, not bothered at all by the two younger men fawning over his would-be love.

I sat and watched, mostly just happy to be in their company. My grandfather died before I was born, and my grandmother passed away when I was nine. There were no elder Northbys left in the world, and we were missing these gentle, happy relationships.

I looked up to find Iris giving me an assessing stare.

'Oliver, be a dear and grab me a bottle of water.'

'Of course, Iris.' He stood and walked out, an eager servant.

'Now, dearest. Are you going to tell me why you are so reflective and pensive, Nicholas?'

'I don't …' I looked into her crystal-blue eyes and realised they were Abbey's. I dropped my gaze to the floor before looking up and meeting them again. 'Actually, I'm worried I've upset Abbey.'

'Why? Things seemed to be going rather well between the two of you last night.'

I shrugged. I avoided telling Abbey's grandmother that I'd hit up her granddaughter for two weeks of sex and had managed to make Abbey feel cheap and used.

'If you have upset Abbey, that upsets me a great deal, dear. If it is worrying you, perhaps you should start by apologising. Abigail is far more forgiving a person than either Kate or myself. She very rarely holds grudges, Nick.'

'I'm sorry.'

'Not to me, dear …'

I smiled and nodded. I needed to apologise. Maybe it would go some way to remove this dreadful feeling in my gut.

Oliver walked back into the room and handed Iris her bottle of water. 'Good Lord. Rose, two doors down, just grabbed my arse.'

'You mustn't blame her. Her husband died forty years ago and instead of living again she fell into the grave with him, dear.'

My brother met my eyes briefly. I felt Iris's gaze on me again and got the feeling she didn't miss much. *Fuck.* Is that what happened to me? The thought hit me like a cricket ball to the ribs. I was winded by it.

'You know what you boys should do? It is a fine day. You should go and have lunch at that nice pub at The Rocks. What is that one called, dear, the one that I like? With the man on the guitar.'

'The Fortune of War,' Lionel said.

'Yes, of course. You should go there and drink in the sunshine and eat, and then at some point, a man with a guitar will come and sing to you.'

'Fortune of War?' Oliver said, putting it into his phone. 'I could do that. Nick, what say you?'

'Well, if Iris says we should go, we should certainly go.'

I slid my sunglasses onto my nose and ran a hand through my hair. It was almost winter, but other than a week of rain, Sydney had this beautiful, golden take on the season. The sun was belting down, making it warm, and I was drinking a cold beer. I'd had worse summers at home. I was thankful I had popped a T-shirt underneath my jumper, which I'd shed about an hour ago.

Like all things about Australia, the winter felt optimistic. I find it to be a distinctly positive, auspicious sort of country. It's the Abbey of the world.

Of course, Australia also felt like a 'young' country, though it was home to one of the oldest civilisations on earth. The pub was

Sydney's oldest, dating back to 1828, and it had a distinctly English feel about it, a reminder that, for a lot of people, the country's history dates from English colonisation. How wrong they were. Across the street, gallery windows were lined with Aboriginal art for tourists to purchase; the great divide told through this simple streetscape.

Ollie walked back with two more beers. I watched women and a couple of guys look at him appreciatively as he wound his way through the tables and chairs out the front of the pub. He placed the beers down and went to sit, but then his hand shot out in a wave to someone to his left.

I looked behind him and then stood as I saw Abbey and Kate walking down the street towards us. Abbey's hand reached out quickly to Kate's wrist, but she was not quick enough.

Her sister sang out to me, 'Nick Northby, as I live and breathe.'

People looked over at us, briefly interested because she'd yelled this from ten metres away, and I felt a grin come over me. However, Abbey's obvious discomfort quickly eradicated it.

I have to fucking fix this.

My need to sort it out immediately just overrode my control, and I walked until I ran into her, instinctively wrapping my arms around Abbey in an enormous hug.

I could feel her stiff and tense. Christ, I want never to feel that when I hold her, ever again. I created that tension. Abbey does *not* feel like that in a hug. She's normally pliable and bendy, possibly even floppy. Never stiff. I kept holding her, waiting and hoping for her to relax, and experienced a moment of panic that it would not happen.

Beside us, I barely listened as Kate introduced herself to Ollie.

'Fuck. You are very attractive.'

'Thanks. As are you.'

'I'm Kate. Abbey's sister. I don't think she mentioned you were this hot.'

'Oliver Northby. Nice to meet you, Kate. I met your grandmother today.'

'That's weird. And you should watch yourself. You are just her type, and I know she's hunting for a new husband.'

Ollie snorted, but looked pretty pleased with himself.

'Uh, wait, did she tell you to come here?' Kate said.

'She suggested it, yes.'

'Abbey, she bloody well set this up. She's a handful, and this is just her style,' Kate said to Ollie. 'She once set us up with two tradies here. Abbey was married with a child, but Gran was never a fan of her husband and thought this random electrician she'd met was a better fit – but that was years ago, and I didn't think. We got a text message saying she had bought us lunch at the Fortune of War. That we were to go and drink and think of her.'

I had not stopped hugging Abbey, and she was still stiffly standing in my arms.

'I'll go get us a drink,' Kate said, giving us a quick side eye.

'We have a table,' Oliver said. 'I'll grab a couple more chairs.'

When we were alone, I whispered into Abbey's ear for her only. 'I am so fucking sorry about last night. I respect you enormously and it has been eating at me that I got it so wrong. I misread this situation. I fucked up. I'm so bloody sorry, Abs. I did not mean to make you feel cheap. I bought that dress because I had to and for no other reason. I bought that dress because I wanted to see you happy.'

She smelled amazing, like the shampoo I knew she used, which I now stock in my shower. My fingers itched to run through her hair, to slide under her jumper and feel her skin, but she had not spoken or moved. I took comfort that she had not pulled away either.

When I moved my head ever so slightly, I watched a single tear run down her face and I felt heartbroken to be the cause of it.

'You are a real fucking arsehole. Do you know that, Nick Northby?'

'There is no one that knows that more than me.' I gave in and pressed a kiss into the side of her head. 'I would never want to tarnish what we have shared.'

She nodded, and finally her shoulders dropped. She put one hand on my back, a small hug. The relief that this tiny gesture brought me made me want to sink to my knees and collapse.

'Beers,' Ollie called out.

I grabbed Abbey's hand and led her back to our table. I couldn't stop looking at her. She wore jeans and a sparkling jumper and boots. A leather biker jacket and beautiful pearl studs at her ears. At the table, I let go of her hand as she sat, but slid my knee out so it touched hers the entire time. I made certain I never let her go for the rest of the day and the entire night.

Chapter Nine
Abbey

The light streamed through the curtains and the fluttering breeze made them dance. I was dreaming of the island. I was sweating from the heat and his warmth was behind me, his arm wrapped tightly around my waist. I brushed my hand along the hair of his forearms.

As I reached down for his hand, I realised I still had my jeans on in this dream. Weird that they were exactly the same jeans I wore yesterday. I was also wearing my fuzzy black jumper, which probably explained why I was so fucking hot. I pulled my damp hair off the back of my neck and wrestled myself out of my jumper.

My tongue was stuck to the roof of my mouth, and I reached out for a glass of water and then it dawned on me. *Oh, Jesus Christ. This is not a dream.*

At least I wasn't naked. I did not completely capitulate to him after he apologised.

The day before comes flooding back. The double date set up by my grandmother. Me seeing him and trying to get Kate to turn around and leave. Him engulfing me in a hug that I did not want, but could not seem to move out of. His apology.

After that there was alcohol (a lot), food (I insisted on paying for everything and he let me) and some bloke on a guitar, who did marvellous renditions of Oasis and Mumford and Sons' songs. I am almost certain I danced and sang to Ed Sheeran. I am almost certain that Kate and Ollie made out with each other, before both making out with other people. Nick and I did not kiss. We were just attached, connected. If I moved, he moved with me. We danced and sang, and then we piled into a taxi and came back here.

Ollie was asleep on my couch before we went to bed. Kate crawled to her bedroom as we came in. I marched Nick to the kitchen, put two ibuprofen into his hand and made him drink a glass of water before pulling him into my room.

'Do you forgive me?' he whispered into the dark.

'You are a fucking walking red flag,' I replied.

He took a huge, shuddering breath. 'You make me want to break all my rules.'

'The thing about it, Nick, is that you don't seem to understand that you are the risk and not me.'

'That's because you undervalue yourself.'

'So do you.'

I closed my eyes, he closed his ... and here we were.

They left after a surprisingly un-awkward coffee and toast, Kate and I both heading back to bed for a bit.

Monday brought my first day at work without him, and it was odd not to be constantly aware of his presence in the office. Oliver and I were busy that week with a couple of high-end meetings, along with the preparation for his business trip, but I missed Nick.

He messaged me every day, checking in, making sure we were both okay. Actually, his messages gave off not even remotely hidden, completely out of control parental-anxiety vibes – and they came thick and fast on the Monday.

How's he going?

Make sure he remembers to eat.

Let me know how the sponsorship meeting goes at 9. Remind him to sell the benefits of our international chain too. It's going to be a big factor for the corporate travel market.

There were at least three more messages like this before I phoned him at eleven.

'Is everything okay, Abs? What's he done …?'

'Nick, you need to calm the fuck down. You are driving me nuts and it is making me anxious,' I whispered.

He surprised me by laughing. 'I'll admit it is actually killing me not being there.'

'You don't say.'

'All right, all right. I take your point. I'll go …'

'Get a life? Stop hanging around your multi-million-dollar penthouse being a total loser?' I suggested.

'Yes. Both of those things.' I could hear his smile and imagined his eyes crinkling, which made my stomach flip. 'Thanks, Abbey.'

On Wednesday night, he rang me at six. We spoke on the phone until my battery ran out a couple of hours later. The conversation was mostly about work, but it flowed easily as he filled me in on what he had been doing the last few days, playing tourist in Sydney.

He sounded so happy and relaxed, and I wished he was in front of me so I could see it.

On Friday, I'd planned Oliver's last meeting to finish at eleven so I could get him to the airport, in a car, for his flight to Brisbane at one. The two senior EAs I'd sorted to assist him were already up to speed, with very strict instructions on how to best support him.

The meeting with Mike and the finance team finished on time. I'd had a running text commentary from Mike throughout, letting me know he was feeling serious, *serious* heat for the new CEO. He wasn't the only staff member to notice Oliver's appeal, not by a long way. Women were fanning themselves in lifts and offices, and he had groupies everywhere, several of them unnecessarily making their way to the top floor in the lift to catch a glimpse of their new, hot, single boss.

Oliver had been a tremendous success in week one of flying solo. I picked up my phone to text Nick, but then had the thought that I might call him that afternoon instead, or maybe even catch him for a drink the next day.

Oliver came out of his office after sending a few emails and asked me to walk with him downstairs to the car. I took his laptop bag, leaving him free to carry his luggage. He stopped several times to say hello to some employees whose names he had memorised.

When we were in the lift, he looked at me directly. 'Why are you smiling at me?'

'I'm super proud of you this week. It was a fantastic start. I think you are going to be great at this, Ollie.'

He smiled a chuffed, dorky grin, and I could tell he was pleased with my praise. 'Thanks, Abbey.'

'Hmm ...'

'What?'

'It just occurred to me that you set us up.' His grin deepened. 'On the holiday. Nick and me.'

He inclined his head, raising an eyebrow. 'I'm amazed you didn't realise that earlier. You were both pathetically sad, but I also thought you were similar in ways. There was certainly some manoeuvring to be done to get you both to the restaurant and especially to keep other couples off that bloody trip to the island. You both insisted on not being around couples. Weirdos. He is my brother and I love him. But he needs someone like you in his life, Abbey. The only person who doesn't know that, is him.'

I moved on from that, as it was stirring up feelings that I didn't want churned up.

The lift doors opened, and we crossed the lobby. I shielded my eyes against the sun as we walked out onto the busy city street. His car was ahead, the driver waiting by the door to open it for him. My phone vibrated in my hand and, seeing Nick's name flash up with a message, I stepped back out of the sunlight to read it.

Oliver kept walking to the car. The driver opened the door, standing behind it.

A high-vis shirt caught my eye, and it seemed as if everything slowed down. I saw the bike rider, who was wearing a black helmet and a lime-green high-vis jacket, jump up onto the curb to avoid a bus and then swerve to avoid the opening of Oliver's car door. As he did so he hit Oliver, careening into him at speed.

The cyclist flew off the bike through the air like an acrobat, with his head, protected by his helmet, clattering as he hit the footpath. But Ollie's head wasn't protected by anything, and he crumpled, after hitting it first on the open car door and then on the concrete path as he fell backward.

Fuck.

I ran forward, screaming at the driver to ring an ambulance, which, thank God, he was already doing. I ripped off my navy-blue cardigan to stem the blood coming from Ollie's head, applying pressure, and cradling him in my lap. He was in and out of consciousness. At one point he looked me straight in the eye and called me, 'Sad Abbey'.

It was clear his leg was also broken, given the weird angle it was at and the strange limpness of it. I avoided looking at it, not wanting to add vomit to the mix. Several pedestrians were assisting the cyclist. I sat there holding on to Oliver, feeling the urge to sob at how long it was taking for actual professionals to arrive and take over.

Minutes felt like hours. My heart was pounding in my chest. There was so much blood that my cardigan was wet, the little mother-of-pearl buttons red. I became fixated on weird details, like the driver's name being Keith and that Keith had a tattoo of a spider which appeared on his wrist every time his cuff rose.

It felt like a lifetime before I heard sirens and then the paramedics were there, taking him off me.

I wanted to ride in the ambulance, but they wouldn't let me. So I grabbed our things and jumped in the back of the car, and Keith and I followed the ambulance to St Vincent's.

I called Kate first, knowing she was in the emergency department. Then I called Nick.

He picked up on the second ring, as if he had been waiting for a call.

'Abbey.'

I could not answer. I attempted to, but my voice choked, and he spoke again.

'Abs, are you okay?'

'Nick.' His name came out in this strange, hoarse whisper. He was waiting for me to continue, but the emotion was still robbing my voice.

'Abbey. What is it, sweetheart?' His voice was so tender I felt my chest ache as my heart split.

'Nick, it's Oliver. He was in an accident. I think his leg is broken, and he hit his head.' My voice cracked again as I choked on tears. 'It's really bad. I'm in a car behind an ambulance. They're taking him to St Vincent's Hospital.'

'Ollie's hurt?' I could hear the emotion and panic in his voice. 'Tell me you're okay, Abbey,' he demanded.

'I'm fine, Nick. I'm okay.'

He took a deep breath. 'I'll meet you there.'

Keith dropped me off at the front door of Emergency and I arrived in time to see the paramedic stretcher Oliver into the hospital. After that I was by myself. I sent off messages to Peter to pick up Ella from school and then to Liz, one of the EAs I'd sent to Brisbane, to let her know Oliver did not need to be picked up from the airport. Once I found out what was going on, we would look at cancelling next week. Or the next month, I thought, as I sent the message.

Nick burst through the door of the emergency room about ten minutes after I sat down. His eyes scanned the room, landing on me. His face was ashen, and concern was already deeply etched on his handsome face. I stood up and we both just walked towards each other until we collided.

After a long moment, he stepped back from me, checking me for damage. There was blood on my blouse, and, though I had attempted to wash it off, Ollie's blood was on my hands and under my fingernails.

He pulled me back into his chest, whispering questions. I explained what had happened, and that I didn't have any more details, but that Kate was here and would give us an update as soon as she could. It would likely be several hours before we heard anything at all.

The two of us sat, stony-faced, holding hands. Nick would sometimes get up and pace the hall, while I worried obsessively for him and Ollie. When Kate finally emerged, several hours later, she refused to speak until the doctor was with her, which I suspected meant it wasn't great news. I thought I would throw up, expecting her to tell us that he had lost too much blood and hadn't survived.

The doctor was young. Younger than I expected him to be. *Was he even a doctor?*

'I'm Dr Hayden Tan. I work in the ER. You're Nicholas?'

Nick nodded once. Economising his energy.

'Okay, your brother is a bit of a mess, Nick. He has a spiral fracture to his left leg. His pelvis has a hairline fracture, but we are not too concerned with that one. The head injury is the priority. He has a laceration and a small haematoma. We've placed him in an induced coma. We need to monitor him very closely to ensure the bleed does not get worse. If it *does* we may need to create a burr hole, or perform a craniotomy to control the damage.

'Right now, he's about to have his leg treated. The ortho team will put a titanium rod from his knee to his ankle and then allow the break to heal on its own. We'll keep him in an induced coma for twenty-four to forty-eight hours and then, if the bleed is resolving, we can attempt to bring him out of it. He's in the ICU, you can visit with him for a few minutes. Only one of you, though,' he said, looking at me.

Nick seemed frozen under the weight of the doctor's list of his brother's injuries. I reached out to him to rub his arm and then circled mine around his back as Kate also instinctively grabbed his hand.

He nodded. 'Yes, I'd like to see him, please.'

He followed the doctor and Kate and I stood, watching him go.

'You should go home, Abs,' Kate quietly implored. 'You look exhausted.'

'I'm not leaving Nick. I'll take him home when he's done.'

'Abbey ...' Kate started.

'I'm not leaving him, Kate.' The caution in her tone made me want to bite her head off. I breathed through my annoyance. I needed to know what the worst-case scenario was. 'Kate, is he ... Is Ollie going to be all right?'

'The next forty-eight hours are really important. We don't know yet,' she said.

It felt as if hours passed, but it was only ten minutes later when Nick emerged. His face was frighteningly pale, but I saw the relief on his face when he saw me, which made my heart contract. I stood up and wrapped my arms around him, holding him.

'Abbey. I ... I don't ... I don't think I want to be alone.'

There was not a chance on this earth that I was leaving him anyway.

We didn't speak in the Uber. He gripped my hand so tight across the seat that I moved into the middle so my body was touching his, offering silent comfort and support.

His hold on my hand continued as we exited the car and went to his apartment door, never breaking contact. He used an electronic keypad to gain entry to the foyer and steered me towards the lift, swiping again and pressing the button for the top floor. When the lift opened, there were only two doors in the foyer at the top. He walked to the one on the left.

He put his keys into a wooden bowl on a marble-topped console table at the entrance and walked into the flat. I walked down three steps, which led to an open-plan living area that was bigger than my entire house. The kitchen was white marble, the furniture tan leather. Huge black-and-white artworks decorated the walls. It was masculine, but somehow managed to still be comfortable and homely. There was glass everywhere and high ceilings and the glittering lights of Sydney harbour for the view. It was beyond beautiful.

He walked through the lounge and down a hallway, opening a door.

'This is my sister Evelyn's room. There should be some of her clothes in the drawers, and you should find something that fits you. She has a bathroom in there.'

Sister? I walked into the room, which was also beautiful. All cream with coral accents. The bathroom was done stylishly in black-and-white subway tiles with black taps.

There was a mirror, and I looked at myself briefly. My face was pale from the day, and I looked drawn. My makeup had held up pretty well, despite the tears, but there was a streak of blood across my cheek. Oliver's blood. I took a shuddering breath.

I undid my buttons with shaking hands. Oliver's blood had stained through my navy shirt onto my skin. Turning on the shower, I stood under it for a good five minutes before working at washing the blood off me. There was a heavenly scented body wash and, after ten more solid minutes under the running water, I reluctantly stepped out and dried myself off on the fluffiest of white towels.

I tentatively peeked into Evelyn's drawers and there looked to be a basic supply of odds and ends, things that were evidently left behind whenever his mystery sister – who I had never heard of until a few minutes ago – was last in Sydney. I found some trackpants that fit me and a stretchy singlet, which would mean I didn't need a bra.

I headed down the hall in the direction I thought was the lounge room. As I walked past a door, I heard another shower running and stopped, putting my ear to the wood. Part of me wanted to go in, to comfort him, and give him anything he needed to feel better. The decision was made for me when I heard glass shatter.

I marched straight in, ready to fend off whatever demons he was fighting. By the time I reached him, the shower had stopped, and he was standing there naked, dripping wet and bleeding. He had put his hand through a glass shelf in the shower; it lay shattered on the dark-grey tiles.

'Jesus,' I muttered.

His hand was bleeding, and a shard had nicked his leg.

I handed him a bath towel, and then reached for the hand towel and held it to his leg to staunch the bleeding of a Northby brother for the second time that day. He started sobbing then: hard, harsh cries that echoed in his chest and throat.

'I'm so scared, Abbey, I'm so fucking scared.' He was shaking, his eyes on the ground. 'What if he's not okay? I put too much pressure on them. I'm not a fun brother. We are all that we have. I don't say I love you enough. I cannot bury another person I love. I cannot do it; I will not survive that. It would break me. I can't do it, Abbey. I never want to be in that dark place again. I cannot lose my little brother. It's my fucking job to protect them!'

I put my body against his, rising up on tippy-toes to put my face to his face, whispering his name, and told him everything was going to be all right, although I did not know that.

I kissed his temple and left my lips there, praying that anything I did would be of some solace to him. This glimpse into how much death had touched his life was illuminating, though.

He rested there against me while his sorrow drained.

I noticed the moment his lips began moving against my throat, his grip changing from taking comfort from me to needing me, his fingertips digging into my sides, pulling me into his body further. I must have given some indication of need too, although what sign it was, I would never know, but he picked me up and carried me to his bed.

When the back of my legs met the mattress, he placed me gently back down on my feet with reverent care. His beautiful, bereft eyes looked into mine and an unspoken conversation between us took place.

I reached up, taking his face in my hands, placing my lips firmly on his in answer, and he responded to my consent with immediate abandon.

He parted my lips with his tongue, tasting my mouth, biting at my lips. His hands were everywhere, pinching at my nipples through the thin material of the singlet and trying to get my borrowed track pants down.

His erection was between us, and I ran my hand down his chest and then down the length of him while stepping on the cuff of my pants, trying desperately to remove them. He felt exactly as I remembered him, and his eyes closed at my touch. He pressed his forehead into me, kissing my jaw, his nose in my cheekbone. He took off my top, his mouth claiming my nipples, making me issue involuntary noises. My knees were growing weak with desire, and I slid down onto the firm mattress, parting my legs for him.

He continued to lick and nip at my body while he positioned himself and then plunged into me as deep as he could.

'Nick,' I moaned his name.

'Do you have any idea how hard it has been, being near you, under the same sky, in the same city, and not doing this? I think about you all day. You haunt my dreams at night.'

I was so turned on; I knew if he moved an inch, I would come.

I tried wriggling myself, but I was pinned to the bed by him.

'Do you know what is terrifying, though?' His voice, normally commanding, was uncertain, throaty, raw, and somehow made my chest ache. 'It's not the thought of the sex, Abbey. What terrifies me are the thoughts that I want to take care of you. I want you never to worry about anything, ever again, or face any challenge by yourself. The thought that I want to come home to you, cook your dinner, watch you eat the entire meal, be a great stepdad to your kid. Paint your fucking walls. Be the kind of man who is friends with your sister and loves your gran.'

I was ready to confess all. I wanted these things too and so much more. That he wasn't alone in his dreams, that I cared for him. That I loved his brother like he was my own. That I had fallen in love with him.

'But it's not who I am, Abbey. That's not who I am. I made a promise to myself. Never again, not anymore. I cannot take the risk.'

Jesus Christ, who was he trying to convince here?

My heart went down like a punctured balloon, flying around the room.

'I know.' And I did know that. He had told me. He couldn't fall in love in the real world. The unknown demons of the past were haunting him still. I knew he had been married before, but he didn't reveal himself easily and I hadn't pressed him on it. But whoever she was, she had clearly done a number on him.

He started moving then, in and out of me in long strokes. My head told me there was no way I could get back into this enough to be where I was a few moments ago, but he knew me. He knew what I liked. He knew exactly when to speed up and where to touch me. I came apart under him with such force and he poured into me, breathing my name like silk and chocolate.

He rolled off me and then pulled me into him. Our breathing settled face to face, we let our bodies recover from each other. When I heard his stomach rumble, I hopped up, throwing on his heavenly smelling tee, and then padded out to his kitchen, making him a cup of tea and toast.

I brought it back to bed and insisted he eat something. I made him drink his tea. He was grabbing his head, a tension headache caused by the stress, and I found painkillers in his bathroom and some Band-Aids to dress his cuts, before lying down and holding him, brushing his hair with my fingers until he slept in my arms.

He was possessive of me in his sleep, never letting me move where his body could not go with me. I acclimatised to the extra heat and eventually I slept too, tucked into him, wishing I could sleep here with him forever.

When I woke in the morning, the bed was empty and cold. The harsh daylight was streaming through the window. I was naked under the covers, his T-shirt dumped on the floor beside me.

My eyes adjusted to the light, and I looked around the room properly for the first time. It was a spacious room, the bed a king-size with a whisky-coloured padded headboard. There was a wall of books and a black desk in the corner with his laptop on it. Photographs were behind it, a picture of a baby, and a family picture of his mum and dad and the three kids.

He was recognisable as a little person, freckles spattering over his nose, his cheeks rounded, his jaw not yet defined. The photo had caught him mid-laugh, his brother and sister both tiny. There looked to be about five years between the kids, and I realised they must be twins, Ollie and Evelyn. From what Oliver had said, Nick had raised him when their parents died. What I didn't know was that he had raised two of them whilst running a company.

I only had one kid, and it was fucking hard. How did he do that?

My phone buzzed with a message. It was from Ella saying that Peter was going to drop her home at midday. It was Saturday morning, and I had to restock the groceries before my child came home, so there was no more time to hang out in this harbourfront penthouse, belonging to the emotional abyss of a man I had fallen in love with, who was currently missing in action.

I walked silently down the hall to Evelyn's room, grabbing a pair of jeans and a black T-shirt I'd seen last night, and quickly got dressed. I took deep breaths, trying to quiet my head from the emotionally compromising sex last night, as well as the apparent fact that Nick was nowhere to be found possibly because he was regretting said sex.

I took a second to look at myself in Evelyn's mirror. I pinched my cheeks: there was no point in feeling emotional about it. Nick was in the middle of a crisis. We were at worst friends ... or colleagues ... or acquaintances ... who'd had sex on a holiday. Either way, I had made myself available to him. He had asked and I had chosen, and now I had to be an adult about it. It wasn't the time to assess my growing feelings for him.

I silently crept into the lounge room.

'Hey. I was just about to bring you tea.'

'Oh, hey. I, uh, thought you weren't here.'

'Kate called me to give me an update on Ollie. I didn't want to wake you. She said his leg surgery went well and the bleed has started to reduce on his brain, so the plan is still to wake him up tomorrow.'

'That's wonderful, Nick.' I paused, looking at my feet. I felt incredibly exposed today, concerned that if I looked him in the eye I'd confess my undying love and beg to be by his side forever more.

'Are you headed to the hospital?' I asked. Keeping my composure would have been a lot easier if he hadn't been here, looking relaxed, making me tea in his kitchen.

'Yes. I'll head off after a shower. You coming?'

'I have to get home to Ella. I need to get some groceries, you know, boring run-of-the-mill shit. We're having a *Pirates of the Caribbean* night tonight. She wants tacos.' I shrugged and paused because I could hear a forced note in my voice. I took a deep breath, trying to remember to just be myself. 'I'm worried you don't have anyone to lean on. So I wanted to say that, um, you should come to mine if you need to. Oh, but ... I, uh, haven't had a guy stay in my room since Peter left and unless that person is going to be around, you know, a lot, I'd rather not introduce that situation to Ella.'

I watched his reaction to that; it was his turn to drop his head to his feet.

'But I do have a fold-out lounge, which you are welcome to. I don't really want you to be alone.'

He looked up and studied me for a second. Then he moved around the counter and grabbed me into a hug. It was warm and comforting and almost made me cry into his chest.

I nuzzled a little and held him close. 'I hope Ollie's okay,' I said, muffled.

'Me too.' He lifted my face, pressing a gentle kiss on my lips before grabbing his phone and ordering me an Uber.

In the car, I felt the tears escape as I watched the city out the window, annoyed at being a sook. To distract myself, I went back through the messages on my phone. There were quite a few I just hadn't seen in the chaos of yesterday.

The first was a passive-aggressive text from my ex-husband, about picking up his daughter from school for me on a day he wasn't scheduled to.

You should thank me cause I'm doing you a huge favour.

Dick.
Kate had messaged me on her break at nine last night.

Abs, I think you have feelings for this guy. I'm not sure he's not a commitment-phobe. DO NOT HAVE SEX.

Too late.
I scrolled down further. There was an unread message from Nick. I had completely forgotten it; the reason Ollie had been hit and not me. I opened it.

I know how mad you are with me and that things are strange, but I'm struggling not to beat down your door just to be near you. Please tell me you will have dinner with me before I leave. N xx

I smiled at that, closing my eyes, the grin spreading across my face. I read it again and as I read the last line, another came through from him.

It's just occurred to me that your ex-husband's name is Peter Parker. Is he a superhero by trade?

I laughed out loud at that, earning a look in the rearview mirror from the cabbie, and typed back:

God no. His mother swears blind she has never read the cartoon or seen a Spiderman movie. Sometimes, if she came over for dinner or whatever, I would just have it running in the background to see if I could trip her up.

He responded with a bunch of laughing emojis and then a love heart, before adding:

My sister is on her way to Sydney. She should arrive tomorrow. Any chance you could have dinner with us on Monday night?

I'll check with Kate and see if she can look after Ella.

Great. N xx

For two people not in a relationship, this felt very relationshippy. *What the fuck was happening here?*

Nick

What the fuck was happening here? Pirates of the Caribbean night?

If I went, surely that indicated I wanted to meet her kid. Which I did. I just didn't want any confusion about our relationship.

Admittedly, last night may have been confusing. I was just emotional. She was just comforting me. We were just comforting each other. *Right?*

I could not think about the possibility that Ollie wouldn't be all right. He had to be. *No way Ollie goes down like this.* I saw his teenage years when he was doing seriously dumb shit and we had to implement the Northby rules. Don't die. I should make that a fucking Northby rule.

When I'd walked into that hospital (for the record, I fucking loathe hospitals) and seen Abbey covered in blood, I was so panicked. I wanted to strip off every item of clothing she had on, just to check it wasn't coming from her. I was so relieved she was okay, but then the dawning realisation that the blood on her belonged to Ollie almost made me collapse.

Northbys. Are we fucking cursed?

I needed to set some rigid boundaries with Abbey. She was under my skin and I was under hers, but she was not setting any boundaries, except when it came to her child. That was completely understandable. But I cannot allow myself to fall in love with her. I won't.

It should be easier then, to stop. But there are still feelings I am unable to control and the impulse to be near her … it is terrifying for me, for both of us.

There was no point thinking any further on it. My priority was Oliver. I had to be there for my brother. And she was the only person I knew in this city, and the only person who gave a shit, and she was right. I shouldn't be alone. So *Pirates of the Caribbean* night it is.

Chapter Ten
Abbey

I was far from certain whether I expected Nick Northby to rock up at my house for *Pirates of the Caribbean* night, but I spent the entire grocery trip running through ways to break the news to my child, in case he did.

Ella and I were close and in a way that had nothing to do with Peter. Pete managed to be a good dad, despite often being a massive prick to me. But Ella just preferred her mum at times. When she woke up in the middle of the night, she would come to my side of the bed. If she was worried about something, she would confide in me. I knew about all of the important stuff. Friend dramas, boyfriends, broken hearts, teacher drama and period dramas (as in feminine reproductive, not the travesty of Matthew getting killed off in *Downton Abbey*). Nothing was off limits, but we had simply never discussed me inviting men she did not know to our house.

After getting back with the groceries, I cleaned the house with anxious thoroughness. When Ella came through the door, I noted that, for the first time – and as requested – Peter dropped her off and did not come in, which was a relief. I hated making small talk with him. I mean, what was I supposed to say? *Hey, thanks so much for being a massive, lying cheat and forcing me to recognise that I'm not sure I ever loved you.* Also, this wasn't his house any longer and after the dress night, I finally realised he was crossing a boundary, coming in as he had. It felt surprisingly good to have got it off my chest and to have him respect the new rules. My rules.

I timed the Nick talk for when Ella and I were preparing vegetables for the tacos. I popped down the knife on the wooden benchtop and stared at the white-and-green checked tiles on the wall, running what I would say through in my head and trying to get the amount of casual right. I picked up the knife again and started chopping.

'Ella, the reason I couldn't get you from school yesterday was that my boss, Oliver, got hit by a cyclist. It knocked him over and he hit his head and broke his leg. He's in Aunt Kate's hospital. It was very serious.'

'Is he okay? What bone in his leg was it? Is he awake?' Ella's love of *Grey's Anatomy* meant that (currently) her dream career was to be a doctor.

'Umm, he will be okay. He's in an induced coma at the moment. He had a bleed on his brain and they are monitoring him. They may need to remove a section of his skull to—'

'To relieve pressure, Mum.'

'Yeah.' I looked at her, impressed that Meredith Grey was providing such an excellent pre-med-ucation for my child. 'His brother, Nick, is my friend. Obviously, he's extremely worried and stressed about Oliver. They're from England, so they have no other family here. I told Nick that if he needed some company, he could come here and watch the movie with us and sleep on the couch. I hope that's okay with you? I don't know for certain if he will come.'

Ella looked up from grating cheese. 'He shouldn't be alone, Mum. I would be worried sick if something happened to you or Aunty Kate.'

'I agree.'

Ella was getting to that great age where you had moments of thinking your kid might just turn into someone you'd like to know.

'Is Nick your boyfriend, Mum? You can just tell me if you have a boyfriend. I'd tell you if I had one.'

'Umm, he's not my boyfriend, Ella. We're just, umm, uh, you know, friends.'

Ella insisted on a circular platter of pre-made tacos, laid out exactly as she'd seen on a TikTok video. When I finished it, the likeness to the video both surprised me and left me chuffed. I gave myself a pat on the back for being a fucking cool mum and ran out to show her, but her interest had wavered, and she gave me a polite nod.

We popped on the movie, and I quickly drank my nerves in the form of a glass of red with each taco I consumed. The knock on the door made me jump and slop a little red wine onto my fingers, which I indelicately licked off. Despite me preparing Ella for just this eventuality, I was weirdly freaked out. Ella ignored the door, already engrossed in the first *Pirates* movie.

I hopped up and walked down the hall, nervous energy flitting around my stomach. The hallway blocked off the lounge room, and I shook my shoulders. *Be cool, Abbey.* When I swung open the door and saw him, my coolness completely escaped me. Nick looked pale and haggard, new lines of worry were etched into the side of his eyes and his stubble was bordering on holiday stubble. His eyes were big, sad Nick eyes, which made my stomach do a weird curl and the need to take care of him overwhelmed me for a second. He had on a backpack and a grocery bag sat beside his foot.

I reached for him, pressing him into me. He wrapped his large arm around me and pressed back. I think he smelled my hair.

'How is he doing?' I whispered, kissing his cheek.

'They say he's getting better, but it's hard to see.' Nick pulled back a little and his hand flew to his forehead, tears filling his eyes. 'He looked the same amount of unconscious to me.' He pressed his lips into my cheek and then nuzzled his nose into me. 'Jesus, you smell good,' he said, inhaling.

'Like tacos? Come in. I'll get you a plate. You need to eat.'

He nodded and walked close behind me. In the lounge room, Ella paused the movie as we came in and bounced off the couch.

'Ella, this is Nick.' I was trying hard not to be the most awkward person in the room, introducing my lover to my daughter. It wasn't the least bit surprising that I was not pulling it off. My cheeks were crimson, and I was sweating. I pulled my jumper away from my neck.

'Hey, Nick. I'm sorry to hear your brother is in hospital. My Aunt Kate is a legend, though, and so are her colleagues,' Ella said, in a strangely mature way.

I looked at her, marvelling again at how grown-up she seemed lately.

'Thanks, Ella. It's nice to meet you. I appreciate you guys letting me hang out tonight.' Nick looked in his bag. 'I bought popcorn and chocolate for your movie night. Oh, and I bought your mum some rum.'

'Rum?' I said, puzzled.

'Pirate themed? It's Caribbean spiced rum.'

'Yum, well thank you. Now, there is a plate on the coffee table for you. Help yourself to the taco platter. Ella and I have already eaten our fill, so don't be shy. Beer or wine or, er, rum?'

'Beer, please.'

Ella restarted the movie while I grabbed Nick a drink. I held the beer up to my forehead for a second in the dark kitchen, collecting myself, before heading back.

He had sat down on the lounge. I put his beer on the table next to him and then sat beside him. Ella was sprawled on our three-seater, so we were on the smaller sofa. I popped a cushion over my lap and let my leg touch his. I was having a hard time concentrating on Captain Jack Sparrow.

'Nick,' Ella said, 'did you know my mum had the hots for Johnny Depp in the nineties?'

I nodded a confirmation of this while taking a sip of my wine.

Nick snorted his amusement. 'I did not know that, Ella. She told me she had a thing for heroes.'

'Mum says she has a thing for tall, dark, handsome men.'

Nick laughed at that and then raised his eyebrows at me, mouthing, *Is that right?*

I thought my heart was going to leap out of my chest. I was insanely pleased the colour was back in his cheeks and that he was smiling. If we could ease his mind for a few hours, that was a good thing.

Nick wolfed down the remaining tacos and then asked for Ella's help to make popcorn, the two of them chatting away in the kitchen while I tidied up dinner, stacking the dishwasher.

Ella peppered Nick with questions. She was extraordinary, significantly more forthright than me.

'How old are you, Nick?'

'Forty-one.'

'Ooh, my mum is forty-two. Where do you live?'

'In the city at the moment, but in London I live in Hampstead near an enormous park, called a heath.'

'Do you have kids?'

'I have a ten-year-old daughter. Her name is Summer.'

My hands stilled in the sink at this new information. *Why on earth would he have not told me that?* I refused to look at him, but I could feel his eyes on me.

'Where is Summer's mum?'

'Ella ...' I interrupted my daughter's interrogation, deeming this line of questioning way too personal, though I was desperate to hear the answer.

'It's okay.' He paused. 'She died. She had been sick for a long time.'

My heart cried for him. Jesus Christ. How much had he been through in his life? At the same time, I'm not sure that excused him for not telling me about his daughter.

'Oh, I'm sorry,' Ella said quietly.

'Summer was staying with my sister while I was away, but she's coming out to Australia now. I hope you guys will have dinner with us one night?' Nick asked quietly.

'That sounds so nice. Can we go somewhere we have to dress up? Mum always looks so beautiful when she dresses up, Nick, and she got this beautiful dress the other day.'

'Let's finish this movie, Ella,' I said, being non-committal about the family date, after only just finding out there *was* a family. I was a little annoyed. Nick seemed hell-bent on feeding me his life in dribs and drabs, when I had been honest from the start. It was bloody infuriating.

We sat back down with the popcorn and other snacks; I kept my leg to myself. My phone buzzed the minute Ella became engrossed in the film again.

You're annoyed with me.

I looked across at him and his eyes slid towards me, raising his eyebrows, a knowing smile on his handsome, smug face. He was insanely pleased with having read me.

I'm not annoyed. I'm delighted you came.

He shook his head and fired back another text.

Liar. You are annoyed. Ella is a sweetheart, Abbey. You're an amazing mum.

Okay. You are a little annoying.

Pirates eventually finished. I wound up Ella's grand plan of settling in for an all-nighter to watch the trilogy and sent her off to bed. As she was walking out, she unexpectedly interrupted her grumbling at me to throw her arms around Nick.

'I hope your brother gets better. I'm glad your sister and little girl are on their way. You can stay with us until your family is here. My Aunty Kate can be cranky, but deep down she's an angel. She will take good care of your brother.' She pressed a kiss into his cheek, which made me feel strangely emotional, and I followed her from the room to tuck her in and give her a kiss.

Ella's room was maybe my favourite in the house. It reflected all the phases of her life, from the little cream bunny she had slept with since she was two, to the Taylor Swift and Alex Karev posters donning her walls.

She hopped into bed, leaning over to turn on her twinkle lights, and I kissed her on the head.

'You really are the world's best kid,' I said to her honestly.

'You really are the world's best taco maker.' She kissed me back. 'I think Nick likes you.'

I snorted.

'Seriously, Mum. You should date. It would be good for you.'

An Iris/Kate in the making. That's all I need.

'Goodnight, Ella.'

'Goodnight, Mumma.'

Nick was out in the backyard taking a phone call when I came back. I assumed it was the hospital, so I cracked the rum and prayed for good news while pouring it into two tumblers with some ice and leftover lime from our dinner. Then I headed out the back to get some wood onto the fire.

By the time he finished the call, the fire was crackling and warm, and he sat down beside me, close, on the outdoor lounge. I handed him the rum, and he drank almost the whole thing in one gulp.

'That was Kate. She said the scans show the bleed has reduced again. He's doing well.'

I swallowed the rum and the tension, feeling it unwind in the muscles of my neck. I threw my arms around him and held him.

'He's going to wake up tomorrow, right, Abbey? Tell me he's going to wake up.'

'Of course he's going to wake up.'

He breathed into my neck. 'Did you bring the bottle out?'

'Hell yes, it's delicious.'

'That's my girl.' He gave me one of his rare laughs, wiping his eyes, and I was so moved to hear him laugh, that my eyes filled with tears, too. His face became concerned. 'Are you okay?'

I took a deep breath and a huge sigh. 'Yeah, it's just been a big couple of days.'

He put his arm around me, and I snuggled into him.

'I am sorry. I don't mean to upset you. I just don't share easily with people. The fact that you know some things should tell you how highly I regard you.'

'I'm not annoyed.'

'You are annoyed. You shouldn't be afraid of saying it. And you are right as usual.' He kissed my hair.

Fine. It is annoying. I don't really understand why you wouldn't tell me you had a daughter. But your brother, who I adore, is in ICU and I feel bad for you, arsehole.

We sat and watched the flames, a beautiful silence surrounding us. We were both quiet people and there was just so much shit going on. I felt peaceful for the first time in a while. Comforted in his arms.

He yawned. He was exhausted and, though he argued he was happy just sitting there, I insisted he rest.

Nick pulled out the sofa bed while I grabbed sheets, blankets and pillows. I watched him take off his jeans and pull a pair of comfy jersey pyjama shorts from his bag, putting them on so they sat low on his hips. He looked so good in clothes – he looked good naked too, but clothes sat on him as if they were made specifically for him. He climbed into the bed, and I turned out the lights.

I let the sudden desire to curl up with him win. It was overwhelming, my need for him, so I laid down on top of the blue-and-red-checked quilt cover and the soft grey blanket next to him. We both rolled onto our sides to face each other. He pushed my hair back from my face and then grabbed the waist of my jeans to pull my hips closer to him.

'You are so warm, Abbey. Your home is so warm and welcoming. Everyone loves you. You are light. Pure light.'

I sighed and pressed my lips to his gently, my heart thumping hard. This was getting serious. I knew now, without any doubt, I was at risk of having my heart completely crushed by him. But when he said stuff like that it made it difficult to care or worry about any future heartbreak at all. He spoke like someone who loved me. Whether he was ready to admit it or not.

I lay awake with him until his breathing fell into a steady rhythm, then I softly padded to my room.

If his wife had died and he had lost his parents young, it was clear that grief had made him build this tight construct around his heart. It would take time to bring it down. Time, I knew I was willing to give to him.

He left earlyish. A call had come through from Oliver's doctor, confirming they were going to attempt to wake him up that morning.

Nick had had a moment of crisis when he realised he needed to be at the airport at exactly the same time to pick up his sister and daughter. But that was easily solved. I lived around the corner and had a child who adored trips to the airport.

Ella, as expected, did not need convincing, so we packed off Nick to the hospital and then jumped in the car. She had always been obsessed with planes, ever since she was little, as the proximity of our house to Sydney's Kingsford Smith Airport meant the flight path was directly above us most of the time.

I took care with my makeup and casual clothes. I wanted to make a good impression on Nick's sister and little girl. It seemed important getting to meet them, despite not knowing that either one of them existed three days ago. Nick had sent me photos of them, and I studied them again as I waited at the arrivals gate. I shouldn't have worried because even in the busy international terminal they were instantly recognisable.

Evelyn was the female equivalent of Oliver. Beautiful olive skin, intelligent blue eyes and light-brown hair with caramel highlights. She was around my height and build, but slightly finer. She had a gorgeous warm smile and waved at me as she guided her suitcase and her niece out through customs.

Summer was also a little beauty. She was all Nick; she looked just like him. Her wavy dark hair was shiny and fell into soft curls, and her eyes were a greener version of his. She seemed to be a quiet, solemn little thing who did not smile easily. She was wheeling a matching suitcase in miniature to her aunt's and was dressed in a comfy-looking velour tracksuit in a willow green that matched her beautiful eyes. She was carrying a copy of *The Secret Garden* and I knew we would be friends based on her excellent taste.

'Abbey,' Evelyn called out as if we'd known each other for twenty years and were meeting after a long absence. Her voice was earthy and low, but her rounded vowels and crisp accent matched her brothers'.

When they both made it around the railed-off area, she beamed at me and threw her arms around me.

'Oh, my goodness, of course you are Abbey. You look exactly like Nicky described and, of course, that beautiful picture of you both from the holiday. God, I don't even know how to thank you. But thank you so much for looking after my brothers.'

I was astonished that Nick was Nicky and that he had sent her a picture of the two of us on holiday. I didn't have any pictures of us together, but I remembered him snapping a couple of selfies over the two weeks.

'Oh, Evelyn, it's so nice to meet you, too. I must admit to completely adoring your brothers. I'm so sorry for the circumstances, though.'

'There is no way on earth Ollie goes out like this.' She sniffed.

'I have faith that he will be back being an absolute pain in our arse soon.'

I pulled away from her, giving her a sympathetic smile before turning to Nick's little girl.

'I'm Abbey. You must be Summer. Your dad has told me all about you. This is my daughter, Ella. Ella, this is Evelyn, Nick's sister, and Summer, his little girl.'

'Hello,' Summer said shyly, earning my instant endearment.

I bent down a little. 'Did you know you are carrying one of our favourite books, Summer? Maybe while you're here you can come over with your dad and we can have a movie night and watch the film.'

'That would be nice. Thank you, Abbey.' She turned to her aunt. 'Aunty Ev, can we see Daddy now?'

'Sweetheart, he's at the hospital with Uncle Ollie. You and Jacinta will go home and Daddy will be there after he and I check in on Uncle Ollie. Okay, baby? Uncle Ollie is poorly.' Evelyn pointed behind them. 'Abbey, this is Jacinta. Summer's nanny.'

'Oh, hi!' I said politely to the leggy nineteen-year-old that was Jacinta. She had long dark hair and gorgeous curves, hips and boobs. *Jesus.* She looked like Salma Hayek. *The nanny is a babe.*

Before we dropped off Ella at her friend Bella's house to 'hang out', she and Summer became best friends in the fifteen-minute drive, exchanging numbers and making arrangements for catchups, much to my amusement. I then drove Summer and Jacinta to Nick's apartment with the luggage. Nick had left me a set of keys that morning. Then, finally, Evelyn and I headed to St Vincent's.

She chatted effortlessly, a welcome relief in comparison to the other Northbys of my acquaintance. Though Ollie was chatty, he never gave me important information, such as Nick having a daughter and being a widower. I learned more from Evelyn in the short drive to the hospital than I had from Nick or Oliver in a month.

Evelyn was thirty-five, divorced, and had a dog called Liam, who was named after her childhood idol, Liam Neeson. She worked in investment banking and had a slew of hobbies: she painted with oils, made pottery, baked, cooked and, occasionally, wrote poetry.

'There is no way on earth Ollie goes out like this,' she repeated.

'You guys are twins?'

'Yep! It's odd. I always felt certain that if something ever happened to him, I would know straight away. We've always been so close, you know? Except during the dreadful foster years.'

'What happened to your mum and dad? The boys have never said.'

'They were on a trip to France for a weekend and had a car accident. It took them both instantly. Our world fell apart. Ollie and I were nine, Nick was fourteen. We didn't have any other relatives left alive. Mum was Australian, but an only child. Both of her parents were dead, and we'd lost my dad's mum, our gran, about six months before that.

'Our nanny offered to adopt us, but there were all sorts of legal ramifications surrounding our inheritance and the control of Mum's company. They separated us into different foster homes. Five horrendous years where we didn't see each other, and Ollie was getting into strife. Then Nick got a judge to agree to let him be our guardian. He was nineteen and responsible for us and the company.'

'That's a lot.'

'I'll never forget him coming to get me. Of course, my older brother, who was fun and funny and awkward, had been replaced by this man, tall and so fucking serious. He hugged me so tightly and I sobbed. Ollie was there, and we just stood on the road outside my foster parents' home, clinging to each other. We lost so much.'

My heart broke for the young versions of the Northby siblings, especially Nick. I couldn't imagine being nineteen and having so much weight to bear. Jesus, when I was nineteen I was drunk most weekends and working at a retail store, where I would turn up so hungover I'd spend the whole day thinking I was going to die.

'Not that Nick was ever particularly emotional,' Evelyn continued. 'I saw glimpses of the old Nick when he met Rebecca, but then her illness ... It was absolutely horrendous; it almost broke him.'

I was so keen to hear details, but somehow Sydney traffic, notoriously terrible, had decided to clear for our benefit and we were at the hospital already. The whole of Sydney had apparently decided to sleep in, depriving me of the revelation of why the man I was in love with had his heart tightly locked up in a vault.

Evelyn kissed my cheek and hopped out while I went to park. Kate came off shift in forty-five minutes and I'd offered to pick her up, seeing as though I was there. She texted me to come up to the third floor, giving me a room number, and I reluctantly complied. I didn't want to intrude on Northby family time, and I was also conscious that, since I had split up with Peter, Kate had been trying to set me up with some doctor she knew.

I knocked on the door and entered. Tears stung my eyes as soon as I stepped inside. Ollie lay propped up on a few pillows, his shaved head wrapped in a bandage. Bruised and battered, he was Frankenstein's exceedingly handsome monster, but at least he was awake.

'Oh, my God, Ollie,' I whispered, my hand on my chest.

'Hey, Abs.' His voice sounded like his throat was sore.

There was no one else in the room and I walked over to him

and put my head down on his chest, hugging him. 'Oh, my God, Ollie. I am so relieved you're okay.'

'Bloody massive headache. Abs, I need water.'

I grabbed a cup with a straw off the pale wooden bedside drawers next to him. I popped the straw into his mouth. Years of practice with a toddler making me an expert.

He sipped for a few seconds. 'Ta … Abbey, thanks for looking after Nick for me. I'm sure he was a fucking nightmare over this.'

'He was just worried about you.' Neither of his siblings seemed to understand that I wanted nothing more than to look after Nick forever.

A throat cleared behind me and the man himself was in the room. My heart beat hard. It was like getting off a roller coaster that your over-enthusiastic child insisted you ride, but then got to the top and changed her mind – relief tinged with joy. The stress and exhaustion clung to him. He was only ever so slightly less fastidious than usual, but it was the most relaxed I had seen him in the last few days, and it was so lovely to see. He practically beamed me a smile and gave me a look that communicated his relief, gratitude and warmth. There was a touch of adoration in it too, and my heart seemed to swell in my chest.

Evelyn came through the door and embraced me again. Kate was behind her, followed by Ollie's doctor.

'Abbey, this is Dr Sebastian Marks, Oliver's neurologist,' Kate said. Her eyebrows were dancing up and down, and I realised belatedly that she was trying to communicate something to me.

The doctor was extremely good-looking, taller than either of the Northbys by several inches, fit and dark. His dark-brown eyes looked like melted milk chocolate and his face broke into deep dimples when he smiled. His arms and chest looked like they were solid muscle.

'Hey,' I said quietly, offering a small polite wave.

'You're Kate's sister. I can see a resemblance. I've been looking forward to meeting you.' Dimples appeared with his closed-mouthed smile as he met my eyes and held them. He seemed to turn back to Kate for reassurance, giving me the impression my sister had arm-wrestled him into this introduction in much the same way she had me.

Across the room, Nick cleared his throat and put on his CEO voice. 'How long do you expect Ollie's recovery to take, Dr Marks?'

Sebastian dragged his eyes back to his patient's brother. 'Nick, it may take a couple of months for Oliver to recover. The headaches should eventually subside. He may have trouble concentrating for extended periods of time initially, but I would expect a full recovery in six weeks or so. We intend on releasing Oliver home at the end of the week if there are no complications. I've spoken with your orthopaedic surgeon, Oliver. You'll be non-weight-bearing for approximately six weeks. Then you'll need rehab. I think twelve weeks all up.'

'Thank you so much, Dr Marks,' Evelyn said.

Sebastian nodded. I could feel Oliver's emotion and instinctively reached over and grabbed his hand. A tear ran down his cheek and his sister wiped it away.

'Come on, Ollie,' she said. 'Not so bad.'

'Abbey.'

I looked up, surprised to see the doctor still in the room.

'Uh, I realise this might not be the best time, but do you think ... perhaps you would like to have dinner with me next week?'

Oh, fuck. I looked down at Ollie's hand, which had squeezed mine, and then my eyes locked with Nick's. I caught a flash of jealousy, a swift clench of his jaw, a flare of his nostrils, but it vanished almost straight away. Now he was staring at me impassively, as if he was considering what I would say.

Sebastian was astute at reading people. I suppose doctors had to be. 'Oh, I apologise. I didn't realise you two were together.'

I held Nick's eyes, trying to hold on to him. I tried to communicate my hope, my desire, my love and care with a single look. There was a second, a micro-second, where I saw something flicker in his expression and my breath caught with the thought that he was finally going to name what was happening between us. Claim me as his.

But then it was gone.

'No. We're not together,' he said, dropping his eyes to the floor. Shutting down from me.

I wanted to sink into the ground or maybe just burst into tears or burst into flames and rage at him.

'Oh, okay, my mistake,' Sebastian said, sounding not confident. 'Well ... um, how about dinner then, Abbey?'

My eyes were still on Nick. The man I was certain I was in love with, who did not love me. He was refusing to meet my eyes. His brother's hand flexed in mine, who, though he had been unconscious for several days, somehow understood this situation better than Nick. Thoughts about the time we had spent together filled my head. The sex. The two nights lying in his arms. The comfort I had been able to provide him. The love and care I had for his family. His refusal to let me out of his reach.

Jesus. I could not do this anymore. I needed to implement some way-overdue self-preservation tactics. I had to let him go.

'That sounds great, Sebastian,' I said quietly, finally looking at the hot doctor, squaring my shoulders, and putting on the smile that was expected of me.

Sebastian looked relieved that Kate would not be his mortal enemy for failing to succeed. 'Fantastic! I'll grab your number from

Kate. I, uh, look forward to it.' He bent his head in a weird kind of bow and left the room.

Kate could barely contain her excitement and she left too.

I smiled politely. Everything was fine. Yes, my heart was broken. *And Nick fucking Northby* still could not meet my eyes. *Fucking coward.*

I had to get out of there with at least some semblance of dignity. I turned to Oliver, seeing sad sympathy in his eyes. 'I am so glad you are okay, Ollie. Truly I am.' I pressed a soft kiss into his cheek and then walked out the door.

Once I was in the corridor, I walked slowly, letting the sadness come. I would give it a day or two, no more. He didn't deserve it. Though in his defence, he had warned me. How many times had he told me this would be the case? If I had fallen, then I had done so knowing the risks. It didn't make it feel better, though. I was just devastated.

'Abbey.'

I didn't want to turn, but I did, and I did not bother to hide the tears or the misery. I refused to hide the hurt. I wanted him to see it.

He pulled at the neck of his jumper and ran a hand through his hair, making it stick out wildly. 'I wanted to thank you. For everything. I don't think I could have got through the last couple of days without you.'

Yesterday, I would have tried to find the subtext in what he was saying. Today I was done. I turned and kept walking.

Nick

I watched her walk down the corridor. Stopped myself from calling out to her. She deserved someone like that doctor. Handsome and light. She deserved a chance with someone who could love her the way she deserved to be loved.

It would be easier if we didn't have to see each other. It would be so much easier if I could pick up my life and move back to London, giving us the space we both need. But tomorrow, I need to go be Oliver at Delacqua. And that means I'm Abbey Parker's boss again.

When I walked back into the room, my siblings were staring at me.

'I hope you are not going to allow that very hot doctor to swoop that lovely woman away from you, Nicholas,' Ev said.

'I do not require your guidance, Evelyn.'

'Nick, you might be able to pull the wool over other people's eyes and fool them by being an arsehole, but that does not work with us, dear brother. I do believe you are in love.'

'I'm not in love.' I attempted to sound disinterested in the discussion, but it came out more like a growl. Strangely, the feel of Abbey's mouth kissing my cheek and her kid wrapping her arms around me in a spontaneous Abbey-like-hug flashed through my brain.

'Nick, you are allowed to choose happiness. You do know that, right?'

Choose happiness. What did that even mean? I didn't choose anything here. It felt like life was operating all on its own at this point. I could choose happiness; it meant nothing. It did not mean Abbey would be happy. I chose happiness with Rebecca and look where that got us.

'Do you ever think we are cursed, Ev?'

'Nick, we have each other. We have Summer and Liam—'

'I'm not sure a labrador counts, Ev,' Ollie mumbled.

'We have money, we have our health.' She looked pointedly at Ollie. 'We have so much more than so many people, Nick.

I know you know that. It's what you have always told us.'

'So is Ev right? You are in love with Abbey?' My brother can't open his mouth without it making his skull ache, and his voice sounds strange.

'I do not love her. Nothing is going on.'

My siblings shared a look that screamed *our brother is full of fucking shit*. I sat down next to Ollie and changed the subject.

And though we talked of other things, I was still thinking about how I would not have survived the last couple of days if it wasn't for Abbey.

Chapter Eleven
Abbey

I simply do not know how I managed to drag my arse out of bed on the Monday morning. No, strike that, I do know – I lived in Sydney, and I had a mortgage.

Kate walked into my room without knocking as I was staring at my open wardrobe. 'You know you can call in sick, right?'

'I've got stuff to do for Oliver.'

'You looking in there for something slutty to wear?'

'Professional but slutty ... yeah.'

'Pencil skirt and that white blouse you own. Your boobs look great in it.'

I considered, and then nodded.

'Oh ... wait.' She ran out and came back with a pair of stockings.

'Seam down the back?' I asked.

'Yep, he's going to be looking at your legs all day.'

I kissed her cheek. 'You are amazing.'

Dressed, I grabbed my lunch from the fridge and she looked me up and down. 'Damn, Abs. There is something decidedly Cavendish about you today.'

I was insanely pleased with the compliment. 'Thank you, my lovely sister.'

I wiggled into the office, my feet already killing me from the additional heel height of the shoes I'd chosen to wear. The amount of eye contact men wanted to make with me in this outfit was, quite frankly, alarming. Still, a sweet old guy at the train station barrier had stopped in the peak-hour crowd and said to me 'ladies first', which was kind of lovely.

Coming into work felt odd. Ollie was this ball of energy and even in the short amount of time he'd been there his absence felt like a void. It was my job to look after things for him while he recovered, and it felt good to recognise that as another reason why I'd got up that morning.

It had nothing to do with the other one. The other Northby. He was an inconvenience, nothing more, someone I would simply have to put up with. In three months Ollie would be back, and I would be Nick-free.

I would manage my feelings for him during that time by locking them up. Putting them away. If I had taken anything away from our relationship, perhaps it was simply the lesson he'd provided me on compartmentalisation.

The elevator chimed, and I ignored my traitorous little heart as it beat at the sight of him. *How many fucking bespoke suits could one man own? Suit whore.* His grey suit was one I had not seen before. It had been cut by a master and clung to his legs indecently. He looked outrageously good, and I wondered, not for the first time, why I was cursed to be so attracted to this guy.

I mean, he was just everything I never even imagined in a man.

Smart, attractive, quietly funny. He was an intense person and an intense lover. He didn't have sex, he worshipped with a smouldering reverence I had never experienced before. I was addicted to him.

Of course someone like me would fall for him. What was I? A single mum with an enormous mortgage. A boring, middle-aged woman. Not skinny enough, or not pretty enough, for the likes of him.

I felt suddenly emotional and closed my eyes against it. But then Gran appeared behind my lids.

'Not being feeble, are we, Abigail?' she asked with authority. 'Not just those things, are you? What else is there? You are a—'

Cavendish woman. I am a Cavendish. And I looked tempting as fuck today. I opened my eyes and squared my shoulders.

I had left my hair out in the waves I knew he liked to touch; I pushed it aside, revealing the neck his lips liked to graze and, as I *accidentally* pushed my stapler off my desk, I stood slowly, giving him a cool smile before I bent over at the waist to grab it. My tight skirt and seamed stockings played their part as his step faltered. His eyes skimmed my curves hotly before correcting themselves.

He had a satchel and a brown paper bag in one hand, and was carrying two coffees in a tray with his other. A small smile graced his handsome face. He knew exactly what I was about, and he respected it. He put down a coffee in front of me and dropped his bag at his feet, placing the paper bag on the desk. He pulled out two bagels.

'Apparently,' he drawled, as he pulled a chair to my desk, 'this is tradition. The CEO tells me if I do this today, you do it tomorrow.' His eyes were sparkling with amusement at me. 'He also said you are less inclined to be cranky when you eat.'

'Did he now?' My voice remained cool, even as the smell of the food met my nose.

'Mmmhmm.'

'Interesting,' I said, tearing open the bag, starving.

'Careful, Abs. There is sauce and you do not want it to end up on that beautiful blouse.'

My eyes flashed him a warning.

'You're annoyed with me.'

'Annoyed? Me? No, I'm fine. Not annoyed with you, *boss*. Never.'

'Liar.'

'Nick, I'm not prepared to get into it.'

'That outfit looks like you want to get into it, Abbey.'

'Are we going to flirt or work?'

He contemplated this for a second and then leaned closer to me. 'A little HR birdy told me it's your birthday in two weeks.' He lifted his bagel, taking a bite, amused by my hiss of displeasure.

It was completely fine that I was turning forty-three. I was not freaked out at all about how fucking old that sounded.

'I was thinking of having a welcome-home party for Ollie,' he continued. 'And I had the rather fabulous idea that we could all get together and celebrate both your birthday and Ollie on the mend. It would give me the opportunity to thank you and Kate. So invite Kate, Granny Iris and Lionel, oh, and the hot doctor?'

Interesting. Happy Birthday, Abbey. Bring a date. It seemed he was living in an alternate universe where we were friends. I remembered my self-preservation tactics. *We cannot be friends.*

'Don't forget we have dinner tonight with my sister.'

I went to protest that, but had a mouthful of bacon and egg.

He pressed his advantage. 'Also, we have had a few problems in Melbourne since Friday afternoon, so I'm going to need you to come down there with me to sort it out. I'm keen to look at that hotel, so I thought we would stay the weekend and experience it, see what the customers see. It seems to have some sort of cool factor that the Sydney property doesn't, and I want to know what it is, exactly. I know you don't have Ella.' He reached out and touched my hand.

'Oh, nope,' I said, swallowing a lump of bagel.

'Nope?' This with his best Australian accent.

'No. That's not going to work here.'

'The touching or the coming to Melbourne?' he raised a dark eyebrow in query.

'Either. Or both.' The minute he had touched my hand, it confirmed I had an immense problem. My body reacted to him as if it belonged to him. I had to try, somehow, to get my body to comply with the desire I had not to desire him. 'I'm so sorry. I can't do that with you. I have a date with the hot doctor on Friday night.'

'I need you in Melbourne. We have trouble brewing in the restaurant. The celebrity chef is throwing tantrums.' He gave me a dazzling, disarming smile. 'Mike was telling us that the chef down there finds you compelling. I believe "alluring" was the word he used.'

When he said 'alluring' it was probably the hottest word I'd ever heard spoken by a voice, and I looked at his mouth for too long after he finished talking.

'Jack Fife? Pffft. Urgh, all right fine.' *Why, Abbey? Why? What are you doing? Self-preservation. Self-preservation. Hot doctor. But this flirty work banter... Christ.*

'Ev loves you. You'll come to dinner tonight?'

And there was the problem. I didn't want Ev to love me. I wanted Nick to love me. Also, what was he playing at, being all flirty and charming and extending invitations?

'What are you doing?' I breathed. I needed to be freed of this torture.

'Just working.'

'Are you seriously telling me that is what this is? Just work?

You're flirting. And then spend the weekend in Melbourne? Have dinner with my sister?'

'Abbey, you purposefully knocked a stapler off your desk. I thought *you* were flirting. I'm sorry. I genuinely need you to come to Melbourne. Jack Fife is a prima donna, and you are the one person I'm told can help. I need you there in a professional capacity. You can set the rules. Okay? Also, I told Ev we were having dinner. You are the only person we know here in Sydney, and you have been extraordinary the last week. My sister and I want to thank you. Nanny Jacinta has the day off and Summer wants to come too, so bring Ella.'

'Fine.' *Fucker*. How had I just been talked into the family fucking dinner?

If I'd thought working with him was going to be easy, I was wrong. Bad Cop had left the building, and he was in full charm mode. The turnaround he performed in the exec meeting was next level. Even I was impressed.

The team were naturally wary; he had performed his role in the first two meetings almost too well. But he started softly, earning sympathy and respect.

'Welcome, everyone. We'll get down to business in a few minutes. I just wanted to give you guys an update on Oliver. He is, umm, well he was knocked about. If you knew him better you might know that he is pretty good at most things he puts his head to and knocking it on concrete was no different.

'He's awake and, apart from being in a foul mood from the headache and hospital food, he is on the mend. The doctors say his recovery should take about three months, but he is my brother and I don't want any pressure on him. The important thing is that he gets better.'

I could feel his emotion and wanted to reach out to him to let him know I was here for support. But he had made it impossible for me to do that, so I sat on the hand nearest him and picked up a glass of water with the other.

'I, um, just wanted to thank Abbey. She rendered crucial first aid to Oliver and got him to the hospital as fast as possible. My brother, sister and I have always tried to keep this feeling like a family business, but it has gotten so big that it is sometimes hard to manage. Abbey cared for Oliver in those first few moments like he was her own family, and I honestly cannot express my gratitude.'

I put the water back onto the table with a thud.

He met my eyes. 'Thank you.'

I nodded slightly, or at least I think I did.

Nick cleared his throat and began going around the table, starting with Mike. 'Why don't you give us an update on the finance team?'

'Thanks, Nick. I'm relieved to hear Oliver is okay. I hope you will pass on our regards. We've been busy with the end of financial year next week. I sent emails about what we needed from department heads. If those reports could be submitted by Wednesday at the latest, that would be incredibly helpful.'

'Guys, if we can try to get those to Mike as quickly as possible, that'd be great. Mike, just knock on my door any time or let Abbey know if you need me. I'm completely confident you guys are all over it. Right, who wants to go next?'

By the third manager, I could see the table had collectively relaxed and, as a result, some great discussions and teamwork occurred. I could also see where Oliver had learned leadership, that it wasn't something he knew innately; it was something he had learned from Nick.

The other interesting thing from the exec meeting was just how many things he included me in on, things that were going to be reported to me instead of him, or things he wanted me to sit in on so that even I left the meeting a little invigorated professionally.

However, the different number of Nicks was making me a little wary, too. Holiday Nick, Brother Nick, Sex God Nick, Prick Boss Nick, Good Boss Nick. Abbey's Nick? Cute with Ella Nick? *Jesus*.

I dropped him a report he wanted later that day.

'Abs, I'm a little stretched. I hope you don't mind me handing some things over to you?'

'Of course. I'm honestly a little excited to be included.'

'Abbey, we both know if I weren't here you could run this place on your own. You know this business inside out. You undervalue yourself enormously. If you want to do something different than be an EA when Ollie gets back, tell him.'

I smiled, pleased.

'Will you come and sit in on the marketing meeting after lunch?'

'Sure.'

'You want to, uh, have lunch with me?'

'Lunch?'

'Yes, lunch.'

'With you?'

'Yes, lunch with me. We had breakfast together.'

'Actually, I, um, have plans with Mike.' The sinking feeling in my gut was telling me I was a little disappointed. My head was telling me I was glad to have an excuse to put some distance between us.

'Oh, okay. Well, I'll see you this afternoon.'

I enjoyed his disappointment immensely. Though here we were with our lines blurred again.

The marketing meeting had been postponed because of some crisis Nick was having in his London office in the middle of the night there, so we ended up doing it at the end of the day. I must admit, I was tired when I walked into the meeting. Nick was distracted and had brought in his laptop so that he could continue to manage the issue.

I had been in the initial meetings with Ollie, where he had asked the marketing team for a national campaign and a single catchy slogan that would become synonymous with the hotels.

'Right, let's get started,' Nick said to the bunch of twenty-somethings that had filed in.

'Oh, great. Thanks so much, Nick.'

The spokesman was a young guy called Jake Taylor. He had a practised confidence that told me he'd done this sort of thing at uni and felt his day had finally come. He had on an expensive suit and was handsome in a young, preppy way. He probably did well at Friday afternoon drinks with the ladies. His enthusiasm was palpable, his eyes alight with the excitement of presenting a concept he was absolutely certain would revolutionise the company.

'We've been diving deep into our demographic analytics and psychographic segmentation profiling to synthesise a brand narrative that resonates on both an emotional and aspirational level. The goal was to distil the essence of the guest experience into a succinct, impactful slogan that not only captures the luxury and comfort of our hotel chain, but also speaks to the figurative journey of our guests. After extensive brainstorming sessions and intensive focus groups, we believe we've landed on a tagline that encapsulates this.'

I blinked, because as far as openers go, that was jargon-y.

Jake clicked the remote, and the sleek PowerPoint presentation behind him flickered to the next slide, revealing the words in a bold, stylish font: 'Another Day in Paradise'.

I looked at Nick, but his head was down and he was tapping away at an email.

'We've crafted "Another Day in Paradise" to evoke bliss and escapism,' Jake explained, pacing slightly as he gestured to the slide. 'It's designed to position our hotels as more than just places to stay, but as destinations where everyday stress melts away, and each morning feels like a renewal, a reminder of that vacation feeling. The phrase leverages the imagery associated with paradise, which our research shows has strong positive connotations across multiple demographics, particularly within the millennial and Gen Z markets. By tapping into these emotional triggers, we can drive higher engagement and foster deeper brand loyalty for consumers.'

He paused, looking around the table at the mix of young marketers, Nick and me, establishing eye contact with us. Well, with me, as Nick was still glued to his email. 'We believe this slogan not only aligns with our brand ethos, but also differentiates us in a crowded market. It's fresh, memorable and, most importantly, it tells a story our guests can relate to and aspire to.'

Jake's smile widened as he concluded, clearly proud of the work his team had delivered. 'So, what do you think?'

'Great,' Nick said.

I looked at him and then I kicked his chair. 'Jake, I can see the hard work that has gone into this. But you can't use it,' I said.

As I spoke, Nick finally started listening and looked at the PowerPoint on the screen. A slight flex of his brows was the only change on his face.

'Why is that, Abbey?' Jake was clearly annoyed.

'Because of the song.'

He snorted, 'And what song is that, Abbey?' His hands were on his hips, his snort telling me in no uncertain terms that women my age didn't know more about music than him.

Beside me, Nick had closed his laptop and was barely concealing his amusement. He pushed his chair back and crossed his legs. He sat eagerly and silently, waiting for me to continue.

'Phil Collins,' I said.

'Who?'

'Phil Collins. You know, pop artist? Genesis? Actor? He sang "In the Air Tonight".'

'Uh, nobody here knows who that it is, Abbey. Maybe it's a little irrelevant. We are trying to build the brand's future. You guys always want to get stuck in the past. It's the difference between my generation and yours.'

Oh, Jake.

'Jake, you cannot use that slogan. Regardless of whether you know the song or not, regardless of whether you know one of the biggest-selling artists from the 1980s or not. The song is the reason you cannot use the slogan. The last demographic report that came across my desk two weeks ago suggested that over sixty per cent of Delacqua's clientele were born prior to 1985, so predominantly our customers are Gen X and Baby Boomers. If you had used them in your focus groups, with the slogan instead of just the word "paradise" – which of course people respond positively to – you would understand what the issue is … before you brought it to this meeting with the owner of the company.' I was on a bit of a roll. 'The issue is that the song is about a homeless woman.'

'But that's perfect, Abbey. Delacqua is a home for everyone.'

'Jake, the price tag for a basic room at one of our hotels is $500 per night. I can assure you it is not a home for everyone. The song

"Another Day in Paradise" refers to a woman starving on the streets and asking a man for help. He ignores her and goes about his life, living *another day in paradise*.'

'Oh, I know who that guy is!' one of the young marketing assistants, who had an iPhone in her hand, piped in, clearly having done a Google search. 'He's Lily Collins's dad, Jake. You know, *Emily in Paris*.'

It was Nick's turn to look confused, but I had Ella and Netflix and no life. I knew what they were referring to. Summer was probably a bit young.

'You guys really don't know who Phil Collins is?' Nick asked.

There were a few grumbles and shakes of the head. '"Easy Lover"? "Invisible Touch"?' Nick waited patiently before standing. 'Okay. Well, we are back to the drawing board with this one, team. Let's see what else we come up with. Jake, I'll just get you to run it by Abbey before we meet at this level again.'

We sat as they filed out, dejected.

'Who the fuck doesn't know who Phil Collins is?' Nick said irritably.

'Jesus, are we *that* old?' I said incredulously.

'Good save. I wasn't listening.'

'I know. Are you—' I stopped and attempted to rephrase what was going to be a personal question. 'Is everything okay?'

'I'm a little flat.'

'That's because of everything that's been going on.' I couldn't shift the caring notes of my voice.

'I guess.' He swallowed. 'Why don't you head home. I'll send a car to pick you and Ella up so you don't have to drive.'

I nodded. 'Okay. That'd be nice. Thank you.'

'You know what my favourite Phil Collins song is?'

I shook my head.

'"Groovy Kind of Love".'

I smiled despite myself. I'm not certain what I was expecting, but it wasn't that.

'What's yours?' he asked quietly.

'"Against All Odds".'

He nodded and that smile he had that never quite changed his face appeared. 'See you tonight, Abbey.'

Oh, boy. I was so desperately in love with this man. I was headed in one direction. Heartbreak.

The family dinner was a bad idea. Full stop. I had these clear thoughts as I dressed and prepared to meet him. It was difficult for me to enforce any of the boundaries I tried to implement with him because of how much I wanted and loved him. He was like a tasty loaf of bread on a carb-free diet. I definitely had a bad feeling.

Ella and I hopped into the chauffeured car, which drove us to the door of a cute little restaurant in the city. My child was pretty certain she was rich and famous tonight.

'I feel like Margot Robbie, Mum.'

We entered the casual but elegant restaurant and Family Nick was there. And he … I could tell he would be the most dangerous Nick of all.

Family Nick took everyone's order and chatted to the girls over the menu about what they wanted to eat, listening intently to their thoughts, and then grossed them out by telling them all the weird things he had eaten around the world. I tried not to buy in, but I could not stop smiling at him.

I watched him throughout dinner. He was so relaxed around his sister and Summer. Family Nick and Holiday Nick were the same, but minus Sex God Nick, and I suspected that this was actually him, just Nick. I wished Ollie could have been there too and from time to time the two Northby siblings would go quiet, and I knew they were thinking the same.

Family Nick was indulgent and devoted. He would bend down when Summer spoke, eager to hear anything she told him. He was equally great with Ella. I couldn't stop looking at him. He was breathtaking. Pale-blue jeans and a white shirt. Classic and masculine and beautiful. The waitress tried to flirt with him, but he didn't notice. He was ours. The women at this table.

After dinner, he took the girls next door where there was an arcade place, leaving Evelyn and me to chat.

'How long have you been in love with Nick, Abbey?'

I almost spat out my wine. But I couldn't see the point of attempting to deny it.

'It's hard to define. Maybe straight away or maybe I just realised this week.'

'Rebecca died when Summer was eight months old. You are the first woman I've ever had dinner with. He doesn't do things like this.'

'I don't know what he does and what he doesn't do, Ev. I think if he wanted a relationship or to talk about feelings, he would. But he runs every time I think he is going to say something about how he feels about me. So …' I shrugged. 'It feels like I'm the only one emotionally involved and, frankly, that is not a great feeling. And I know I can't keep doing things like this. He will break my heart. And it's not like I'm some blind teenager walking into this.'

I sighed. 'I want a relationship of love and devotion; I don't want to be the only one in it. I've already pretended my way through a marriage. I know what I want now. I'm not prepared to settle for less. And Nick … Nick gives me no sign that he wants anything more than … what has already happened.'

'Fuck, men are hard.'

'Cheers to that,' I said, clinking my glass to hers.

When they came back from the arcade flushed and grinning, Ella was gushing. 'Mum. Nick, Summer and I played this *Jurassic Park* game and Nick brought down the biggest dinosaur. Summer and I were FREAKING OUT, like screaming. Nick is the best. He's so funny.'

'Hero complex,' he provided, throwing a lopsided grin my way.

I was done. It was one thing for me to be in love with him. Under no circumstances could I allow him to break Ella's heart, too. I stood and picked up my handbag. 'Ella, it's getting late. We should get you home.'

His face fell.

I could not get out of there quickly enough. 'Say goodbye and thank you. I'll meet you out the front, Ella. I'm just going to order an Uber.' I walked hastily out the door, offering his sister a perfunctory kiss on the cheek. 'Bye, Ev.'

When I reached the fresh air, I took in a deep gulp and threw my head back to look at the sky. A tear had come free, and I pushed it away, furious with myself.

'Abbey.'

'Nick, I need to go.'

'Okay, I'll get the car for you.'

'Nick, I don't need your car, or you.'

He took a step closer to me, and I stepped back from him. His eyes had darkened, and a crease had formed between them, concern on his face. He reached for my hand, but I took another step back.

'Abbey.' I heard frustration.

But I wouldn't let him comfort me. I could see his sister trying to keep our girls inside, keeping them engaged with a fish tank just inside the door, to give us a minute.

'You're upset.'

'I can't keep doing this, Nick. I want … I want more than this. I don't want whatever this is. It isn't enough. And I can't have Ella wanting it too.'

I waved to Ella, and she ran out throwing her arms around my boss/boyfriend/love of my life.

'Night, Nick.'

'Night, Ella.'

We hopped into the Uber and went home.

Nick

I looked out the car window on the way home and attempted to make appropriate responses and smile at my daughter.

'I wish I had a sister. Ella is lovely. She's so lucky to have a mum. Abbey is gorgeous too. Ella says they have movie nights, and that she prefers her mum's place to her dad's place because she doesn't like her dad's new girlfriend and her mum has a degree of chill. She said she wants Abbey to have a boyfriend, and she is excited because Abbey's sister, Ella's Aunt Kate, has a friend who is a doctor. An actual doctor. Ella says that doctors are the best.'

Ev threw me a dark look across the car, which I ignored.

We finally got home and got Summer into bed.

'I love you, Daddy,' Summer said, and she kissed my nose. I sometimes try to find Rebecca in her face, but she looks so much like me, Bec didn't get a look in.

'Goodnight, Sum.'

'I like it here. You seem happier.'

'Do I?'

She nods at me solemnly.

'Goodnight, Sum. Love you.'

When I got back to the lounge room, Ev had made us a cup of tea and was looking at me with a stern expression.

'What was tonight, Nick?' There was a distinct helping of attitude that instantly made me defensive.

'I'm not clear on what you are referring to, Evelyn.'

'What are you doing with that woman? It isn't good enough. She likes you. A lot. And she is lovely. And you like her.'

'I'm not discussing it with you, Ev. Quite frankly, it is none of your business.'

'Actually, Nick, it *is* my business because I am a co-owner of the company and one-third of the board that Abbey works for. And I'm your sister.'

'Abbey's a grown-up. She knows exactly what the deal is.'

'Oh, that's why she left upset? After we all had a great time? And you playing happy families with the kids, but not prepared to commit yourself. I love you. That's why I can tell you to your face, you are being a prick.'

'I don't need this, Ev.' I reached for the tea she had made me, not meeting her eyes.

'That's fine. I don't need it either, Nick. I have enough men in my life with the emotional capacity of a small puddle. It's just hard to watch my brother – who, when he lets himself love someone, loves them better than anyone else I know – not allow himself to love. I'll stay at Ollie's tonight. Goodnight, Nick. Fuck you.'

She left, taking her teacup, and I sat in the dark. I finished my tea and then dragged my exhausted arse to bed.

What the fuck was I doing? It was supposed to be a night where Abbey felt appreciated.

I started undressing, undoing my belt and taking off my jeans. The problem was that she already felt like a part of my family. And so did Ella. I'd stopped thinking and just relaxed and it felt completely natural. And I forgot.

I forgot the boundaries. I forgot about Rebecca. Her illness. The day she died and the blackness in the months after.

I can't let that happen again. I was giving mixed signals. I need to protect Abbey better.

I made a deal with myself in the dark that Abbey and I were purely professional from this point on. I would not cross the line with her again.

Chapter Twelve
Abbey

I sat on the plane to Melbourne by myself, Friday at midday, having booked my flight two hours earlier than Nick's. I planned to sort out Jack Fife without Nick and get back home before dinner.

As I sat, staring at the safety leaflet and the tray table 'in the upright position', I could not stop thinking back on the week that was. As far as weeks of my life where everything was a fucking nightmare went, this one was right up there.

Tuesday had been awkward after the family dinner. I spent the day avoiding him, only for him to amp up his charm. He was funny, smart and intoxicatingly beautiful. At work he listened to my opinion like that of an expert. I felt intelligent and important.

In the afternoon, a phone call came through from Ella's school, asking me to submit the paperwork for the junior student exchange program. The principal was a lovely lady in her early sixties and, because Ella never got in trouble, we had an uncomplicated relationship.

'Hi, Sue. I'm so sorry I haven't returned them or the deposit. I've been busy at work, and it slipped my mind.' In truth, I'd had to wait for a pay cycle to come around to scrounge together half of the deposit.

'Abbey, that's no trouble. One of the reasons I'm calling is to let you know that we've had a donation from a business, who is offering to cover the costs of the program in full.'

'What? Really?'

'Yes. The school always delights in finding benefactors.'

'That's amazing, Sue. You guys must be thrilled. Which business?'

'I'm sorry?'

'Which business donated the money? Did they just cover Ella's?' I turned and looked through the glass at the man sitting at the desk behind me. *No way he did this. Right?*

'It was an anonymous donation, Abbey. And, no, it wasn't just Ella. They covered another student as well.'

'I see. Well ... I'll get those forms to you, Sue. But now I've got to get back to work.' I hung up and stood. I was rigid with a fury I didn't believe I had ever felt before.

First, I did not need to be fucking rescued by him, or Kate, or Gran. It pissed me off that they thought I was weak. Second, paying for my kid to take a life-changing trip because he was worried I couldn't afford it ... told me there were feelings. More than that, it told me there was love. And it was pissing me off that he would not admit it.

I walked into his office without knocking, marching straight past his desk into the kitchen. It was that or the bathroom, the only places in the office that would afford me the privacy I needed. I walked to the back wall and leaned my head against the cool marble surface.

'Abbey, are you okay?'

'Did you pay for Ella's student exchange program?'

'I'm sorry?'

'You heard me, Nick.' I spun around to look at him accusingly, my arms folded against my chest.

'Abbey, I ...' His eyes were shining, but he was not cleanly shaven and he looked tired, as if he hadn't slept.

I had the urge to feel him, to feel his breath on me, to feel his lips on me, yet at the same time I wanted to rage at him – such was the nature of our relationship.

'Yes, I did,' he said. 'I didn't mean for you to find out.' He leaned against the bench behind him, sagging a little on it.

'Why?'

'Why what?'

I took three purposeful steps towards him. 'Why did you do that?'

He swallowed and looked up at the ceiling, avoiding my gaze. 'Because I can.'

'Can you hear yourself? The things you say and the things you do tell me different things, Nick.' I closed the gap between us, placing myself in front of him. I put my hand on his heart and felt it thud comfortingly underneath me. 'I do not want your money. I do not need saving or to be rescued by you.'

He breathed out and shook his head before placing his forehead on mine. 'I know that, Abbey.'

'Then tell me why, Nick? Let me in. Tell me why you do these things. For me.'

He put his hand over mine on his chest and we stood there for an age, simply looking at each other. He pushed a strand of hair behind my ear, leaving his hand there, and I leaned into it. But I could not make him speak.

'I need you to stop.' I stepped away from him and left the office.

After work, I brought Gran home for dinner. Her and Kate's chatter was sufficient to keep my mind entertained as I chopped salad and popped crumbed chicken into the air fryer. But it wasn't sufficient to lift my mood.

'Abigail, how is that lovely man of yours? I've not seen him this week.'

'I'm not sure who you are referring to, Gran,' I said. The absolute last thing I wanted to do was to think about him. I took a sip of wine.

'You know, he came by a few times.'

'Yes. They don't have any family left. I think he just wanted to feel close to a family.'

'You seem sad, Abigail.'

I turned around to them, heat in my cheeks and my heart rate thumping in my chest. 'I am sad. I'm in love with him. He does not love me. Or he does and won't admit it. Are you happy?' I put my wine down on the bench. 'So I have two choices: leave my job or put up with him and this situation until Ollie returns. It's just … you know, difficult for me to be near him and not be with him.'

'But, Abbey, you have the date with Sebastian. And, honestly, he is a significantly better option than Nick. I mean he is taller, more handsome, a doctor,' Kate said. 'He's not a total commitment-phobe with more money than sense.'

'Maybe you should date him then, Kate,' I offered, sick of her shit and feeling exhausted.

She didn't respond.

'Abbey, you know, in the *Duke's Dark Desire: The Adventure to India* – not my favourite, but still – the heroine, the Honourable Romola Le Monde, implements a set of rules to resist the duke's brother Rufus St Morten. Perhaps that's what you need?'

'Rules?'

'Yes, Abbey. Rules. The attraction, when it is so strong, is an exceedingly difficult thing to combat. I certainly felt it for your grandfather, Harry, while I was still married to his best friend, Ray. It felt stronger than anything I've ever felt, then or since, like somehow the earth had made two people who were meant to fit together, whose souls would call to each other no matter the circumstances.'

'Did you have an affair, Gran? With Grandad? I don't think I've ever asked.'

'No, child. It has never been my style. I was married, and that felt permanent. Ray wasn't blind, though. It is difficult to hide from destiny, I'm afraid.'

'He died in a car accident, didn't he?'

'Ray? Yes, child. I married your grandfather a fortnight later.'

'Were people shocked?'

'No one that mattered.'

I pulled out plates and the cutlery, while my grandmother continued her lesson.

'Now, Abbey. Rules. You must implement lots of rules to ensure you don't accidentally have sex.'

Ella walked into the kitchen at that exact moment and, without pausing, turned straight around and walked back to her room.

'Rule number one ... no skin-to-skin contact. No angsty, prolonged hand touching or grazing of fingers as you pass each other things.'

It was as if she had been a fly on the wall.

'Rule number two ...' Gran took a sip of her wine. 'No confined spaces. If you are in his office, keep the door open. If you are in a lift together, opposite walls.'

'How does that work while I'm on a plane?'

'Abbey, the last time I checked, it was your job to book the travel. Sort it out.'

I had been dreaming of our bodies being in close proximity, but the truth was that I would fly economy and he would not, so it would not have happened, anyway.

'You must avoid extended eye contact. Holding a man's gaze too long can suggest that you want him, the same as looking at his lips. It will not do. You must remove all of the period-drama tropes, my dear girl.'

I sighed. 'I love those.'

My sister drank her wine and rolled her eyes at me.

'Also remember, the less time you spend alone together, the less chance there is of having sex. Unless you want to add additional partners, in which case other people around might still make you want to have sex. I must say, Abbey, I tried group sex in between marriages during the eighties and found it highly overrated.'

Oh, my God.

On Thursday night, I'd had the rescheduled date with the hot doctor.

I made the bare minimum effort for my dinner with Sebastian. I had agreed to go, but, beyond that, I knew deep down my heart wasn't really free to find love or even companionship with another. Still, a girl had to at least *pretend* to move on.

He had picked this dodgy-looking Turkish restaurant in Alexandria, which looked awful but served the tastiest food. The tables were the 1950s aluminium kind, and the chairs were in mustard and orange vinyl, which reminded me of my mother's Tupperware drawer in 1987.

Sebastian was confident, intelligent, funny, apparently carrying these personality traits with a grace and humility that defied his handsomeness and his profession. He was dressed in jeans and a Henley shirt in a soft caramel colour, which suited his eyes and fitted against his firm, gorgeously muscled chest. Other women could not help but stare at him, which was vaguely disconcerting, especially since he didn't seem to notice.

He reached over the table to touch my hand when he was making a point about something. And when he drove me home, he got out and walked me to my door, before planting a kiss on my cheek, which was sweet but didn't alter my pulse.

Kate was waiting expectantly in the kitchen; a weird nervous energy radiating off her.

'Well, how was it?'

'Where's Ella?'

'She's doing her English assessment in her room.' Kate was packing her bag for work and stopped to fill up her drink bottle, which was absolutely enormous. How she drank that much water in a day was frankly bizarre. All I could think was that I would constantly be on the loo.

'How was it? He's lovely, right?'

'It was fine.'

'Fine?'

'Yeah, um, nice … I guess.'

'Nice? You guess?'

Her accusing tone instantly pissed me off.

'What do you want me to say, Kate?'

'Abbey …'

'What?' I walked into the kitchen and started to unpack the dishwasher. I was tired, emotionally raw, and if there was an edge to my voice and an immediate defensiveness, then it was warranted.

'Sebastian is the perfect guy,' Kate pushed.

I handed her the cutlery rack. 'Maybe you should date him then, Kate, since you seem to think so.'

'I see what you're doing. You won't give Sebastian a chance because you think you're in love with Nick fucking Northby. He who refuses to commit, and leads you on, all while telling you he cannot love anyone. Doesn't stop him from having sex with you, though, does it?'

Kate softened her voice, putting down the cutlery rack on the bench so I could see she was genuinely worried. 'He's a commitment-phobe, Abbey. He's never going to say he loves you. Also, he's being a massive prick, because you can't hide the fact that you are in love with him, so he knows, and he still keeps leading you on.'

I felt heat climb up my face and my heart start to race. I hated that other people could see that, but I was also furious that she was just cruising on into my feelings and my relationship with Nick, as if I needed her opinion.

'Kate, enough.' My tone was warning her to back off, while I concentrated on putting the plates in the cupboard.

'No, Abbey. You need to hear this. Sebastian is a good guy and Nick is a fucking arse.'

'Nick is not a bad guy, Kate.' My voice was still calm, but I could feel the adrenaline kicking in.

'Abbey, you are being pathetic. He's leading you on.'

He's leading me on? Hang on, where's the Kate that had G & Ts with him and bullied me to go to that fucking party in that fucking dress?

'He's not leading me on Kate. Fuck.' I whipped around to face her, and my voice rose. 'He's not commitment-phobic, Kate. Every single person he has loved has died on him. He's fatalistic and realistic and he associates love with risk. He doesn't want to feel like that again. He doesn't want to feel broken. He is terrified of everything he loves and being invested in a person who could leave him.

'And, yes, I love him. I am wrecked with love for him. My heart beats only for him. And if he could say he loves me too, which I think he does, then you would have to just get over yourself and get along with him and respect and love him too. But don't worry, because that's not going to happen. I know this. I also understand that I need to move on. I'm trying. I don't need you to fucking rescue me. I'm fine. So stop railroading me.

'Also, stop advising me. You are four years younger than me and your longest relationship is six months. Also, I think it's time for you to find your own place. I love you, but Jesus, Kate. I need some space.'

I had not meant to let all of that out at once and Kate, naturally, did not take any one part of it particularly well. She had packed her things the next day and moved out.

So everything was fine. Just fine. Swimmingly fine. At least I had the Nick thing under control.

Having successfully implemented Gran's rules at work with Nick, I wasn't entirely sure what he made of my new distance, as I had been busy avoiding his wounded eyes. I was pretty proud of myself. I mean, he wasn't *that* attractive. I could definitely resist a moderately hot Englishman with murky eyes and floppy hair. No problem. I was a fucking Cavendish woman. It was all about the rules. *Just stick to those rules, Abs.*

I was surprisingly calmer on the one-hour flight from Sydney to Melbourne than I had been on the eighteen-hour trip to the Maldives and, with all the other business people on board along with a couple of girls-weekends-away groups, I felt competent and mature.

When we touched down, I hailed a cab to the hotel. I had packed lightly in a single carry-on in case of disaster, but had absolutely no intention of staying and had a return flight booked later tonight. The idea of hanging out with Nick for the weekend was not a good one. In fact, it almost certainly would involve the breaking of all the rules, which was completely fine if I wanted to have hot sex and a broken heart.

Melbourne has a distinctly different vibe to Sydney and, over the years, I'd built a deep love for it. It is more artsy than Sydney, with interesting sculptures and design points throughout the city. Without the glittering harbour, which most people could not help but fall in love with, it had somehow evolved a funkier, edgier quality to it and the river was still beautiful, despite its muddy colour.

The Delacqua Melbourne was my favourite of all of our hotels. It sat at the Paris end of Collins Street and had been a hotel for over one hundred years. Eric commissioned a renovation and extension back in the early 2000s, and the hotel was meticulously brought back to life. It was opulent and charming.

The original hotel had five stories of art-deco features, which had been expertly repurposed. Floors one and two held function rooms, in which Melbourne's most fashionable and discerning brides wanted their weddings. Floor one was in particular demand because a section of the hotel was partitioned out into an atrium with a garden inside, a feature that looked magnificent on Instagram (or so I was told). On level three was Australia's most sought-after restaurant. An additional eleven storeys of hotel rooms were built on top of the old girl, but the American architect had managed to achieve an eclectic art-deco vibe to the additional floors.

I climbed the marble stairs and walked behind the check-in counter, saying hello to the staff I knew and introducing myself to the ones I didn't. I noticed the staff all looked extremely polished, and the place was pristine, setting a shining example for their new owner.

One of the many benefits of keeping the original building was the classic, ornate lift that came with it. The black wrought-iron gate and white marble floors were beautiful and old-fashioned, distinctly Parisian, with gold-coloured mirrored tiles decorating the inside.

Iris had once told me that she had been on stage in the theatre down the street back in the sixties and had stayed in the original hotel. She talked of ball gowns and orchestral bands and, frankly, you could easily imagine it just by standing in the lift.

I checked my makeup in the mirrored wall. Sometimes a woman could use dress as an arsenal and I would need every single weapon available to me for my meeting with Jack Fife. I wore a high-necked black dress which clung to my curves and tied at the neck, with a white blazer. Jack Fife was notorious: short-tempered, talented to the point of arrogance, horrendous to any staff not meeting his exacting standards and a renowned womaniser.

The elevator opened, my heels making an impressive noise as I stepped out from the marble of the lift onto the marble of the corridor.

'Why did you book an earlier flight than me?' His voice was crisp and authoritative, but held a faint trace of exasperated humour. His arms were folded across his chest, and he was leaning on a wall, feet crossed at the ankles.

I let out a huff and Nick gave one of his rare laughs. 'Abigail Parker, I think you're trying to avoid me.'

His tie was off, and he had a few undone buttons revealing his glorious neck. I forced my eyes from his throat and the memories of how he tasted there, how the soft skin and coarse hair felt against my lips, how much heat came from him. I dragged my eyes up to meet his, only to be caught in the river-current colour as he held mine captive for a few seconds.

He reached for my arm, walking us towards the restaurant, and despite the warmth of my jacket, my skin erupted in goosebumps. *Goddamn it, the rules are failing all over the place and it's been two minutes, Abbey. Two fucking minutes.*

He reached his mouth down to my ear. 'I know what you're doing, Abbey.'

I stopped walking and turned into his chest. 'What does it matter to you, Nick? What are you doing? And more to the point, *why* are you doing it?' I put my hand over his heart, and he covered it with his.

'Have dinner with me tonight?'

'I'm not staying here. I'll sort Jack and then I am on a flight home.'

He dropped his eyes to his feet, but not before I saw concern in them. I lifted my chin higher and continued towards the restaurant.

The egotistically named 'Fiefdom' was completely black; black walls, black leather furniture, black bar. Warm white LED lights ran around the edge of the ceiling. The only relief from the black was the brushed, light-grey limestone floor tiles, which had been custom cut into enormous squares for the space. A huge black-and-white image of Jack hung above the bar, his arms crossed in front of him, a larger-than-necessary knife in one hand, which I'd heard him say was a not-so-subtle symbol of the size of his cock. His rugged, handsome face was unshaven and lined. The restaurant was imposing as fuck, completely outrageous and the hottest seat in town. There was a three-month waitlist for a table.

'Abbey Parker.' His voice was deep and coarse like a carpenter's hands and his eyes wandered over me as if I was a piece of meat.

I had actually been to the market with him once and seen him pick meat, and it was exactly the same.

'Jack.' I kissed him on each cheek.

His hand claimed my wrist. 'You look like a cool glass of water on a searingly hot day, Abbey.'

'Hmm, you have such a way with words. I'll take that as a compliment, Jack. This' – I pointed to Nick – 'is Nick Northby.'

'Oh, Abbey, I'm disappointed.' His hand that wasn't on my wrist went straight under my blazer and he rubbed my back, not bothering to look in Nick's direction. 'What fabric is this? It feels delicious.' He raised an eyebrow at me and, when I did not take his bait, he added, 'You know I don't like other roosters in my henhouse, gorgeous.'

Arrogant fucker.

I remembered the first time I'd met him; I'd been a little starstruck and flattered by the attention he paid me. Eric had noticed straight away that I got a lot more out of Jack than he or any other guy did, so from then on they sent me down for everything to do with the build of Fiefdom. I lived in Melbourne for about six months. I'd just met Peter and had put my romance on hold to come and project manage Jack, though I was never paid accordingly.

Jack had done a brief stint in the UK on a cooking game show, which had skyrocketed him to fame, and he came home demanding a restaurant from the fanciest hotel in Melbourne, which happened to be us at the time. Conceited and overconfident, he was the kind of man who would look at other women while he dined me, but he took me to great restaurants, introduced me to wine, kissed me a few times, and tried to have sex with me frequently. Despite what my sister thinks, I am not naïve about men, and I knew that holding back sex gave me leverage with him. There were plenty of other women who would sleep with him. But in the twenty years I had worked for Delacqua, I was (proudly) not one of them.

As such, I was the road not taken. The mystery never solved. That was all it was. The *allure* was that I had never bedded the man while thousands of others ... had.

'Oh, Jack darling. Nick isn't another rooster.' I used my hip to bump Nick and ran a hand down his arm, which earned me a confused, semi-heated look. He was watching Jack with distaste, and I desperately needed him to play along here. 'Nick is not a rooster. He is the farmer, Jack. The fucking farmer, who owns the fucking farm. So why don't you sit down with us, tell us all your problems, and then let us know how we can make your coop nicer, Jack?'

Jack sighed, crossing his arms in front of him, mirroring the pose of the picture above the bar, cock-sized knife sheathed. Then he extended his hand to shake Nick's. 'You'll come to see that I like Abbey, Nick. She's a straight shooter, and she never takes my bullshit.'

'She doesn't take mine either,' Nick said simply.

Utter bullshit. I put up with so much of his shit, it's not remotely funny.

It took Nick approximately an hour to sort out Jack. The chef wanted a Michelin star for Fiefdom and had a list of demands that came along with the attempt to get it. Nick had no objections to Jack's plan, so there was no real argument. They both knew they would have to put significant pressure on Michelin to make it happen because, geographically, they chose not to assess restaurants in Australia. Nick was prepared for some manoeuvring of the budget required to obtain it and they detailed out a six-month plan, which I took notes on.

Once everything was resolved, to Jack's satisfaction, we were offered a table at the restaurant that night, which Nick declined.

The civilised nature of the conversation and the business objectives aside, I could clearly see that Nick disliked Jack. He had that effect on people.

Jack walked us to the foyer. 'Abbey, I hear you are single again, babe. I finish at eleven tonight. If you want to come to mine? I bet you're a minx in bed. I'd love to get under that pencil skirt. I'd want you in black lace underneath, though. How do you feel about bondage, babe? I can just imagine using that tie around your throat—'

Nick turned and grabbed Jack by the throat of his chef whites, pushing him up against the nearest wall.

Jack's shock turned to laughter. 'Uh, I've obviously overstepped.'

'Do you think I give a shit about who you are, Fife? Everything here is *mine*, not yours. If you do not like it, you can sod off. If you decide to stay and I ever hear you disrespect another employee of mine or hear a whisper of sexual harassment, a breath of inappropriate behaviour, I will put you out on your arse and find another fucking cook. Do I make myself clear?' Nick's eyes were glittering, and his voice was like ice. 'Apologise. Immediately.'

The silence hung in the lobby. My heart was pounding so loudly it was all I could hear. Jack looked as if he desperately wanted to be defiant. He wasn't an idiot though, and he knew power when he saw it.

'I apologise,' he said to Nick.

'Not to me, idiot.'

'Abbey, I'm sorry if I offended you.'

Nick released his grip and stepped back. He then turned and walked to the waiting lift, and held it for me.

Jack held my gaze for a beat too long, the thought clearly occurring to him that I might be sleeping with Nick. But then he shook his head, remembering he'd never managed the conquest, so Nick could not possibly have. He walked back to the restaurant, and I turned to the lift.

Once we were inside, Nick went to step towards me, but I pointed to the camera, and he stopped moving. His breathing was heavy, a flush underneath his stubble.

'Where is your bag?' he growled out raggedly.

'At reception. Why?'

'We're not staying here. There are too many eyes.'

'I'm not staying, Nick.'

'Abbey. I'm asking you to stay.'

The doors opened to the main lobby. I noticed everyone looking at him, then the murmurs of 'new owner' and his name being whispered. I felt suddenly protective of him. It was a fishbowl at Delacqua. He couldn't stay here and be enraged over another man being disrespectful to me without everyone knowing something was going on between us. He walked to reception, grabbed my bag without speaking to anyone, and then headed out the front to where his driver was waiting.

The weather had turned wild, and wind was gusting up the street. It was forceful. It pushed me sideways.

'Nick, I am not coming with you. I'm done. I cannot do this with you anymore,' I shouted over the top of it.

'Abbey, please. Get in the car. We can't speak out here.' His hair was whipping about wildly.

'What is there to say?' I shook my head and went to grab my bag.

He held it out of my reach. 'I will drive you to the airport. Get in the car.'

'I can get a cab, Nick.'

'Abbey, please,' he yelled. 'Please.'

I could hear the heartbreak in his voice, and I felt his emotion in my body.

I nodded, and he opened the door for me to get in. I sat in the welcome silence out of the wind and closed my eyes against the feeling of giving in to him; I placed my palms on top of the leather seat and tried to centre myself while he walked around the car and got in the other side. Once he was in, he gave me a long assessing look and then spoke to his driver.

'Steve, I'm so sorry, I realise the weather is wild, but can you give us a few minutes, please? Go get a coffee or something?'

'Of course, Mr Northby.' Steve exited the car and the minute the door closed, Nick turned to me.

'Abbey. What is going on? You left dinner Monday night upset and now, trying to deal with Fife without me, which quite frankly makes me absolutely bloody horrified now that I've met the prick ... Why are you trying to put distance between us?'

'Are you blind?' I asked him. 'Or are you choosing to ignore what should be absolutely clear to you. Which is it?'

He went to speak, and I cut him off, unable to hold on to it for a second longer. 'Nick, I am in love with you. I love you. I want you to love me. And I want you to let me love you.'

His eyes went wide, and then his face softened.

'I knew. I mean, I know what you think and where your boundaries are, but I haven't told you mine, Nick. I haven't made those clear and we are so fucking past them, it isn't even remotely amusing. I think I was in love with you before I left the resort.' My voice dropped to a heartbroken whisper, and he reached out, taking my hand in his. 'I honestly think I was. But now this constant having you near but not having you thing. The sex whenever *you* feel like it. The fucking perfect, perfect family dinner with our girls. You keep doing nice things for me, but denying you feel anything. My body and my heart respond to you as if you are mine. You will break me if it doesn't stop. And I can't.

Not anymore.' Now the honesty was flowing, it was kind of hard to stop it.

'Is this about the doctor?' he whispered. A flash of jealousy escaped that we both knew he had no right to.

I snorted. 'I need to move on from this. And it isn't about someone else. But it's not going to work with the doctor, it's not going to work at all. He's fine. He's perfect. Most women would love him. Hell, I think Kate may love him. But it doesn't matter to me. It's not going to work because he is not you, Nick. I think about you all day. I dream about a life with you at night. I worry about you endlessly. I love your family like they're my own. I love you with a fierceness I do not recognise. I haven't felt like this before. Ever.

'And I'm not even sure you deserve it, because you give me nothing. You keep everything so compartmentalised that you are unknowable. And I'm done. I feel like I'm dreaming or imagining there is something between us because every time you get the opportunity to declare your feelings, you don't. I cannot do this anymore.'

Nick

There was this huge part of me screaming to tell her the truth. It was making my mouth water at the thought of saying it to her. I was salivating. *I love you too. Please do not ever, ever leave me.*

I shut my eyes against it and tried to find the darkest day I could. It was two weeks after I had buried her. Oliver had come through the door and the house was as dark as I was, even though it was midday. Summer was screaming. She was screaming so much she was taking these outraged breaths in between because it had gone on so long. I was collapsed against a wall, unable to move. It had been four days since I had slept, and I had not changed my clothes or showered in that time. I'd fired all our staff, telling them to get the fuck out. I remembered the shock on Ollie's face and him running to Summer to hold her. I remember him coming back into the lounge, shouting my name. I'm not sure I could hear him. But I remember Summer. She was sweating and red and her little body was convulsing with these stuttering breaths, and she pressed into Ollie as if she could not get close enough to him.

'I'm sorry, Abbey.' I opened my eyes and forced myself to look at her. There was no surprise in her face. Hope had not been there. She knew I would shut her down even as she spoke. *How fucking brave is that?*

Her phone vibrated in her lap.

'Fuck,' she breathed.

'What is it?'

'They've just closed the airport. All flights are cancelled.'

I looked outside the window at the gale-force winds. Somehow, the world was conspiring for us to be together.

Her hand reached for her grandmother's pendant and the other hand, which was in mine, was limp.

'I'm sorry we lost Grandma Iris's necklace on that adventure, back at the waterfall. But I'm not sorry for what happened between us over there,' I said quietly to her. 'I'll never be sorry for it. I care about you so much. I care more than I can ever tell you.'

She looked at me and nodded. Her eyes were a grey colour reflecting the sky outside.

'Stay. Delacqua will pay for a hotel room. I want you to stay. You make the rules, okay. You decide everything. I'd like to hang out and talk some more.' The hopeful note in my voice was painful.

She looked at me for a long time and then gave a very slow nod, squeezing my hand and I sagged a little. I was relieved I had twenty-four more hours with her, at least. I would spend every second with her she would allow and then, when she decided she'd had enough, I would respect that too.

Chapter Thirteen
Abbey

It felt good having the 'I love you' off my chest. The weeks of holding it in had become a burden, and now I'd said it, I felt dramatically lighter. There had been this second, this brief moment where I thought he was going to confess everything to me, but then that crease had formed between his dark brows, and he withdrew to the sad place.

But we were together for the next day at least. What if I used this time? Made him tell me the things he wouldn't so far? Made the rules so that I could learn everything I could about him? If there were *two* days on offer, why wouldn't I take two days?

'I make the rules?'

'Yes.'

'Fine.' I took a deep breath. 'First, we will stay together. Second, there will be absolutely no sex. Third—' I paused because after looking initially thrilled, he then looked crestfallen. 'You will tell me *everything* about *anything* I ask.'

He was silent for a second, and then he gave a half smile. 'Can I touch you?' I raised an eyebrow at him, and he clarified,

'Can we hold hands? Can I kiss you? Can I hug you?'

'Yes.'

'You drive a hard bargain, Ms Parker.'

'Is that a yes, Mr Northby?'

'Yes.'

He messaged his driver to let him know we were ready and gave him the name of a swanky hotel that was as far away from Delacqua as we could get in the Melbourne CBD.

He opened my door and took my hand as we walked into the lobby of the hotel. I'm not entirely certain what about him screamed money other than the colour of his Amex, but the receptionist fawned over him and offered him the biggest suite available, which he took. I shook my head disapprovingly. He ignored me.

It was so easy to slip back into couple mode with him because it felt like the most natural thing in the world and our holiday had been spent exactly like this. But neither of us could quite bridge the void between us, no matter how close we held each other. One of us had declared ourselves and the other had not.

The room was, *ah Jesus*, it was exquisite. It was a soft mushroom colour, instantly soothing. There were two bedrooms, he pointed out, letting me know I had the option not to share his, and then he went and dumped his things in the smaller of the two. French chairs were dotted about the lounge, which had a gorgeous view of the river. There was a dining room and an office. The bathroom looked like a freaking day spa. The last – and only – time I had been in a room this fancy was the last time I stayed with him.

I changed, getting out of my dress, thankful for my disaster planning and that I at least had a change of clothes and toiletries with me. Emerging, I had a moment of doubt he'd be there, but there he was on the sofa. He had his feet crossed at the ankles and was drinking tea. Part of me had expected him to run and hide from the crazy lady who did not understand that sex was sex, and that when a man said he would not fall in love with you, he literally would not.

He extended a hand to me, and I walked to him, sliding into his lap. He looked as exhausted as me, and the crease between his eyes told me he was worrying.

'Are you all right?' he asked. I nodded. 'Are you certain you want to stay? I will get you home if you've changed your mind. I can have Steve drive you.'

'Nick, I love you. Two more days is two more days. If this is it, I want them.'

His grip around my waist pulled me to him tighter. I was reminded again just how freeing it was to have told him how I felt. Finally, I did not have to pretend.

He kissed my cheek. 'I ordered you champagne. I thought we might head out on the town, get drunk and then we're going to find a guy playing a guitar in a pub and sing along with the rest of the crowd, to music we didn't even know we knew the words to, until they turn the lights on and kick us all out. Yes?'

'Okay.' It sounded like the perfect evening.

He emerged from the shower, a champagne glass later, in just a pair of trunks. I watched him through his open door as he slid on a pair of black jeans and threw on a navy T-shirt. He added brown accents, a belt and boots. It shouldn't work, but it did. He sprayed on the Hermes scent I loved, and I sniffed appreciatively at its herbal lemony notes. He reached down into his bag, emerging with a navy jumper. His movements were graceful for a man, elegant somehow.

I poured a second glass of champagne for me and one for him

and handed it to him as he walked across the room to me. He clinked my glass and though I could still see sadness in and around his eyes, I also saw affection, warmth and respect.

'Jesus, Abbey, you are so lovely. You do know that?'

I was dressed all in black. Black jeans, black turtleneck, black woollen coat and a cute pair of lace-up boots. I wear a lot of black. I have pale skin and golden hair. It sets them off.

I attempted to lighten the mood. 'Not Jacinta-the-nanny lovely though.'

He almost spat out the champagne, laughing, delighted and I watched as his shoulders dropped an inch. Relaxing. 'You should have seen Ollie's face when he got home and spotted her. It was the first time I knew for certain he was on the mend. Summer's old nanny retired recently. Ev hired Jacinta for me,' he clarified, so that I knew *he* had not hired the sexiest nanny since Fran Drescher.

My stomach made a loud grumble and my eyes pulled away from him for a minute.

He grabbed the waist of my jeans and pulled me to him, rubbing a hand across the fly of my jeans. 'Are you hungry?'

'I'm starving.'

'Let's go feed you.'

We grabbed sunglasses and his coat and walked out of that hotel hand in hand. A regular couple on the streets of Melbourne.

I led us towards the Yarra River, and we found a restaurant with a view of the busy riverside. Heaters sat above the table keeping us warm, but when I shivered as the wind crept in through gaps, he leaped out of his chair, putting his coat across my knees. It was hard when he was nice; my need for him overwhelmed me and I'd glimpse a future life of being cared for like this. It was heartbreaking to have found him and not have him as mine.

'Right,' I said, looking intently at the menu and avoiding his gaze, which had become concerned. 'What to eat?'

'Abbey.'

'Yeah.'

'Can you look at me for a moment?'

I rolled my eyes and put down the menu.

'You're upset. When I first met you, you were the most honest person I'd ever met. It bothers me immensely that you're withholding your thoughts and feelings from me.'

'That is a huge double standard, Nick. You conceal so much, mostly from yourself, ironically. And me.' I sighed. 'Of course, I'm upset. I love you and I tried to establish some boundaries, and I allowed you to move past them. I don't want people I love to walk over me in life.'

'You undervalue yourself.'

'You keep saying that and it is frustrating. How do you think you see me so clearly, but you do not see yourself? *You* undervalue me. You undervalue my love. You undervalue yourself. Do you know that?'

'I know my exact value, Abbey.'

I shook my head. 'Nick, you think you are an abyss and a figure on a bank statement. You are also a loving brother, a wonderful, loving father. You do nice things for people you care about. Why don't you factor in that stuff?'

I knew I'd hit a nerve because he looked away from me. A wry smile flashed, and he pulled at the neck of his jumper.

'What I am terrified of is being undervalued by the people I love,' I said. 'So this relationship is pushing some buttons for me.

The two of us are here together when we both know we aren't what we need from each other. I know I stayed, it was my idea, but I'm not sure how I feel about it. I guess a part of me is living in hope.'

'For what?'

'For you to admit how you feel about me. For you to put aside the things you lost and choose the things you have.'

The waiter approached, and I ordered a bowl of wings, sweet potato fries and a salad. He ordered the wine. When it arrived and the waiter poured two glasses, I tasted the wine and looked at him, impressed.

'How did you learn about wines?'

'My first girlfriend.' He swirled the glass and sipped the wine. 'I was eighteen. She was thirty-eight and a sommelier. Her name was Louise Carlow. She gave me an education in more than wine. We were in a relationship for a year or so, casually. As soon as I got custody of Oliver and Evelyn, that was that. I didn't have time for a girlfriend.' He said this softly with a shrug.

'Evelyn said that Ollie was acting out in the foster home.'

'He got into strife with a credit-card-fraud scheme. He also stole a car.'

'Was he charged?'

'No. I managed to sort out what everyone needed.'

'You paid them off?'

'Yes.'

'Wait, Louise Carlow? *She works for you.*' I was slightly shrill, I'll own it. I'd spoken to the woman on the phone. Also, it was kind of pervy, her preying on a young boy. A loaded young boy.

'Yes, she is in her sixties now and our head wine buyer. We are still good friends.'

I was a little bothered by that, but I attempted not to let it show. Jealousy seemed a weak sort of thing. I wondered if it weren't for

Jack Fife would we even be here ... I was grateful when our food arrived, and I tucked in heartily, but his words came back to me about being honest and I put down a wing to ask a question.

'You like control. You were very bothered by Jack Fife. If he had not been an arse, what was your plan for this weekend?'

'Abbey, I ... adore you. Worship you. I do ... I guess, I feel compromised ... emotionally. By you.' He put down his chicken and closed his eyes. 'I don't mean to control. But this feels constantly out of control and where things are out of my control ... it stresses me out.'

'Having feelings for someone is not an emotional compromise. You feel out of control with me?'

'Yes.'

That's because you are in love with me, idiot.

I watched him demolish a wing, absorbed by his mouth, licking the sauce from his fingers.

'You promised me answers, Nick,' I reminded him. I wasn't letting him get away with avoiding truths. 'You wanted me here for the weekend. What was the plan?'

'I know, I know ... Christ.' He bit his bottom lip. 'I didn't really have a plan. I could feel you trying to put space between us this week after dinner on Monday, and that was hard. I didn't like it. I thought, after our meeting, I would spend time with you. I do feel it,' he conceded, quietly, 'the connection between us. I haven't been able to put boundaries in place either ... with you. I'm sorry. My plan was just to have you to myself for the weekend. I wanted that. I want you. I wanted to spend time with you.'

'You want me? But you don't want a relationship? Or to be in love with me?'

'Abbey, I cannot have other people hold my heart. My family I have no choice with, but other than that? No.'

'I would cherish it ... if we are being honest. I would hold your heart and protect it for as long as I could.'

His jaw tightened, and he reached for my hand. The long look we gave each other was interrupted by the waiter coming to check on how our lunch was.

Nick watched me demolish the remainder of the wings and fries, and I washed it down with the last of the wine.

'Honestly, watching you eat everything on your plate is the strangest thing I think I've ever been attracted to. I cannot say I have ever, ever noticed a woman eat before.'

I shrugged at that. 'It never occurred to me to try to impress you, in any way at all. I am who I am.'

'I know.'

'Where to next?' I asked.

'Art gallery?'

'Yes.' I took out my phone.

'Are you googling?'

'Yes. There is a Turner exhibition on. I love Turner.'

'I have never seen you google anything.'

'I google things. Just not people. That seems like a weird thing to do. If we cannot accept each other at face value and allow the time needed to get to know one another, what is the actual bloody point? I cannot imagine there is much truth in social media.'

'You are incredibly wise, Abigail Parker.'

'You are starting to sound like Gran, Nick.'

'There are worse ways to be.'

'After the gallery, we'll go to the footy.'

'Footy?'

'Yep, let's go, we'll pub crawl from the art gallery down to the MCG. We need to have the full Melbourne experience, so AFL it is.'

We were walking side by side in the winter sunshine, pushed along by the gale-force wind, up to the gallery, when he grabbed my hand and gave me a boyish smile that made my heart contract and my stomach flip. I lifted our joined hands to my mouth to kiss his.

I had never really paid attention to art until I was a teenager and through drama class, where I had this kick-arse teacher, I learned about different art movements and became absorbed. It wasn't my fate to paint or draw, just to admire.

Joseph Mallord William Turner was a favourite, and I was absolutely delighted when we walked in, to the point where I may have squealed like a little girl at my good fortune. I dragged Nick into the building and practically ran to the exhibition and then slowed down, becoming silent and absorbed in every single painting on display.

We read about Turner's life. How he had fathered two daughters, but had only had a casual relationship with their mother, Sarah Danby, who he never married and how, after the death of his father, he had suffered through bouts of depression.

At every painting, Nick would pepper me with questions. What did I like about it, specifically? What didn't I like? What did it make me feel?

'Why are you so interested in what I like about them?' I finally asked him as we sat in front of one. If there was a perfect time to see the popular exhibition, half past three on a Friday was a winner. Apart from four old ladies, we were alone.

'Well.' He gathered the thought in his head. 'Art is rather subjective. It's like perfume or cologne. It's quite individual. What appeals to one person is not what appeals to another.'

'Art is not that subjective,' I argued. 'People a lot wiser than me have decided that this art is worth more than other art. It appeals to the masses, it's not that subjective. I think you're right about perfume, though.'

'You don't have paintings like this on your wall at home though,' he said, pressing his point.

'I would find a spot for one if I had one.' I went back to looking, but then something occurred to me. 'Wait a second, moneybags. Please do not tell me you own one of these?'

'Own one? No.' He snorted. 'I have three.'

I giggled at his joke, and he laughed along, too. 'Are there any other artists you love?' he asked.

'Degas. Most of the impressionists. A little romanticism too.'

'My wife was the same.'

My head snapped towards him and I looked at him in awe, stunned at this offering, to the point where I felt tears sting my eyes. 'Will you tell me about her? What was her name?'

He met my eyes and then turned back to Turner. I could see him wrestling with his choices and the decision to offer this to me; the reason why he was broken. The reason he wasn't whole. The reason why he couldn't take chances with his heart anymore.

'Her name was Rebecca. I met her in Leicester Square one day. It was like a scene from a movie. A meet cute. This huge downpour started really very suddenly, and I didn't have a brolly. I ducked under the cover of a cinema entrance, and she did too.' A small, sad smile graced his face. 'That was it. We made eye contact. I said something … forgettable. One day I was alone and then the next day I wasn't.' He breathed as if he had forgotten it was required. 'We had this whirlwind romance. I married her within six months of meeting her and we were happy. About three months later, she was pregnant with Summer. She was having what we thought was just severe morning sickness, but she also started fainting and just having periods of acting a little odd. She fell down some stairs in the garden carrying tea out for us. I took her to the hospital. They ran some tests, and they found it ... a brain tumour. It was early days ... in the pregnancy ... and I ...'

His voice caught and I took his hand, moving closer so that my body was completely against his. This was like lancing a wound, or at least I hoped it would be.

'I begged her to terminate. They could have operated on the tumour at that point, and I couldn't imagine not having Bec in my life. But she refused to risk Summer and it was completely out of my control.

'Summer was born and Bec, *Jesus*, she was so sick already. I took time away from work, but it didn't matter what I did, it wasn't enough. I had to hire a nanny for Summer and a nurse for Bec at the same time. It was just so fucking horrendous and no matter how much I tried or how many doctors I dragged her to, the tumour kept growing. It killed her within twelve months. She didn't see Summer's first birthday. But it changed who she was, too. And this ... other person replaced the person I loved.'

His face lost colour, as he said this, and his voice became a hoarse whisper. 'She would rage at me, Abbey. I couldn't leave her alone with the baby. It was like all the light parts of her personality got consumed by the tumour and all that was left were the dark parts. I felt the grief hardest then, while she was still alive, and I didn't recognise her anymore. She hated me, hated our life, hated our child. When the doctor said she had to go into palliative care, I felt relieved that it was almost over. What kind of man feels that, about his wife, about someone he loved?' He squeezed my hand tighter. His other hand rose across his chest, and I could feel the ache in mine like it was my pain.

'Abbey, I loved Summer from the minute she was born. Honestly. But I missed Becca so much I just couldn't function. It was my job to protect her. My wife. I promised myself I would protect my family the minute Mum and Dad died, but I couldn't. I could not control any of it. I was in this black, cavernous hole. I didn't want to be in a world where Rebecca was gone, and I let the grief consume me.' His breath shuddered, and he pushed away a tear that would not obey his desire not to cry. 'Ollie and Ev were so great, they got me some help and looked after Summer while I was sick. They looked after me. I don't think I'd be here if it weren't for them.'

I wrapped my arm around him.

'Whenever I feel overwhelmed, regardless of what is happening in life, I lean on them. I do my best every day to recreate the Rebecca that I loved for Summer, who doesn't have a single memory of her mum. I hope I'm doing a good job of that. On the anniversary of Bec's death, I force myself to go on a holiday. I go to the resort that was the first one my mother bought. Hartwell was her company, her maiden name. This year was the tenth anniversary of Bec's death.'

'Our holiday?'

'It's the first one … the first one I have been on where I met someone who made me feel … not sad.'

I put my head down on his shoulder and he pressed a kiss into my hair, and we sat there together, in front of a William Turner painting called *Shade and Darkness*, while I processed the tragedy that had been his life. Was it any wonder he was terrified of letting it happen again?

I startled a little about ten minutes later when he spoke.

'C'mon, Abs,' he sniffed and wiped his eyes again. 'I need a drink. Let's pub crawl.'

When we stood, I hugged him suddenly and, with a deal of force, kissed his bristled cheek. 'I'm so sorry you have been through so much in your life. I cannot imagine what that was like, Nick. I love you. You are a good man.' He kissed my head again. 'Let's get you a beer,' I said.

As we emerged into the late afternoon, the temperature outside had plummeted, and a frosty wind raced through the city. I loathed the cold, and I buried my nose into his warmth while he teased me, calling me and all Australians 'children of summer'.

'Have you ever been to England?' he asked.

'I did a Contiki tour once.'

'That doesn't count.'

'I slept with a guy from Essex.'

'That definitely doesn't count.' He laughed. 'Abbey, I don't know how you would survive an English winter.'

'Oh, I'd survive. I am a survivor and I never complain.' My lips were shivering.

He shook his head, but he took pity on me, dragging me into the first pub we spotted. It was warm with a mass of bodies, and he joined the queue for drinks. By the time he emerged, two miracles had occurred. I had ducked next door to buy us a little something, and I had found a table.

I reached into a bag and handed him his gift and he looked at it, puzzled. I clinked my glass onto his, feeling quite pleased with myself.

'Don't you believe we should have discussed which team we were supporting tonight?' he said.

'No. I decided. You need to deal with it.'

'Sweetheart, if you are going to pick teams for me, you are going to have to give me a reason.' His voice was low and flirty.

Jesus Christ, this man is fire.

He leaned over the table and took my hand, running his thumb over the cheap silver flower ring I had on, causing electricity to course up my arm. 'So, Abigail, why this team? Why am I an Essendon Bombers fan tonight?'

'Well, Nicholas ... admittedly, I don't know heaps about AFL, and I would never normally dream of being such a controlling person to make decisions for *you*.' I paused for emphasis, and he rolled his eyes, grinning. 'But what I know for absolute certain, mostly because it is a well-known fact amongst Australians at large, is that Collingwood supporters are the worst. So, by elimination, we are indeed now Essendon fans. C'mon the Bombers!' I did my best Lleyton Hewitt impersonation.

I reached over and wrapped the scarf around his beautiful throat, pulling him close and pressing a kiss onto his lips. 'Now drink up, gorgeous man. Google tells me there are at least three more pubs on the way. And this game will be fucking packed.'

He looked at me with devotion, which made my stomach flip over itself. I wanted this man in my life. Permanently. Anything less than that was simply not enough.

Nick

I woke the next morning feeling significantly better than I had expected when I went to sleep five hours ago. I rolled over in the unfamiliar bed, trying to find her in it and did not have to look too far, for her head was on her pillow and she was facing me.

She had my T-shirt on and a small crease between her brows that I knew from our holiday meant that she would wake with a headache from the alcohol. Her chest was rising and falling in peaceful slumber and her hair was absolutely all over the place. The most beautiful disaster I had ever laid eyes on.

I felt an ache deep in my gut at the thought of not seeing her again. It was very difficult to imagine, and I knew it would cause me untold pain.

We had got home at three in the morning, after approximately seven thousand beers, forced to drown our sorrows because the mighty Bombers got fucking smashed. A Collingwood fan had taken against me in the crowd and had called me a 'fucking whingeing Pom' at which Abbey (the most peaceful woman on earth) had taken offence.

'Oi,' she had said. 'You shut your goddamned mouth.'

I'd looped an arm around my little Valkyrie and gently guided her to the bar.

We'd pub-crawled back to the hotel and then had a hell of a time trying to find the key. Abbey was pawing at my pockets and then fell over with her hand in the rear pocket of my jeans, taking me down as well. We both lay on the floor in the corridor, crying with laughter.

I eventually found it in my jacket pocket, picked her up over my shoulder and carried her in.

I put her down, and we just looked at each other and then she reached forward and kissed me. But her rules from earlier in the day and knowing how exposed her heart was made me attempt to slow her down. Her kisses though were forceful, urgent and needy – and don't get me wrong – I want Abbey all of the time and I have not had enough sex in the last ten years for my cock not to be hard when this woman who I desire above all others is shoving her tongue down my throat and trying to get us both naked.

Not getting the response from me that she wanted, she pushed me away and then stripped off every layer she had on, standing there naked in front of me. When I didn't move, she walked slowly towards me. She slid her hands into my hair. *Fuck. This woman.*

'Baby,' she whispered, pressing the full length of herself against me. She had never called me that before and it had my stomach turning and my cock twitching against my jeans. 'I have needs, Nick.'

I smiled at that, and she gasped as I placed my icy hands on her waist. 'Needs?'

She nodded at me and then my fucking little temptress licked her lips. I closed my eyes and let images flood my brain of the many, many ways I could satisfy her needs.

'You were rather specific earlier today that it was not to happen, so I can't let it, sweetheart. As much as I would like to take care of your, uh, needs.'

'Urgh,' she groaned into my neck. 'It's not fair for you to use that against me now. I know what I want.'

'I'm not disrespecting Sober Abbey. Drunk Abbey is a flirty little minx.'

'Only with you, baby.'

I swallowed the unexpected emotion that came over me when she said that. 'Still. I'll make you a deal. Once we both wake up and recover from the hangover that is sure to come, if Sober Abbey has needs and decides she would like my assistance, then I am her servant.'

She looked me in the eye – her eyes are the kind of blue artists would want to paint – and she bit down on her rosy full bottom lip. One last attempt at drunkenly seducing me. *Fuck me if it wasn't working*. I could feel myself raring to go.

'Fine.' She sighed. 'But I am going to sleep in your bed naked and press my arse into your cock all night and you are going to be hard and not be able to sleep.'

'Fine,' I said, deciding to live with the torture rather than cross the line.

I made her drink water before she went to bed and rummaged

in her handbag for pre-emptive painkillers and found some, *thank God*. I climbed into bed, her arse pressed into my hard cock as promised. A few minutes later, she was still shivering from the cold, so I pulled my T-shirt off and put it over her head before resuming the tucked position we were in. Two question marks curled, the answer unspoken in the peace of the position.

'Nick,' she had whispered into the dark.

'Yes?'

'It wasn't your fault, you know.'

'What wasn't my fault, Abs?'

'Rebecca dying. Or your mum and dad dying. Or foster care. None of that was your fault. You did your best every single time, babe. There was nothing else you could have done. It wasn't your fault, Nick. None of it.'

There she went, shining her light on my darkness. Offering me absolution, I desperately wanted to believe. I pulled her closer and cried silent tears into her hair before the alcohol forced me to sleep.

The sleep I have when Abbey is with me is peaceful and dreamless, the best sleep I have had since forever.

She finally woke, her eyes fluttering open to meet mine. I loved watching her wake up. She was snuggly and warm and liked cuddles and coffee in the mornings.

'Hi,' she said quietly.

'Hi.'

'Were you watching me sleep?'

'You snore. It's like a gorgeous symphony.' I reached for her, and she snuggled into my chest, fingers straight into my chest hair, while mine were in her golden curls. 'What do you want to do today? I think the wind has died down. Do you want to go home? More footy?'

'God no.' She shook her head vehemently. 'I just want to be near you. I don't care what we do.'

My hands stilled. Now that she had declared her love, I kept feeling it in everything she said and did. It was like this solid, warm glow in my chest. There was something comforting and yet astounding about being loved by her.

'Actually, I need breakfast,' she said. 'And I desperately need Panadol. But apart from that I don't care what we do. Let's go buy a book each and lie in the park. Or stay in bed all day and watch crappy movies. I wonder what degree of freezing it will be today. I don't have many clothes.' She rolled over to check her phone. 'Ah, fuck. I forgot to charge it. It's dead.'

'Here, I'll charge it.' I grabbed it off her and connected it to the charger on my bedside table.

She settled back into my chest. Her breathing became regular, and I wondered if she would fall asleep. My fingers fell into her hair, and I felt so connected to her, almost as if our two souls had merged and become something whole.

'Abbey, I want you to know—'

Her phone ringing interrupted me and that was probably good timing because I had no idea what was going to come out of my mouth.

She went to ignore it but then said, 'It might be Ella,' and climbed over me to pick it up. 'It's Peter.'

I sat up because I heard anxiety in her voice.

'Hi Pete. Is Ella okay?'

I watched as she instinctively wrapped her naked bottom half in the sheet, covering herself as if she didn't want her ex-husband to see her. I wondered, not for the first time, who this guy was. I obviously thought he was a bit of a prick and, honestly, Abbey brought out jealousy in me that I had never experienced before.

The envy is interesting and probably had to do with not being able to say she was mine, a problem of my own making. But I didn't like that he made her beige.

Abbey had told me on several occasions that he never called her and was a text-message-only guy, even through their marriage, so his phone call made me worried that something was wrong. I have stood at too many graves. I stress about phone calls from guys like Peter Parker.

'Hey, Abbey.'

I could hear him through the phone, though he wasn't on speaker. He was speaking slowly and I felt the urge to shout, 'Come the fuck on,' though I managed to suppress it.

'Umm, Ella's fine. Sorry to bother you. I know you're away on a work trip. Abbey, the nursing home can't seem to get in touch with you or Kate and they said Iris had a fall. She's okay. They said that her heart is playing up, and they wanted to let you know. I guess I'm still the next contact.'

'Shit. Okay. I'm going to come home.' She closed her eyes tightly, and her hand gravitated to her throat, where her pendant should have been. 'Thanks for calling me.'

'Of course, Abbey. Of course.'

I watched her internal crisis as her eyes filled with tears before they spilled over, and I wrapped her into me. I had started to feel her pain as if it was my own. *I'm so far gone.*

I wanted to fucking rage at myself and anything in the world that hurt her. I couldn't keep denying these feelings I have for her. They wanted to spill out. I wanted to shout them from the top of the tallest building or Oprah's couch. I have two options here. And the only one I think I can live with is to walk away at the end of this weekend.

Sometimes, when I was being particularly cruel to myself,

I imagined I hadn't been through what I have been through. That I met Abbey, but I was a different person. That our relationship was out in the open. Our families barbecued together, our girls played Taylor Swift songs and danced around her house. That I got to wake up to her every day, that I told her I loved her so often she'd started to roll her eyes when I said it.

I needed to get her home to her family.

'Sweetheart, let's get back to Sydney. Let's get you home.'

Chapter Fourteen
Abbey

Sweetheart. We. Home.
Oh, God, I want to sink into that fairytale.

I tried to control the sheer number of emotions attempting to overwhelm me. Chief amongst them was the fear that I was not home – not close enough to check on Gran. I had to channel my inner Nick Northby and deal with the rest later.

'Gran has had a fall,' I said, though Nick had clearly heard that part of the call. 'Kate must be working. I don't know, she's uh … not speaking to me.' My voice caught in my throat. *Everything is a fucking mess.*

'Is Iris okay? Wait. Why is Kate not speaking to you?'

'We had a stupid fight about the hot doctor and you …' He looked genuinely horrified by that. 'And then I just downloaded on her. I unpacked every issue I'd had with her over our whole lives. She's been living with me to help me, but I need to be alone sometimes and her desire to have an opinion on every facet of my life has been bothering me lately. Instead of saying this like a normal person, I waited until I was backed into a corner, exploded and told her to get out. She was super upset.' I put my pounding head into my hand. 'I'm her big sister. I should have handled it better.'

He gave a soft laugh through his nose. 'That sounds familiar.'

I looked at him, realising for the first time that we both had that in common. 'Duty.'

'Yup, duty. Tell me, Abbey, did someone force the duty on you? Or is it just who you always were?'

'I don't know. I know I shouldn't whine when you lost your parents so young and then literally raised your siblings.'

'You're allowed to share complaints about your life without comparing them to someone else. You're allowed grievances. You're allowed to be angry or annoyed. The way you feel is valid. And it is important to the people who love you.'

Does that include you?

I sighed, thoughtfully. 'I've always done it. I'm not certain where the expectation came from. She was allowed to be Iris, and I was expected to be mature, the grown-up one, the bigger person, the boring one. I don't know if I did that. Or if it was a role I was given. Is it because I'm quiet? I don't know, but either way I find it hard to say "enough" or "no". And there are bigger questions. Is that what attracted Peter? My submissiveness? Is that what attracted you?'

'Abbey, what attracted me to you was your self-assurance, your self-possession. You seemed to know exactly who you were, and you seemed completely comfortable with it.'

'I am comfortable with who I am. I just don't want to be passive or submissive in my life anymore. I don't want to have to bend my expectations to meet somebody else's anymore. I need someone who bends for me too. I just hate the way it exploded out with Kate.'

'You've been accommodating for forty-two years and putting your foot down for a minute, Abs. It might take some getting used to.' He pulled me into his chest. 'Just give yourself a bit of time. And rate yourself significantly higher. You are important to everyone important to you.' He pressed a soft kiss into my hair.

'I know it's selfish, but I just wanted to be with you for what little time we have left.'

'I'm not going to let you walk out of here and deal with this alone, Abbey. I thought I'd come with you. We'll fly home, go check if Iris is okay, and sort out this stuff with Kate. I'm not leaving you. We've still got one more day. Peter has Ella. I'll just stay at yours tonight.' He tilted my chin up to look at him. 'If that's all right? Abbey, if that is what you want?'

He'd checked in with me, showing me he respected the new boundaries I was trying to establish. I could have laughed until I cried because he was looking at me as if he was offering nothing at all. As if the idea of spending a whole day and night with him meant nothing. The truth was, it was everything. It was going to be what kept me going into a lonely old age. And maybe one day, if I had granddaughters, I would tell them – as Iris has told us about her life and her loves, some great, some not – but I would tell them about the time I had a great love and I got to spend this one last day with him. And maybe they would ask me how I recovered from my great love and maybe I would tell them that I didn't. Ever. But at least I had one. Maybe I would tell them that I found myself at the same time. 'The Greatest Love of All' Whitney Houston called it. And if they asked me if it were possible to fall in love after forty, I would say it is easier than one could possibly imagine.

I didn't know what to say to him. Everything felt inadequate. I swung around and wrapped my body around his and whispered an emotional, 'Thank you.'

Automatically, I switched into EA mode. I headed to the lounge, pulled out my laptop and attempted to book urgent flights. The problem was there were no flights, not until late that night, and I was genuinely stressed that my gran might not make it. The more I thought about not being in Sydney for that eventuality, the more stressed I became, and I broke into sobs that were silent but made my whole body shake.

'Hey. Hey now.' He squatted in front of me. 'Abbey, please let me help?' he urged gently.

I needed help. He took my hand, and I nodded. I needed him.

He made three phone calls about the flight. That was all it took, and we were leaving in, well, as soon as we could get to the airport.

Unable to get on a commercial flight with enough speed, he'd hired a private one. He arranged for the driver who picked us up at the hotel in Melbourne to have bacon and egg rolls, coffee and painkillers. He rang St Vincent's Hospital and had Kate paged, leaving a message for her. He then had Evelyn head to the hospital to pick up Kate and get her to the nursing home, where we would meet her. He arranged for his driver to take us from Sydney Airport to Iris's nursing home.

By some miracle (also known as Nick Northby) we pulled up in front of Ashford House on a cold, rainy Sunday, not more than three hours after I had received Peter's call.

In the parked car, I experienced the overwhelming desire to freeze time. Stop. Right this very second. Nick beside me. Gran alive.

'Remember the day we lost it?'

My hand was at my chest where my pendant should have be. I offered him a sad smile.

'Yeah. You made me get on that bloody boat again.'

'Yes, because fears are there to be conquered.'

I scoffed at that. This man had absolutely no insight into himself. 'Are they?'

'Yes.' He looked at the window, a small, resigned smile on his face. Maybe he had a little insight. 'Remember, we swam, we drank, I kissed you under that waterfall again and I made you tell me about your sister and the boat.'

'You did more than that.'

He nodded, smiled, and I was surprised to see his eyes shine and a crease between his eyebrows. 'I'm so sorry we lost it, Abs. Truly, I am.'

'Me too.'

I got it though … what he was trying to say. Fears were meant to be conquered. Don't be feeble. I had to get out of the car and face what was happening.

We climbed the stairs and walked down the corridor to Iris's room. The light from the grey day was streaming through her window, making me squint at the glare. My grandmother was tucked in her bed, dressed in a nightgown, so white it almost caused as much blinding light as the window. Her hair was in a loose braid that fell over her right shoulder and her eyes were closed.

She looked altered, suddenly frail. The fall had left an enormous bruise on her right arm and there was a gash on her temple, with another bruise underneath her cheekbone which looked like badly applied contour, a Kardashian's face before blending.

'Abigail Cavendish. I hope they did not call you back from your holiday in Melbourne with your Nicholas over this little bruise. I hoped the two of you would finally forget all of your nonsense, make love and then declare yourselves.'

Jesus Christ. I cleared my throat.

'Hello, Nicholas.'

'Iris.'

'Well, dears? How did it go? Did you sort each other out in the physical sense and the ever-after sense?' She peered at us closer. 'Dear me. Neither?'

Oh, my God. 'Gran, are you all right?'

'Dearest, it's all a big kerfuffle. I was simply trying to make tea.'

'Gran, if you use your buzzer and call a nurse, they will bring you tea. Remember, I told you?'

'Lionel proposed last night, and I think I was just overwhelmed, dear.'

'Lionel proposed?'

'Marriage, dear.'

'Yes, Gran, I gathered … And are congratulations in order?'

'Abbey, dearest, it would seem that I … I don't want that. I'm terribly worried I have upset him, and I just feel …' She reached for her chest and I took her other hand and buzzed for a nurse. 'I just do not wish to marry again.'

'I'm sure Lionel is all right, Gran. Would it ease your mind if we checked on him? They're worried about your heart, and I don't think you should be stressing about anything at the moment.'

'Perhaps Nicholas would be a dear?'

'Of course, Iris. I'll go check on him. Man to man.'

I threw him a grateful smile, and he left.

The nurse came in and clucked over Gran, propping up her pillows and reminding her to try to stay calm.

'Abbey, I feel quite upset, dearest.' I had seen my grandmother cry twice in my life. The first time was when we lost our mum, and the second was when we lost our father.

'Hey now,' I said, sliding onto her bed and putting my arm around her. 'There is no need to worry. Lionel will be fine. He's a big boy. Besides, how many men have you turned down over the years? You should be an old hand at this.'

'Fewer than you would imagine.'

Hmmm.

Kate flew around the door and bolted to the bed, lunging at us, hugging us both tightly.

'Oh, my God, Gran. I am so sorry. I was in the bloody theatre for three hours and did not get the message. I'm so sorry. Nick's sister just dropped me off.'

To my astonishment, my sister burst into tears.

'Oh, Kate. Shh. There now. Gran's fine, aren't you, Gran?'

'Yes, dear. Completely fine. Very silly, really. Come now, Kate – don't be feeble.'

'You … need … to … use … your … buzzer, Gran,' Kate sobbed.

'Gran also turned down Lionel last night. He proposed, and she's a bit upset,' I said to Kate.

'You shouldn't worry about that, Gran. He asked. You declined.'

'That's my girl.'

'Gran, they are worried about your heart. It is racing. The specialist is coming tomorrow,' Kate said, a little calmer now. 'You need to keep settled, so no more stressing or getting up to make tea.'

'It's all a lot of fuss over nothing. They're acting like I am going to die. But if I am to be treated like a prisoner and kept in bed, you'll have to top up my Kindle and audiobooks dearest.'

'No steamy romances,' Kate said with authority.

Gran looked at me, rolling her eyes, and I laughed. We sat and chatted together for about fifteen minutes when Nick came around the corner with Lionel.

Lionel walked slowly to Iris's bed and Kate and I cleared off to give him room. He extended a slow hand to her, gave Gran a radiant smile, and held out a single pink rose. She took it, holding it to her nose and inhaling, squeezing his hand. She then went to swing her legs out of the bed, making us all jump forward to stop her.

'Good lord, stop fussing. It makes me think *you* all think I'm going to die.'

'Gran, it is serious. You cannot get out of bed.' Kate was red in the face and had her hand over her chest.

'So what? If I die, I have had a good life. My gorgeous Harry gave me your father and your father gave me nothing but grief, but then eventually, he gave me you two. The greatest gifts of my life. Cavendish women. I don't want any nonsense grieving from the two of you. No funeral. You will have a party and play lots of Ella Fitzgerald and Billie Holiday. I expect dancing and cake, lipstick and heels. Is that understood? You will invite gorgeous men to serve cocktail food. No tears. Kate will, of course, not cry, but Abbey, you are far too soft. Nick, she'll need help that day.'

Nick nodded solemnly.

'You are a good boy. I can tell. Do you know I have been married several times? I fall in love with the idea of falling in love. Remember, girls, there is not just one great love in your life. You should love wherever your heart leads you. You must. Otherwise, what is the point of it all? I do not regret a single husband of mine. The love is worth the pain.' Iris patted Lionel's hand. 'Lionel, if we had more time, but not right now, dear, not right now.' She closed her eyes, exhausted.

We stood there and looked at her for a few minutes. Sensing us watching her, she opened one eye.

'Well, get out, dears,' she said.

There was an amount of mumbling as we all started collecting ourselves and our belongings to give the old folks some privacy.

'I'll be down in a sec,' I said to Nick, and he placed a supportive arm around Kate, who was silently sobbing again, leading her from the room.

I walked back to Iris's bed, bending to hug her. 'I love you, Gran.'

'I love you too, Abigail. You look very thin by the way, I do not approve. I've always been exceedingly jealous of your curves.'

'I did not know that!'

'Boobs … you either have them or you don't,' she said, holding her flat chest.

'Love you, Gran. Stay in bed, please?'

'Yes, dear.'

In the foyer, Nick was consoling my sobbing sister, his arms around her, her head tucked under his chin. He spotted me and a sad smile appeared. He flung out an arm for me to come and join them and I went happily, wrapping one arm around Kate and one around Nick.

'I'm genuinely worried she is going to die, Abbey.'

'It's going to be okay, Kate, no matter what.'

'I'm so sorry, Abs, for that fucking stupid argument. For being overbearing, for everything.'

We were talking nose to nose, pressed against Nick's chest.

'I'm so sorry too. I should have never let it burst out like that. Where are you staying? Are you okay? You can come home.'

'I, umm, yeah. Well, I'm uh, I'm actually staying with someone from work.' She paused, pulling back from Nick. 'Actually, it's Sebastian.' She blushed furiously.

'The hot doctor?' I said, smiling and nodding encouragingly. I grabbed Kate back in my arms. 'I'm happy for you, Kate.'

'Thanks, Abs. Sorry for trying to project him onto you.'

'That's okay.' I snickered, finally letting her go. 'He's very hot and perfect. You have to bring him to meet Iris. She will be beside herself.'

'Yeah. I'll call ahead, though, and make sure she can put on her lipstick.' Kate smiled, sniffling.

'Come home if you need to, okay? And at least come round for dinner one night this week, all right?' I squeezed her hand.

Nick had ordered her an Uber, and we walked outside to see her into the car. She hopped in, waving to me through the window as they drove away.

Our driver was still waiting for us outside. Nick opened the door for me, and I climbed in, but only to the middle seat. He slid in beside me and I curled into him for the time it took us to get back to my place. He gave his driver a few instructions when we arrived and then he grabbed our luggage, carrying it into my house. He headed straight to my room and dropped our suitcases on the floor as if we had been on holiday a thousand times together and this was our routine. He then went back to the car and reemerged with groceries.

I pressed my back against the door after closing it, relieved to be home but overcome with emotion.

'Nick,' my voice was raspy with gratitude and love for him.

'Yep?' He popped his head around the corner after taking the groceries to the kitchen and walked back into the hallway. His shoes were already off, his long legs clad in blue denim, a plain white T-shirt adding to the homely perfection of having him there. 'You, okay?'

I marched forward, gently wrapped my arms around him, and pressed a tender kiss on him.

'Thank you for today. I don't think I have ever been more grateful in my life.' I kissed him again, this time deepening the kiss, exploring his tongue, inhaling him.

He let out a noise, a contented sound, and tightened his grip on my waist, pulling me into him. I reached for the bottom of his

T-shirt, but he stopped me, a firm grip on my hand.

'Abbey, sweetheart, are you certain? I never want to cause you pain again.'

I needed him, I wanted him, I loved him.

Iris was right. The love is worth the pain. I loved him more today than I did yesterday. I knew if there was a dawn tomorrow, I would love him even more again. There was nothing that could change that. Not him, not his immovable boundaries. Not me and not my new firm rules. I could not change any of those things, but – by God – I wanted to. I had tried to make him see that, together, we made perfect sense. And while there was still time left, I would continue to try to get him to see that he loved me, too. And if this was the last time, well, I wanted that memory.

I put my mouth against his ear and breathed, 'Yes.'

He took off his T-shirt and then reached for my hand, leading us into my room. We would block out the world, pretending for one more night. In the morning he would be gone, and I would make certain that us being thrust together at work was no longer an option.

Nick

There were twenty-four perfect hours. And then there was a void, a chasm.

Our lovemaking was slow, and it felt … meaningful and poignant. It also felt like goodbye.

She napped in the afternoon, and I made myself at home in her kitchen. My driver had gone for groceries while we were with Iris, and I showed off a little with a lasagne recipe I knew by heart. Ev often cooked when someone was worried or stressed. I could not tell you the number of times she had landed on my doorstep with freshly cooked meals, especially with Rebecca's illness and especially through those dark times after. The beef ragu was her recipe.

When Abbey awoke later that day, the smells of tomatoes and garlic wafted through the house and she came out sniffing appreciatively, taking the glass of Shiraz I handed her and sipping it slowly. I had put on a playlist of our favourites from the holiday, but acoustic versions where I could find them and they were playing softly in the background, while we snuggled on the sofa.

Wrapped in a fluffy red jumper, Abbey was very touchable, and I spent an enormous amount of time running my hands along it throughout the evening.

She cleaned her plate of my lasagne twice, making the most delightful noises that landed on me with force and then made my chest ache because I knew this was it.

When we were tired, she blew out candles while I finished cleaning up. We met in the bathroom where I watched her wash her face and moisturise before we both brushed our teeth. The peace in the domesticity was something I had forgotten.

Abbey, never one for lots of clothes in bed, insisted on my stripped-off T-shirt but it was covered in pasta sauce, so I fetched another from my suitcase for her, which she described as 'buttery goodness'. We hopped into bed, faced each other and she hooked a leg over me, and I had the perfect eight hours.

She made pancakes on Sunday morning and fantastic tea.

Ella messaged her, letting her know she was headed home … and that was it.

I waited for her tears, but they did not come. She was resolved and certain.

'Nick, I'm only going to ask one thing of you,' she said seriously.

'What is it?'

'I need you to help me by letting go, too.'

I nodded my head. A pit in my stomach. I knew exactly what she was planning on doing. I kissed her one last time and headed home.

There are rules to being a Northby. A code of conduct if you like. It was something we had developed over the years as a way of being able to not piss each other off too much. We were all we had. We had to stick together. Even Summer knows the rules.

Number One: Always be honest.

Number Two: Always ask for help if you need it.

Number Three: The business is our livelihood, and we must always act to protect it.

Number Four: Never let a Northby down.

Number Five: Nick is the boss.

I messaged them from the car saying that I needed help and they both responded quickly, as I knew they would. We were to meet in an hour, so I stopped in at a bottle store and bought their best whisky. A Northby did not confess to the breaking of several of the rules without a gift.

I opened the door to my apartment and was met by footsteps pounding towards me and my child launching herself from approximately two metres away into my arms.

'Daddy.'

'Hello, my little beauty,' I said, my voice muffled by her neck.

'How was Melbourne?'

'Very …' I searched for a word. 'Tiring.'

'Dad, do you think you could buy me this game I want on my phone?'

'Of course. Just get it.'

'Okay.'

'Wait, wait. Sum, it isn't violent, is it?'

'Not really.'

That would have to be good enough for now. I had other things on my mind. 'Okay.'

She ran off, and I had the feeling I'd been swindled. My sister was standing there, shaking her head.

'Nick, if someone had told me that you would be such a fucking pushover as a parent, I would have fought them.'

I frowned. 'Is Ollie here?'

'Present.' He wheeled himself into my line of vision and his injuries shocked me again, though I was happy to see him upright, and some purple and yellow in his bruising.

'Jesus Christ, Ollie. You look like shit.'

'I'll have you know I have taken absolutely sensational drugs, and I am feeling rather robust. This should last approximately forty-five minutes.'

I left my suitcase at the door and walked down the stairs. I held aloft the bottle of whisky.

'Can you drink this?'

'Yes,' he said.

'No,' Evelyn said.

I handed it to him and put my hand on his shoulder before hugging my sister. I went to the kitchen and grabbed three glasses from the cupboard.

Ollie studied the bottle and then had an unspoken conversation with his twin, before turning to me.

'What the fuck did you do, Nick?'

I handed the glasses to Ev before pushing him over to the dining-room table. When we were all seated, I poured.

I sniffed the glass appreciatively. It smelled both sweet and earthy; I felt I could smell hay and perhaps brandy. I took a large mouthful. It was as sweet, smoky and smooth as anything I had tasted before. It was an excellent whisky to fess up to breaking Northby rules.

'I spent the weekend with Abbey.'

'No shit,' Oliver said shortly.

'And??' Ev said.

'And she is in love with me. She told me.'

'Well, that is wonderful, Nicky. I'm happy to celebrate the drought being over, brother.'

'I can't do that, Ev.' I drank again. 'I told you guys I could never do that again. You both remember it. It was a fucking disaster and I ... I almost didn't recover.'

My sister put down her drink, the heavy crystal base making a solid thud. 'So, let me get this straight. This lovely woman who you adore, and we *all* adore, tells you she is in love with you and you – what? Just say nothing?'

'I told her I couldn't. Right at the start. I said I can't. She knew the lay of the land. Jesus, Ev, you make me sound like the world's biggest prick.'

'You know what, Nick? If you felt nothing and you have been behaving like you have, then you are a *big* fucking prick. Do you think Ollie and I don't know about that dress? About the payment to her kid's school? About the salary increase? Your visits to her grandmother? Those things – *they* say that you are not being honest. Still. And outside of your relationship with her, she is our fucking employee, Nick.'

'She's about to resign.'

My brother clenched his jaw and then winced from the pain it caused in his skull.

'I'm sorry. I know you're angry, Ollie.'

'Do you, Nick? You have been dishonest, and we did not call you out on it because we thought you were finally going to let yourself love again. Your behaviour has been *off the charts* unacceptable. You have put our business at risk time and time again. And your eyes are still not open. You want to cut yourself off? Just focus on work? The one thing you are good at … how many fucking times have I heard that? Meanwhile, you raised us. You raised Summer, who is a little fucking legend, by the way. You are so much more than our business, Nick. You deserve a loving partner. You deserve to live your life with love and support.' He paused for breath. 'I am so fucking mad at you. Abbey deserves so much better than any of this.'

A lump formed in my throat and tears stung my eyes. I could feel heat flooding my face as I became incredibly interested in the woodgrain pattern on the table.

'I'm going to step aside. At Delacqua.'

'Perfect. Should we send Summer in?' Ollie asked, his sarcasm biting.

I swallowed the misery, got my shit under control, and lifted my eyes to him. 'Actually, I have another solution.'

Chapter Fifteen
Abbey

I stayed in bed after the alarm on Monday morning. I could smell him in my room, and I was calculating how long I could keep these sheets on my bed before I would be considered a huge grot. I should rip them off, put them in the wash and get rid of his scent, but like his T-shirt that I had not returned to him, I knew I could not part with them yet.

I had very decisively written my resignation, asking for the necessary month's notice to be waived due to personal reasons. I knew as well as he did, he had no choice but to let me go. He'd crossed too many lines. So today would be my last day at Delacqua. I estimated I would be home within two hours.

I needed a change. Working with him every day was not conducive to ever being able to move on. I knew that unless one of us gave the other space, we would be in this dance forever. This routine we had would become destructive.

I wondered whether that was always what happened when love was denied. Maybe love could turn into something a little dark and sinister. I didn't know and, honestly, I did not give a fuck.

I would not trade a day I had spent with him. And though I did not genuinely believe my heart could recover, a tiny part of me could conceive that, maybe in the future when he had faded in my head a little, maybe then I might.

I had taken this train journey almost every workday for the past twenty years. The faces of strangers who hopped on like I did to stand in this overcrowded train compartment each morning were familiar. Some faces had disappeared over the years, women had children, people retired. Sometimes there were moon boots and crutches from adventurous holidays or weekends. Sometimes there were partners or children accompanying them. For the most part, little changed.

I had a tiny bit of leave saved and some long service leave, which I knew the Northbys would honour. It would give me some time to decide what to do. Nick was right. I had unknowingly become bored professionally, so maybe it was time to branch out a little. Attempt to look for a role in management. Try something new.

There was a part of me that was terrified, but I also recognised another newer part that was excited by the idea of walking to the edge and leaping. Maybe the new part wasn't new, maybe it was just restored. I felt as though my life was in my control for the first time and, whatever risks I took, at least they were risks I had chosen to take.

I arrived at work on time, disappointed that Nick wasn't in the office. We needed to rip off the Band-Aid. The prolonged goodbye would kill me otherwise. I loved him, but I had given him every opportunity I could to declare his feelings, and he hadn't. He was in this enormous ocean of denial, drowning and in need of rescuing, but I had tried and, if I continued, he would pull me in too. I simply wouldn't let myself drown.

Forty-five minutes later, I was annoyed he wasn't here. I was hoping to be able to do this without the masses being present, just in case one of us cried – namely me.

My phone buzzed, and I smiled as I saw it was Ollie. His vision had been blurring in the hospital, but his texting suggested his recovery was progressing.

> I know what you are about to do. I won't be accepting your resignation, Abbey. Check your email. I expect you to be there when I get back. Also, we are having your birthday party here on Saturday at 11 a.m. Do not bring anything but yourself and Ella.

I bristled at the Nick-like authority contained within that message. In fact, I suspected it wasn't from Oliver at all.

I rose from his desk where I had been sitting waiting for Nick and walked out of the office to my desk, turning on my computer. I tapped my foot impatiently as it booted up. And then, finally, waited for my emails to load.

Ever since I'd had Ella, I had refused to install workplace emails on my phone. The root of the entire problem with the world was our phones, as far as I could see. Neither Eric nor a Northby could possibly need me that badly, and if they did they had my number. I did not respond to emails out of work time. The only exception to this rule was Sunday nights when I would check them on my laptop, but that was just to know what I was walking into on Monday morning, not so I could reply. But last night I had been having a personal crisis and writing a resignation, so my routine had gone out the window.

I had flown out in the middle of the day on Friday, so there were quite a few emails downloading. There was one at the top, which had been sent late last night. It had gone out to the entire company, from the owner, Nick Northby.

My heart began beating incredibly fast. What on earth was he doing?

I opened the email; it was a company memorandum, attached as a PDF.

MEMORANDUM
TO: All employees of Delacqua
RE: Abigail Parker appointment

As most of you know, my brother was in an accident a little over a week ago and thankfully we expect him to make a full recovery. In the meantime, it is imperative that the business remain on course with the vision that Hartwell Holdings has planned for it, the building blocks of which Oliver had only just commenced implementing.

Temporarily, Hartwell Holdings is appointing Abigail Parker as Acting CEO of Delacqua Hotels. Abbey's extensive knowledge of the business is unparalleled in the organisation and makes her the best candidate for this caretaker role. We expect that Oliver will be back on board in three months. In the meantime, it is the expectation that all staff will look to Abigail for leadership and guidance, offering her the support she deserves by delivering your continued excellence. Abigail will conduct this business as she sees fit during this time, independently and with the full support and backing of myself and my board.

Sincerely,
Nicholas Northby
CEO Hartwell Holdings

Jesus fucking Christ. I put my head down on the polished wood of my desk. *Fuck.*

My phone buzzed again. It was Ollie.

> Okay, welfare check. Deep breaths Abbey. Deep breaths. You can do this. The three of us had a board meeting last night over a 20-year-old bottle of Scotch. My brother confessed his sins. We decided that this was the way forward. I know you will do an amazing job. Your new EA starts at 8. Her name is Monica. Text me back in five minutes, so I know you're okay. Also, make sure you're not sitting at your old desk when people start coming in. Power is perception, Abbey.

Power was perception. He was certainly right about that. I instinctively looked down at my outfit. I had on a burgundy suit today, with a conservative black top, an attempt on my part to make sure that nothing would distract Nick and I from the conversation I'd been planning. Did I even look like someone who could run a company?

What were they even thinking? *Oh, my God.* I was prepared to admit to having a moment of panic. But it was important in situations like this not to be feeble. *You are a Cavendish woman, Abigail.*

I stood on legs that felt as if they had not been used for some time. I logged off from my computer, grabbed my handbag, the photo of Ella that sat on my desk, and my favourite pen. I felt a thousand years old.

I opened the door to the huge office. Eric's office, Nick's office, Oliver's office and now *my* office? I pushed in the visitor's chair I had been sitting at while I waited for Nick and walked around to the padded tan leather chair that, when I sat down, I realised I would have to adjust because my feet would not touch the floor.

There was an envelope on the keyboard that I had not seen from the other side. Purposefully placed so I would have to be sitting in this seat to see it. My name was scrawled on it in Nick's heavy handwriting. He wrote the way he conducted himself, with authority and purpose, his penmanship bold and black. I opened it slowly.

If I could give anyone everything, every part of me, it would be you. N xx

I brought the paper up to my face and closed my eyes, letting myself feel the heartbreak of that for just a minute. I swear I could smell him on the paper, though that was probably in my imagination. A huge, hollow, achy lump was in my chest.

The phone on the desk rang, making me jump, and I looked at it for a second before picking up and said, 'Abigail Parker' with as much authority as I could muster.

'So you are alive. Security says the first of the execs is on the way up. Time to get your head in the game, Abbey. I have full faith that you can do this and kick arse. I'll call you Friday, but if you need me, I'm here.' Ollie hung up.

I turned on the computer. Time to focus. I wasn't certain if I would still need to reschedule Nick's meetings for today or what would happen.

There was a knock on the door. An extremely well-dressed woman in her mid-fifties entered. She had a beautiful, friendly face, her skin a lovely milky colour, and she wore bright-green glasses, which set off eyes of the same colour. Her red suit was cut perfectly, and I had the innate sense we were going to get along, just from looking at her.

'Ms Parker,' she said with a regional British accent I couldn't identify. 'My name is Monica Galthorpe. I'm Mr Northby's EA in London. I was in Australia delivering something that he needed. He's asked me to stay and support you in your new role here for the next few months.' Monica stopped before she added politely, 'If that is agreeable to you?'

'It's nice to meet you, Monica. Thank you for agreeing to do that. I hope it hasn't inconvenienced your family?'

'Oh, not at all. My son, Michael, is at university now, he's twenty. He can manage on his own for a few weeks. It was Mr Northby who got him his position at university anyway, so I owe him one. Anyway, should we get to work, Ms Parker?'

'It's Abbey, Monica. Just Abbey is fine.'

'He said you'd say that,' she said, laughing. 'I've rescheduled all your meetings for today except for the executive meeting, which I've moved back an hour to give you time to prepare. You ready?'

'Yes,' I said, and my voice was firm and confident.

I left at half past six that night, exhausted but exhilarated. There was naturally more than a little interest amongst my fellow employees in my promotion, but having worked with most of them for a long time, they accepted it with grace. If they talked about me or my relationship with the Northbys, they did so behind my back.

Having planned the schedule with Nick last week, I was as prepared for the meetings as he would have been and I spent the day writing notes for myself on delivering the key messages, in a tone that reflected me and not him.

There was, thankfully, not much spare time for reflection on just how much I missed him. Bathroom breaks and a very sentimental pot of tea were all I afforded myself.

I missed him as if someone had cut off my arm, though. Weird, then, that in gifting me this role, I also felt incredibly loved and valued. But somehow that made it all the more heart-wrenching.

I made a quick call to Ella in the lift to let her know I would be late, but there was dinner for her to reheat in the fridge. She was planning on eating while watching a video of a lung transplant, which was being live-streamed on YouTube. I told her that was gross, but she seemed happy.

Of course, one of the perks of the top job was Keith, the driver, and the car. It was a privilege that overwhelmed me, but it was extremely convenient tonight because it meant I could head straight to Iris before heading home.

Dinner was being cleared from the resident's rooms and the slightly unpleasant smell of overcooked vegetables and purees filled the hall. Iris was lying on her bed with her headphones in. The flush in her cheeks, the slight shake of her head and knowing smile told me she was listening to something racy.

She looked thinner than she had even yesterday; she was wearing the shirt she had on the last time I took her to the café, and it was swimming on her. She was paler than yesterday as well, fading into the white shirt.

Her eyes opened, her eyebrows raised, and her smile lit up when she saw me. 'Abigail.'

'Hi, Gran.'

'You just missed your boy.'

'My boy?'

'Yes, Abbey,' she said, frustration creeping into her voice. 'Nicholas. You know, English, rich, lovely bum.'

'Nick was here?'

'He brought me lunch and then spent the day here. I think he was anxious today and I think he is lonely, poor man. Doing it all by himself. He doesn't have any older people in his family, your boy.'

'He's not my boy, Gran.' I tried, unsuccessfully, not to let the heartbreak come through in my voice. 'He doesn't want me like that.'

Iris looked at me, shaking her head. 'Abigail, if you genuinely believe that you are a fool. The problem with men is that they don't cope with their emotions as effectively as we women do. He is simmering along, though. He'll get there, eventually. You trying to force the issue will not help, dear. I would recommend patience.'

'I just can't be with him if he is not all in, Gran. It's too much. My feelings for him. They're not like anything I've ever felt before. I feel like I'll implode. I can't do casual with him. I'm way too in love.'

'Abigail. I might have had seven husbands, but some of them meant significantly more to me than others. What you are experiencing is rare, darling, but it is real. Cavendish women aren't fee ...' She paused and then it seemed like she changed tack. 'Don't be afraid to feel it.'

'I don't want to feel *it* if he isn't. I don't want that. It exposes me far too much. What if I don't recover from him?'

'Dearest, that's *exactly* the same argument he is using to not be with you. Isn't it?'

My grandmother is a sorceress.

'Abigail, your face reads like an open book. I can assure you, child, I am no master of the dark arts. I've just lived. Please make certain you do as well.'

'I love you, Gran. So much.'

'I love you too, child. Now it's late and I have a saucy book to listen to. Off you go, Abbey. Everything will work out, darling girl.'

I kissed her cheek softly, scared of harming the horrid bruise or her bird-like frailness. 'Gran, are you sure you should be listening to steamy books with your heart playing up?'

'Dearest, if I die listening to a sex scene, it would almost be my perfect death. So, what's not to be happy about?'

I chuckled at that. 'Bye, Gran. Love you.'

'Love you too, my girl. I'll leave them all to you, darling. My saucy books. You might need them until your Englishman is ready.'

Nick

My alarm had gone off at four. I looked at the time. I had to get to the airport.

One day. One miserable, bloody day. I was supposed to stay two more weeks, to make sure Ollie was all right. To make sure Abbey was all right. Simply, I could not be in the same city as her and not see her. So I was running from her, running from us.

I had realised, at about ten on that first Monday without her, that I was a miserable old bastard. It was as empty as I'd felt since before the holiday. No, since I met Abbey on the holiday.

I'd been an anxious fucker on the phone with Monica, checking in on Abbey. Make sure she eats. Don't let any of those execs disrespect her in that first meeting. Make sure she remembered to implement the things we'd discussed with that arrogant fucker, Jack Fife, from Friday. Don't leave her alone in a room with him. Ever. Monica had called me at eleven and told me to back the fuck off.

So I'd headed to Iris. I debated whether hanging out with her grandmother was an indirect violation of Abbey's rules. But I, the great fucking Nick Northby – master of control – had no willpower. I would be as close to her as I could get. I picked up sandwiches from Iris's favourite café and brought them to her, sitting next to her bed.

'Nicholas Northby.'

'I brought you a gift.'

'And here I thought your brother was the flirty one. Well, let's see it. I'm genuinely hoping for diamonds.'

'Sadly, it's only a sandwich.'

She opened up the cloche on her tray and looked at it with distaste. 'Sold,' she said, holding out her hand.

I moved the foul-smelling tray outside and then opened up the salad, avocado and cheese sandwich, laying a napkin across her lap. It was actually enormous, I realised. I was confident I would finish mine easily and Abbey could one-hundred-per-cent finish it, but Iris currently weighed as much as my left boot, so I cut it into quarters for her.

She bit into her sandwich and, though the bite was tiny, she moaned a little, which reminded me of Abbey and brought a smile to my face. Then I remembered I may never hear that sound again, and it fell off my face as I almost cried into my lunch.

'Nicholas, you are not normally so easy to read.' She wiped non-existent crumbs from her mouth. 'Why aren't you at work?'

I finished chewing the mouthful I had, and it went down in a lump. 'I've let Abbey take over until Ollie is well.'

'Abigail has always been exceedingly competent at whatever she did. Swimming lessons, school, boys through her teenage years.' I snorted a laugh at that. 'She will do the job you want her to do.'

'I hope she will do the job *she* wants to do,' I said quietly.

'Why are you denying you are in love with my granddaughter, Nick? Or are we to have untruths between us?'

'I care for her,' was all I could manage. 'Very much.'

She looked at me thoughtfully and I was certain she was going to call me out on my absolute bullshit, but she seemed to see something, and she held back.

'Tell me about your wife, Nick. Tell me about your life.'

And so I did. I told her about my whole fucking life.

The police coming to the door to tell us that Mum and Dad were in the accident. Ev's heartbroken cries and terrified screams as they took her away from me. Oliver's stoicism in comparison. The lovely people who fostered me and how I was a little prick to them – sullen and silent. How I left them the day I turned eighteen and took possession of my inheritance. The first judge, a guy in his fifties, who told me I was too young to have custody of my teenage siblings. Oliver setting up this credit-card-fraud scheme with his schoolmates and how much money I'd had to pay to cover it up. The second judge, an old-timer, who ruled that if I was old enough to own a multi-million dollar company and vote, I was old enough to be the head of my family. Kids went to war at that age back in his day.

I went to tell her about the day I got married, the light that poured in through the church's stained-glass windows, but that wasn't the story that came out. Instead, I told her about the funeral. Details that I did not think about anymore. The flowers – blue hyacinths. The rain. Summer, crying through the whole thing so that the nanny had taken her, and how I had watched her crawl around the grass amongst the gravestones getting mud all over the little white outfit she was wearing instead of watching my wife's coffin lowered into the ground. How I delivered an economical speech during the funeral service that made it sound as if I only knew Bec in passing. How my brother and sister had made polite conversation, while I sat mutely in the corner of the room at the wake.

Strangely, as I was talking, what kept playing over and over in my mind were Bec's insults, as the tumour ate her brain and anger filled her soul.

You fucking cunt.

I hate you, Nick. I wish we had never met.

That child you wanted to kill in my womb that looks just like you. I wish you had killed her.

I left that shit out for Iris, but somehow, I felt she knew.

She asked me questions here and there, but mostly she listened.

I asked her about Harry.

'He was … unexpected. He would sing all the time. His laugh sounded like the perfect song, and he gave the most spontaneous cuddles. He loved with his whole body. He was magic.'

'That sounds like Abbey.'

'The greatest love of my life was my second marriage, Nick.'

In the end, she was getting tired, and I stood to leave.

'Come here, child.'

I went to her, as she held out her arms for a hug. I almost wept. It felt so good to be held.

'Nick, dearest. You are a young man. Please remember that you did not die. You must live, dear child. Living does not mean working. Please remember that, Nick.'

I'm not ashamed to admit I shed a tear.

'Iris, I'm leaving for London tomorrow. I can't stay in Sydney and not be near her.'

She nodded. 'Goodbye, dear boy.'

I kissed her cheek. 'Iris, one more thing. I need you to stop calling Abbey feeble.'

Her stare was assessing, and she was silent, but then the shadow of a smile crossed her face and her intelligent eyes brightened. 'Why?'

'Because Abbey is the strongest person I know. She always confronts her fears. And she's never afraid to be vulnerable.'

'Goodbye, Nick.'

'Bye, Iris.'

Tuesday morning, I kissed my sleeping daughter goodbye. She had argued with me, refusing to return. How dare I change the plans? Did I not know they were having a birthday party for Abbey on Saturday? I promised she could stay here with Ev for two more weeks, and then I wanted her home.

'I think this could be our home, Dad. It feels more like home than home. Or is that just me?'

It wasn't just her.

My flight boarded, and I left Sydney and Abbey on a grey, rainy day.

Abbey

My phone rang at four in the morning. Only five numbers could disturb my slumber: Ella's, Kate's, Peter's, Grandma Iris's, or her nursing home.

It was a nurse on the phone from Ashford House; she said her name, but I would never remember it.

She was calling to let me know that my grandmother, the wonderful, irreverent Iris Cavendish, had passed away overnight, peacefully in her sleep.

Chapter Sixteen
Abbey

The darkness surrounded me as soon as the light from my phone shut down. I took a deep breath, and it stuttered in my chest. It almost felt impossible that she was not in the world anymore. How could someone so large in our lives be suddenly gone?

We had lost people before, Kate and I. Our mum passed away the year before Kate left school. She'd had a stroke in her sleep and never woke up. Then Dad had a heart attack the year after Ella was born.

The difference was that Gran had been there for us. She had been there every day of our lives.

Grief could sometimes take its time. You could think you were doing fine, only for it to kick your arse unexpectedly, always at the wrong time, like being overcome by tears reaching for pasta sauce or explaining your mum's lasagne recipe to a work colleague. Or, like Nick, grief could hold you and you could build your life around it, protecting its vice-like grip, thinking that in doing so you would never let it touch you again. But, really, it was just that you had never let it go.

I unlocked my screen and my hand hovered over his name. The temptation to call him and let him comfort me almost overwhelmed me. I knew he would come. He was in love with me, he just couldn't say it. I would bury myself in his arms and I could let him take care of the details. Let him rescue me, save me, prop me up. It would not change anything between us, though.

It was not enough for me to know I was loved. I wanted to hear it and feel it every day. I wanted his bravery *and* his vulnerability. I wanted him fun and sad. Silly and smart.

The walls he had built around his life for his protection were impenetrable from the outside – he had to want to take them down from the inside of his safe, sad space. It was not something I could do for him.

He needed to decide. To choose me. He needed to choose to be loved and to know those choices were worth the risk of losing everything, that I was worth the risk. But only he could make those choices. I could not make them for him.

I had made the mistake of moulding myself and my needs in a relationship before. Pretending everything was fine when it wasn't. Thinking that being easygoing meant letting go of things that were important to me. I was dreadfully unhappy in that relationship, and Peter was miserable. And, I don't know, if he hadn't had the affair, maybe it would have taken me years to work that out. What a bloody, horrifying thought.

I would *not* do the same thing again. It was time for me to find someone in my life who loved me as I was, even when I did not agree with them, even when I needed space. I'd hoped with every cell in my body it would be Nick, but I could not control that he had chosen to avoid a life of being loved, fulfilled and cared for. He had chosen his grief.

I looked at my phone again, deciding to call Kate soon but

not yet, as she would be sleeping. Gran was so wrong about Kate, thinking she would be unemotional. Kate and Gran were sidekicks, partners in crime. Gran thought Kate was the younger version of her, and Kate thought that too, but I knew Kate had this huge molten centre. She would be devastated.

I climbed out of bed, wrapping myself in a cardigan and pulling on socks against the chill of the morning, and padded silently down the hall to Ella's room. I slid under the covers, wrapping my arms around her while she slept in oblivious peace. I watched her steady breath rising and falling, just as I had watched her as a newborn. She had been the most perfect baby: chubby and content. She would yawn the minute I began to wrap her. She loved routine and rules, but she loved cuddles above all things. I felt an ache in my heart for tiny hands and feet, the baby I had grown within me, this perfect, perfect child, who was now growing into this extraordinary woman.

There was a little bit of Iris in her for certain, a little bit of Kate too. There was a little bit of me and then there was just her. I would spend every day for the rest of my life telling her that the bits that were her were the most important and beautiful things in the world and that she should never, ever change them for a boy. Even one she loved. *Especially* one she loved.

Ella's eyelashes fluttered, and she woke up slowly. She had always been a good sleeper, and she took her time opening her eyes, sensing my body and then snuggling into it.

'Hi, Mumma,' she whispered. 'Is everything okay?'

'Morning, baby.' I pressed a kiss into her golden hair. She smelled like strawberries from a body oil she was currently obsessed with.

'Have I slept in?' Ella croaked out, confused.

'No, baby, you don't need to go to school today.' I took a breath, preparing myself to say it out loud for the first time, making it real.

'Ella, Gran passed away in her sleep this morning, honey. I'm so sorry, baby.'

'Gran's gone?'

'Yeah, hon.'

'Was it cardiac arrest, Mum?'

'I don't know, sweetheart. It probably was, though.'

'Too many racy novels.'

'Too many husbands. Maybe her heart did too much loving.'

'Yeah, I don't think medically that is the case, though, Mum. Oh, this is the worst. I miss her already.' Ella snuggled deeper, throwing an arm around me tight. She took a huge sniffle, and I brushed her hair with my hand, tucking her under my chin. 'Will we sit shivah, Mum?'

'We're not Jewish, Ella.'

'Obviously. I know. But they did it on *Grey's Anatomy*. It's seven days of mourning. The family together. Don't you think that's nice?'

'It does sound like a nice thing. I'm not sure about seven days all together. Maybe we'll sit shivah today then.'

'I think you're supposed to have a funeral first.'

'Baby, Grandma Iris did not want a funeral. She wanted a party, with good-looking waiters serving cocktail food.'

'Oh, that sounds like Gran.'

'Yeah.' I smiled and held back tears. 'Are you okay, Ella? You can come and talk to me anytime if you're sad. It's okay to be sad, honey.'

'What happens when you're sad, Mum? Who do you talk to?'

I sighed. 'I guess I have Aunt Kate.'

'What about Nick, Mum?'

Nick.

'I've got to call your Aunty Kate, babe, and then she'll be here soon. You stay in bed snuggled up and I'll bring you a hot chocolate.'

In the end, the call to Kate was brief. She choked out that she would head straight over. I phoned Peter to let him know what was going on and then Monica, to let her know that I would not be in and leave some instructions.

I showered, standing under the water for the longest time, letting my sorrow drain a little.

Kate arrived about forty minutes later, with bags of groceries and floods of tears, determined to cook each of Iris's favourite things for us. Another hour later there were batches of biscuits cooling, a cake in the oven and a soup on the stove.

'Abbey, it's your birthday tomorrow,' Kate said sadly.

'There'll be other years to celebrate,' I said, not even remotely sad to forego celebrating forty-three.

The doorbell rang, and the three of us looked at each other. I could see us all calculating who on earth it could be, given that everyone who was required there by blood was already present.

I found myself getting annoyed, thinking it was Peter, who I definitely did not want to see today, and I marched to the door to get rid of him.

When I opened the door, I stood shocked and then I was overcome with emotion. Ollie was there on the porch, his wheelchair being pushed by Jacinta, the nanny, with Evelyn and Summer behind him and Lionel in between them, resting on his walking frame.

'Oh, Abs. I'm so sorry. She was a fantastic old girl. We're here to sit shivah. Ella invited Summer. I didn't know you were Jewish,' Ollie said.

I scanned their faces, looking for him, but he wasn't there, and I had to swallow my disappointment and grief over that.

'Oh, Abs, I'm sorry. He left for England this morning. I rang him, but he must have already been on the plane. He would have been here if he had known. I hope you know that.'

So he was gone then. Weird. I thought I would be able to feel it in myself when we were no longer on the same continent. *Fuck. Losing the two of them in one day. That was a lot.*

I felt my eyes fill with tears and then I reached over and hugged Ollie, mostly because I couldn't hug Nick, but also because, after everything, I loved him like family. I let them in, greeting each of them with hugs and kisses, especially Lionel. I did not know how on earth the Northbys had broken him out for the day, but I suspected he was better off here amongst other people who loved Iris as much as he had.

Evelyn immediately made herself at home in the kitchen and started making tea to go with Kate's 'lovely biscuits', and when we sat down to eat and drink, the mood became solemn for the briefest of times.

But everyone seemed to lift a little with each bite of biscuit or cake, and Kate and I began to tell stories of Iris from our childhood. Spending summers with her on the south coast, how she was absolutely, fabulously lucky while fishing and how she would just turn up to a wharf with all the equipment, appear slightly confused for about a minute and then some random friendly fisher-bloke would come over and bait us all up. How she took us to the doctor on our sixteenth birthday so we could get birth control and gave us talks about sexual freedom and body confidence. How she introduced us to old black-and-white movies and gothic literature.

Lionel spoke about how the nursing home's book club and artistry association would sorely miss her. And he would miss her for the rest of his life.

The Northby twins shared their memories of childhood and the memories they had of their family and soon they were laughing to the point where they were crying and so were we.

Arrangements were made for the 'Festival of Iris', as her memorial party was dubbed. We would do it the following Saturday.

We spent the entire day together, cocooned. Cooking, eating and chatting like the weird makeshift family we were. Just a group of individuals who loved one another in various ways.

I drove Lionel back to the nursing home in the afternoon, walking him to his room and waiting for a nurse to come to get him settled. I gave him an enormous hug and promised to visit next week.

I walked past Iris's room, but did not go in. I could see all of her things had already been packed up. I could not deal with that just yet.

Once I got back to the house, the drinking began in earnest. I set the girls up with a takeaway and movies on the fold-out lounge, while Kate, Ollie, Evelyn, Jacinta and I sat around a fire out the back. We made plans to drown our sorrows and for them all to stay. Kate in Ella's room, Ollie and Ev in Kate's old room, and Nanny Jacinta on the smaller lounge next to the girls.

The fire was roaring, music was playing, and Nick, he would have loved this. I looked at the sunset, wondering what the sky looked like where he was right now.

When he realised I had not been paying attention, Ollie reached out, taking my hand, giving me a sympathetic smile. I smiled back, widely, as I was absolutely delighted to see him genuinely on the mend. He looked so much better than the last time I had seen him.

'That shaved head suits you enormously, Ollie. The scars are giving you a piratical quality. I think you should make up outrageous stories to go along with them. You're living in Australia, anything could have happened. Nick once said the rest of the world was terrified of coming here. So let's think ... Kangaroo fight?' I suggested.

'Shark bite, while surfing at Bondi,' Nanny Jacinta chimed in from the open door.

'Koala fell on your head?' Evelyn suggested.

'Seagull attack at Darling Harbour?' Kate offered the most plausible one.

He laughed, but immediately winced and we all started fussing, checking if he was okay, but he waved us off.

'Abbey, about Nick.'

'Ollie.' I held up my hand in warning, my eyes pleading with him. The heartbreak was still so raw, and I wasn't ready yet.

'No, Abbey, I need to tell you.'

Kate and Evelyn had gone quiet to hear what he would say. Jacinta excused herself discreetly to check on the girls and give us privacy. It was a kind gesture.

'He was so miserable this week,' Ollie started. Evelyn nodded in agreement, her eyes downcast. 'He said he couldn't stay. That the temptation to be near you was too great, and that you had asked for distance. He agreed to let Summer and Jacinta stay for an additional two weeks with Ev.'

He looked at Evelyn and she withdrew a white paper bag from her tote.

'He wanted me to give this to you tomorrow for your birthday. But I think, given the circumstances, that you should have it today.' Oliver gave me a small sympathetic smile.

I tentatively reached out to take the bag from him. There was no card or embellishment, and the bag was not shop-fresh, in that it wasn't new and it looked as if it had been used before, or worried at. It didn't look like a present.

Inside was a box and a picture frame. I took the frame out first. It was a wooden frame in a light-oak colour, heavy with a soft, black velvet back. I turned the frame over and the photo brought instant tears to my eyes. It was a picture of Nick and me on the beach in the Maldives, at sunset. A lump rose in my throat. My hair was in mid-flight, caught by the wind, and I had obviously been swimming that day, from the amount of wayward curls I had. I was laughing at something he was saying. I couldn't remember what. My right hand was over my grandmother's necklace, the other over his hand. His arm was wrapped firmly around my waist, the other extended to snap the shot. His chin was over my shoulder, sitting on top of a black sleeveless tee I had on, and his gorgeous dark waves were all over the place. He was pulling a face of concentration, trying to get the ocean into the background. It was the perfect, imperfect picture of the perfect holiday.

I felt a tear escape and roll down my cheek and a few more quickly followed. I brushed them away with the back of my hand and passed the picture to Kate, while I reached back into the bag to retrieve the box.

I already knew in my heart what was in it. My hands trembled as I struggled to remove the lid. The white cardboard box had nothing distinguishable about it. Inside were three empty corners and then pooled in the last corner I looked at, was my necklace.

I lifted it out and ran my thumb over the pendant. The chain was new, but the pendant was definitely my grandmother's. A choked sob escaped me, and I clutched it to my chest. That this would come back to me today was the greatest of miracles. A much-needed reminder she was always here, even if she wasn't.

Kate rose to embrace me, wiping her own tears, as Ollie reached for my leg in comfort. They let me cry over the loss of my gran and Nick. Evelyn grabbed tissues and another bottle of wine.

Kate stood, took the pendant from me, and looped it around my neck before securing the clasp.

'How did he …?' I was struggling to speak.

'He had those two kids that own the boat looking for it from the minute you lost it. He got them sorted out with scuba gear and a metal detector. Oh, and the promise of a boat upgrade. He had word from the resort that it had been found on the beach of the private island. He had Monica fly over to pick it up and bring it here.'

Jesus Christ, Nick.

I stood up and hugged Ollie and, in the absence of his brother, it was an enormous hug that went on a really, really unprofessional length of time.

I was so grateful to have met the two of them on the island. The love that I had for Nick was so very much more than anything I had ever experienced, but Ollie and the rest of Nick's family were a gift I had never expected, either.

We had a late dinner of soup and homemade bread that Evelyn had magically produced from random things in my pantry, and then there was more wine and music and laughter and some tears.

It got to just after one and we were fading, the kids already asleep inside. I stood and began to collect glasses, mentally preparing a list of blankets and pillows needed for our unexpected house guests. I took the handful I had to the kitchen before coming back out for another lot. I leaned over Ollie to pick up his glass.

'Abbey.'

His voice came from behind me, and I gave myself a moment before turning around to look at him.

Nick.

His frame filled the back door, and he stepped down to the yard. He looked cosy in a black cashmere jumper and black jeans. The look on his face was one I would never forget. He looked exhausted, yet somehow flushed with colour, as though he had run here.

I think my bottom lip fell, or trembled, or my face showed I was about to burst into tears, and he lifted his palms up to me in a plea to let him speak.

'Abbey, I— Oh, hey.' He noticed his brother, sister and Kate sitting around the fire. 'Everyone's here.'

'Did you get my message, Nick?' Ollie asked.

'Message? I only landed twenty minutes ago. What are you guys all doing here?'

'Shivah,' Evelyn said. 'For Iris.'

Nick's hand flew to his chest. 'Iris died?'

'This morning,' Kate said, brushing away tears.

'Oh, Jesus. Abbey, Kate, I'm so sorry …' He choked on a sob. 'She was such a great lady and I'm' – he sniffed – 'I'm so glad I met her.'

'Abbey,' Kate whispered to me, because I had not moved to comfort him.

'No, Kate. No.' He shook his head, pushed away the tears for Iris. 'It's okay. Abbey is right to be wary. I have not given her very many reasons to trust me. I, uh, I have not given Abbey the one thing she offered me straight away. Honesty.'

I was taking deep, purposeful breaths.

'If I were honest the first night I met Abbey, I would have told her I was completely captivated. Straight away. If I were honest, I would have told her that the first time she agreed to have dinner with me, my heart soared, and I was nervous as hell. I would have told her that I was completely intoxicated by the end of that holiday.

'I should never have let my lawyers interview you. I knew you. I should have defended you, Abbey. I got that so wrong.

'I should have danced with you at that party. I regret that. I will never, ever put my business needs above your needs ever again, I give you my word.' He took a tentative step towards me.

'I have fucked this up in so many ways. I can only profess complete and utter madness. I was in love with you before I got to Sydney and every single second I have spent beside you, Abs, has made me fall even further. I should have told you I loved you every single one of those days, Abbey. I should have fallen to my knees every day and begged for you to be mine. I know it may be too late …' His voice broke, and I watched as his hand moved across his chest as if he was trying to stop his insides from falling out.

'And you may not feel like you can forgive me for being so fucking useless. But, Abbey, if you let me, I will spend every day of the rest of our lives making certain you are cared for, reminding you that you are enough for anyone, respecting every boundary you set. Reminding you that you are way too good for me, and I will love you with my whole being for as long as you let me.'

There was silence as he, and our family, waited for my response. Only the fire behind us dared to breathe.

'You are a real arsehole, you know that?' I said, pushing away my tears.

'Oh, honey, believe me when I tell you that I know I have been the biggest arsehole ever. A complete, an utter dolt.' He took another step closer to me.

'You ran a long way. Further than I expected you to, Nick. You cannot do that again.'

'I promise you, that will never happen again.'

'How's this even going to work? You live in London.'

'I don't know, but I thought maybe we could just talk about it, find a way through together. Abs, I love it here. And, more importantly, I love you.'

'So you aren't back here because your brother left you a message about Iris?'

'No.'

'What changed, Nick?' I couldn't keep the pessimism out of my voice, and I saw him flinch when he heard it.

'I got to Singapore. I was sitting in a transfer lounge. There was an old couple across from me and she started laughing at something he did or said. I don't really know that I can explain it. But it just occurred to me, like an actual lightbulb moment, that you are this for me. You know, my other half, the one that makes me laugh, the person who makes me better, the bloody one thing that makes me happiest. When I am not with you, I'm just a miserable old bastard and I've let that miserable old bastard rule my life for too long, Abbey.'

He closed the distance between us, and I got my first waft of him. He smelled so good, not like someone who had been travelling all day. His stubble was holiday length and, though his eyes were bloodshot, they were shining at me.

His hand rose to my face, and he pulled me into him, pushing his forehead against mine. 'They called for the flight to board, and I could not do it. I could not take another step away from you. I cannot be without you. And I didn't want to admit how very deep I was already in.'

He shook his head once, looking down before meeting my eyes again. 'Abbey, it's like the fucking angry ocean that surrounds this country. That's how deep. A fucking ocean, a big one. Powerful, out of control, knock you on your arse. I love you so much and it's fucking terrifying.'

I pressed into him, my heart thudding and the joy finally being allowed to flood through my body. *Yes!*

'Everyone's afraid of something, Nick.'

He gave a small laugh through his nose. 'Yes.'

'It's exactly how I feel. Terrified.'

'I love you.' His arm wrapped around my waist, and I reached under his arms, pulling him into me, holding him so tightly I could barely breathe. Our lips met in a desperate crush.

'Hi, baby,' he whispered into my ear while our family cheered behind us. 'I missed you so badly. I've been an arsehole and I'm so fucking sorry, Abbey. Please tell me you forgive me?'

My face was wet, but from my tears or his, I couldn't tell.

'I forgive you. I love you too, Nick.'

He picked me up and did a little spin.

'Wait! Shivah?' He frowned with confusion. 'Was Iris Jewish, or was one of her husbands?'

'Neither. It's Ella's *Grey's Anatomy* obsession.'

'Oh.' He shook his head, gave a puzzled smile. 'Abbey, I don't know how this is going to work logistically. But we'll figure it out together, okay?'

'Together.'

'Yes, beloved.'

He kissed my cheek and then found my mouth again in the sweetest of kisses that made more tears come to my eyes.

'Hey, it's your birthday. Happy birthday, Abs.'

'Thank you for my gift.' I reached for my pendant.

'Back where it belongs.' He kissed my temple. 'Wait, do you even have room for me? The girls are here too.'

'You can sleep with me.'

'In your bed? Abbey, are you sure? Will Ella be okay with that?'

'You're going to be around. Right? You are never going to run away from me again. And you are going to tell me you love me every single day. Right, Nick?'

'I am making a set of Nick and Abbey rules. Each one of those is going on it.'

I nodded, kissing his cheek. 'Well, then you can sleep in my bed. We might as well get everyone used to it in one fell swoop.'

'Promise me you will always tell me when I annoy you.'

'I promise.' I kissed him again, smiling into his mouth. 'You are fucking annoying. I could not love you more, though.'

'I love you too, Abs.'

Nick

Peace is not just a feeling, or an ideal, or a place. It can also be a person and a life. Peace is Abbey and the life we are going to build together.

I lay there in the dark of her bedroom – it's still too early to call it our room, but I hope that day is not far away. I was fighting off sleep just so I could watch her breath rise and fall evenly. She was snoring lightly, a beautiful sound to my ears – all of Abbey's sounds are beautiful – and one of her arms was draped over me. She was possessive in her sleep. No matter how hot I got, she would find me in the bed, forcing me to acclimatise to her.

I had this stupid grin that I could not get off my face and I felt … light and unburdened. It was an unfamiliar feeling, and it made me a little anxious, as if I'd lost or forgotten something.

The curtains were fluttering behind me. She likes the window open, even in the dead of winter.

I don't think this house will be big enough for us, nor will my apartment. I want a house where our whole family can be. But we'll talk about that when we sort out everything else.

I am a lucky man. The luckiest man on earth. I cannot wait for our future, even though it scares the shit out of me. *Fuck me, if that is not rather hopeful sounding. Who would have thought?*

I snorted into the dark, a short laugh, which made her startle and wake.

'You okay, Nick?'

'Shh, beloved,' I said, kissing her head. 'I'm sorry. I didn't mean to wake you. Go back to sleep, my love.'

She snuggled closer to me, and I snuggled right back into her. It was heaven. I belonged here. Our family all under one roof. There is only peace.

I drifted off to sleep.

and popped under the tree. *Oh, Nick.* I know everything that is under that tree.

He'll ask. I'll accept.

I cannot wait.

Acknowledgements

Once upon a time, I wrote a book. And the idea that you, the reader, have spotted that book, picked it up, read the blurb, and decided to read it, is a dream come true. I hope you loved it. Thank you.

It does feel like I won the lottery, but I once read that sometimes the book finds the perfect home, and that is certainly the case here. Juliet Rogers, you will always be the person who said yes, which means more than I can say. Special thanks to Diana Hill for listening to my ramblings and for allowing me so much room to operate within; Samantha Miles for fresh eyes and encouragement and for allowing me to love and hate it at times. And Amanda Maclean, Cherie Baird, Maeve Carragher and the rest of the Echo Publishing team, thank you.

My editor, Lauren Finger, thank you so much for everything. My cover designer, the amazing Christa Moffitt. It is breathtaking. And thanks to Wavesound for making my audiobook dreams come true.

Heather Cracknell, my 24-7 gal, my alpha-beta, my friend,

my international penpal. Your friendship and support have been a constant in this book's life, and when you asked me if it was just going to live on my laptop, it was the first time I believed I could send it anywhere. Collette Rice, you pushed me so hard on these characters and their journeys, and the feedback was astonishingly helpful. Thank you for talking me off the ledge and pushing me to aim high, and helping iron out Nick's red flags. Bridgitte Berchtold had fantastic eyes. Thank you also to Maria Maugeri for her detailed notes.

My mum, Trish, thank you for letting me be a daydreamer, and holding my hand when I cross the road (even now) just in case I'm in my head and not paying attention. The rest of my beautiful family, my dad Mark and Maz. My amazing brother Adam. Lauren, Ash, Sara, Sam and Kell for ladies' days, 'lunches' and champagne dances.

To my boys. I love you so much. Remember that you can be anything you want to be in life if you work hard, and that it is never too late to start something brilliantly new.

To my love, Jamie. I told you I wanted to write a book while sitting around a fire, and you said, 'Just do it.' No one has been more significant in my life than you. You are not a romance hero. Ever. Please stop asking me. But thank you for our life, for being my best friend. For always making me laugh. For looking like Eric Bana. For reading your first romance novel and telling me it was beautiful. Love you the most.

And to the booksellers, librarians, fellow writers who have dug deep with a recommendation, I cannot thank you enough.

Amanda x